Praise for Sean Costello's previous novels...

EDEN'S EYES

"The best horror novel I've read since Stephen King's own *Pet Sematary*. ...Costello knows how to tantalize his readers, priming them for the horrors to come...."
—*Rave Reviews*

"Spine-chilling...impeccable research and pacing...a riveting psychological thriller."
—Charles de Lint, author of *The Little Country*

THE CARTOONIST

"A fast-moving read that mounts in tension while mixing horror with psychological anguish...*The Cartoonist* will not disappoint."
—*Rave Reviews*

CAPTAIN QUAD

"Sean Costello is one of the horror genre's brightest new stars and his third novel, *Captain Quad*, will only enhance his position."
—*Other Realms*

FINDERS KEEPERS

Sean Costello

a
RED TOWER
original

Copyright © 2002 Sean Costello
Cover art Copyright © 2002 Amy Bradley

ISBN 0-9731469-0-7

Published by Red Tower Publications

All rights reserved. No part of this publication may be reproduced, stored in a retrieval system, or transmitted in any form or by any means; electronic, mechanical, recording or otherwise, without the prior written permission of the author.

PRINTED IN THE UNITED STATES OF AMERICA

The characters and events in this book are fictitious. Any similarity to real persons, living or dead, is coincidental and not intended by the author.

This book is for Steve, my son.
I love you, bud.

I am so glad to be your dad...

Acknowledgements

To the gracious folks who contributed their time and expertise to this effort, again my thanks. In particular, I'd like to thank my friend Brian for the hours spent on the phone, patiently tutoring me on the inner workings of the police force.

I'd also like to thank Amy Bradley for the cool cover art. And my long-time pal Nathan Abourbih for creating and hosting my website—and for keeping me on the good side of computers.

Thanks to my lovely wife are always in order, and I'm pleased to have this opportunity to thank her formally…mostly just for putting up with me. I love you, Carole.

1

THERE WAS A FEELING Keith Whipple got every time he walked through the door of Rudy's Quik-Mart. It was the product of an array of sensations: the fragrance of strong, fresh-brewed coffee; the aroma of expensive cigars; the pleased sparkle in Rudy's eyes when they met Keith's; the vaguely startling realization induced by this atmosphere that he was retired, without obligation. It made him feel fine, and since he was clear-headed and without serious ailment, it made him feel young again, too.

Rudy turned to the cheerful sound of the bells strung over the opening door. As usual Keith was his first customer.

"Herr Whipple—" he said.

"Stamp your feet," Keith said, dutifully complying. "I swear, Rudy, you need a new rap."

Hiding a grin, Rudy limped over to his percolators. His left leg was a monstrosity, the result of a mining accident thirty years ago, the skin from the knee down like that of an iguana: scaly, a cadaverous looking gray-brown. Keith had actually felt ill the first time Rudy showed it to him.

"Coffee?" Rudy said, already pouring.

"Black and nasty," Keith said, completing the ritual exchange. He joined Rudy at the soda shop-style counter, the only anomaly in the otherwise standard convenience store. Behind the counter exotic brews perked on a half-dozen hot plates and a selection of cigars stored securely under glass waited for the discerning patron. A small magazine rack featured only *Smoke* and *Cigar Aficionado*. It was a personal touch, a nod to bygone days, and Keith felt right at home here. A creature of habit, he'd been coming into Rudy's every weekday morning since his daughter Kate was nine—fifteen years of coffee, conversation and good-natured gossip, Rudy a connoisseur of all three. The only tough part was keeping his mitts off those cigars. Kate had finally browbeaten him into quitting two years ago, after a suspicious opacity on a routine chest X-ray gave them both a scare. It turned out to be scar tissue, the remains of some benign infection he'd picked up as a kid swamping out the hen house on his parents' farm, but Kate had effectively stamped out his pack-a-day habit, including the cigar jones he'd picked up hanging around with Rudy. On the job he'd looked forward to those cigars, comfortable in his chair in the projection booth at the Grande Theater, Sudbury's oldest movie house, alone up there in a haze of flickering light and swirling smoke. When she was younger Kate had often joined him, complaining mildly about the smoke.

He shed his parka and draped it over one of the chrome and red leather stools. Rudy slid over a steaming cup of coffee. "Try this," he said, wiping his hands on his apron, "but be careful. It's a man's brew." He glanced over his shoulder at the tail end of a news item on the wall-mounted TV, an old black and white Zenith that was always turned on; a length of plastic garland was scotch-taped to the consul, Rudy's nod to the Yuletide.

Keith took a cautious sip. "Hot. Delicious."

"So what do you know that I don't," Rudy said, facing Keith now, leaning his big hands on the counter to get the weight off his leg.

"Did I tell you Katie got accepted in the film school at UCLA?"

Rudy said, "You mean not counting the last twenty times?" and Keith grinned. "Gonna miss her, huh."

"Sure am," Keith said. "But it's long overdue. She's a gifted writer. The script she just finished? I loved it. It's a blend of crime, science fiction and black comedy that's really got legs. But she needs maturing. Not to mention the exposure; her work needs to be seen. No way she's gonna get all that up here in Sudbury. Besides, the last thing I want is to see her hanging around town just to keep her old man company." Brave words, Keith thought, picturing life without her and not liking it much. Cancer had taken his wife when Kate was six, a protracted, painful death, and he and Kate had been pretty much inseparable ever since. They shared a duplex on Howey Drive, living modestly but in comfort, the last mortgage payment made three years ago. "She needs to be where the action is," Keith said. "It's the nature of that business."

"I hear you," Rudy said. "But look at the bright side. Come September you can party every night 'til she makes it big, then move down to California and sponge off her the rest of your life. Fraternize with the hired help."

"There's that," Keith said, putting his cup down, a storm warning on the TV catching his attention. Rudy followed his gaze, saying, "More snow. Can you believe it?"

Keith glanced out the storefront window. "I don't buy it," he said. He'd walked to Rudy's as he always did, the winter sun warm on his face, no hint from his joints about lousy weather. But in the Canadian north, you never could tell. He took another sip of his coffee, then got his reading glasses on and fished his wallet out of his parka, the weather forgotten. "Gotta check my numbers," he said.

Rudy spoke to his back as he made his way to the lottery display. "You hear about Howie Gottler's kid?"

Keith said, "The mental defective?" He dug a sheath of tickets out of his wallet and began checking them against the posted winning numbers.

"That's the one. The coppers caught him up at Bell Junior High yesterday, poking his wares through the cyclone fence for the amusement of the teenyboppers. When the dopey bastard tried to run his johnny froze to the fence like a wet tongue. Son of a bitch got a free circumcision..."

udy's voice faded to a drone in Keith's brain, every neuron suddenly focused on the apparent enigma that now appeared before his eyes. There were three sets of two-digit numbers on the ticket in his hand, six numbers in each set. The series in the first two sets were nowhere close to the winning numbers, no confusion there. But what utterly fouled Keith's normal lines of perception was the fact that the third set matched the winners exactly.

The right numbers. The right order. The right lottery. The right date.

Keith realized he wasn't breathing. He commanded his lungs to inflate, but in the same instant his gaze ticked to the dollar value attached to this draw and his throat sealed off completely.

God in heaven, he thought. I'm gonna die before I can spend a dime. Then Rudy's voice came through—"Keith, you okay?"—and his lungs admitted a thin slip of air.

Rudy came around the counter in a hurry, certain his old friend was having a coronary; Keith's usually placid face was beet red, the veins in his neck standing out like cables. But before Rudy had closed half the distance, Keith darted past him in the opposite direction, almost bowling him over.

"Jesus, Rudy, move your ass. I gotta call Katie!"

He grabbed the phone behind the counter and punched in the numbers, staring wide-eyed at Rudy as it rang, holding the ticket up for Rudy to see.

"Ten million bucks, old buddy!" Keith said. "Ten million bucks!"

To avoid the congestion of the main streets Kate Whipple had mapped out an alternate route to head office. It took her through a maze of residential streets narrowed by snow banks and illegally parked cars, the big van barely squeaking through in places, but it suited her temperament better than the ill-mannered, bumper-to-bumper grind of morning traffic. She sometimes felt that all the really crummy drivers in the country had been secretly exiled to her home town, then encouraged to procreate.

Elvis doing "I'll Be Home For Christmas" came on the radio, the King's rich voice bringing a mist of tears to Kate's eyes. "Shit," she said softly and laughed. She turned the radio up a notch and wiped her eyes.

Kate loved Christmas, everything about it. If there was magic in the world, she sometimes felt, it revealed itself during the Yuletide. At twenty-four, she still anticipated Christmas with the same excited yearning she had as a ten-year-old. This year especially she could hardly wait. She'd bought her dad a DVD player, blowing a big chunk of her tuition money but what the hell. He was going to flip.

As she turned onto the last street before the industrial stretch on Kelly Lake Road her cell phone rang. "Panther Courier," she said into the handset. "Kate speaking."

"Katie, it's me."

Kate felt a flicker of alarm. "Dad, you sound all out of breath—"

"Honey, you're not going to believe this!"

"Believe what?"

Keith told her and Kate felt her jaw come unhinged. She veered too sharply into a curve and the rear wheels slewed into the oncoming lane. Kate over-corrected and the van plowed nose-first into a snow bank, sending a huge plume of snow into the air. Unharmed, Kate simply sat there, staring out at the drift.

"Katie? You still there?"

"You're joking, right?"

"If I'm lying I'll do the Shing-a-ling naked on Paris Street."

"Dad, that's incredible!"

"Take the rest of your life off, kid."

"What...?"

"Tell your boss you're retiring. I'll meet you at home in an hour. We're going shopping!"

The line went dead.

Kate sat there stunned, the phone still clamped to her ear, until an old woman in a Volvo wagon pulled up behind her and leaned on the horn; the van was blocking her way. Kate gave the old gal a numb wave, then reversed out of the snow bank.

Her life had changed, just like that.

Like magic...

Kate made it home before her dad. Mo, her boss, drove her there personally. It was incredible how polite he became once she told him why she was quitting. Until that moment he'd never been more than casually rude to her. A big frog in a little pond. She was pretty sure she was going to enjoy being rich.

The duplex she shared with her father overlooked the now-frozen expanse of Ramsey Lake, a large in-city lake banked by some of the most sought after properties in town. They didn't have lake access—the Howey Drive side was separated from the water by a railway track and a steep hill—but the view from Kate's living-room window was no less spectacular. Keith owned the building and Kate paid him a modest rent for the upstairs half. When Kate was between sweethearts, which in the past couple of years had been pretty much a constant, she and her dad spent most evenings together, sharing meals and talking film, then curling up together in front of the entertainment center they'd set up in Keith's living room: a sixty-inch Mitsubishi TV and a full set of Paradigm speakers, an investment Keith sometimes joked he'd still be paying for when Kate was a grandmother. After that, usually between about eight and eleven, Kate sat in front of her computer and wrote. Not counting her earliest efforts, hand-written on yellow legal pads and buried in the back of her closet, she'd completed nine feature-length scripts, five she was still very proud of and one that had netted her a three-year option from a small indie company in L.A. which, unfortunately, had gone broke. Writing was her favorite thing in the world, slipping into that private space in her mind and watching it happen, then finding the words that would make others see it as clearly.

In her bedroom Kate picked up the envelope from UCLA, ragged from her excitement tearing it open, and took out the single, neatly-folded sheet of white Bond. Opening it now, almost two weeks after plucking it from a stack of bills and flyers, she remembered the mix of emotions aroused by her first quick scan of those magic words: The School of Theater, Film and Television, UCLA, is pleased to inform you of your acceptance.... Joy, excitement, apprehension shading to fear...and an unexpected regret. Stepping into the future meant leaving behind the familiar comforts of the present, everything she trusted and loved. But she'd put it off as long as she could, hoping against hope that she might strike it rich, draft just the right script and, somehow, get it into just the right hands. She'd done her share of fantasizing, reading about guys like Quentin Tarantino, the ultimate Cinderella story, and the others coming down the pipeline all the time, unknowns breaking through with spec scripts, earning millions. But these guys were the exception, not the rule; and they all lived in L.A., a city with one of the highest costs of living in the United States. And until now, even with a full-time job and four years of socking away every spare penny, money had been so tight she hadn't even been sure she could afford to finish out the first year, never mind the occasional trip home.

But now. God, now...

Kate squirmed out of her uniform, tossed it onto the unmade bed and pulled on a burgundy Planet Hollywood sweatshirt over a pair of Levis. She considered doing the litter of dishes in the kitchen and said to hell with it, leave it for the maid. The thought provoked an embarrassed chuckle. Thinking like a rich brat already.

She happened to be at the picture window overlooking the street when an all-white stretch limo pulled up to the curb in front of the house. The rear window powered open and her father's head popped out. He spotted Kate in the window and waved her down, grinning from ear to ear.

"Jesus, Dad," Kate said out loud, pulling on her ski jacket and boots. "What are you up to now?"

Bernie, the limo driver, turned out to be a jovial, speed-talking guy in his fifties with curly red hair and a bandit's moustache. Bernie spent the ten minute drive to the downtown core giving the Whipples a tour guide's spiel so enthusiastic, Keith didn't have the heart to tell him they'd lived in Sudbury all their lives.

"As you folks might be aware," Bernie told them, "Sudbury is a mining town. Nickel and copper mostly." He pointed at the huge Inco smoke stack, visible from virtually every vantage in the city. "Right over there is your super stack, floats all that fallout down south where they don't know any better. Ain't she something? And over here is your Theater Center..."

The storm warnings continued on the limo radio, but the sky remained blue and clear. The only hint of foul weather was the wind, a gusting northerly that whipped up all of a sudden. When Bernie dropped them off in front of the City Center, Keith pulled up the hood on his parka and Kate tucked herself into his flank, using him as a windbreak.

"Give us 'til noon," Keith told the driver. "We'll meet you back here."

Bernie gave them a smiling salute and merged into traffic.

Arm in arm with his daughter, Keith Whipple swept through the shopping center doors on a wave of sheer excitement. To his renewed eyes everything seemed freshly minted, and he felt like shouting his good fortune to the high cathedral ceiling. Since the death of his wife—God, eighteen years—he'd lived from paycheck to paycheck, investing what little was left over with the noble intention of handing a nest egg to Kate one day, something extra to get her life started with. But through one minor disaster and another, the kind of things life had a way of throwing at you when you least expected them, he'd been forced to chip away at that nest egg, diminishing it to the point of near extinction, a fact which, until now, had caused him no end of frustration. As they entered the mall he kept stealing glances at Kate's beaming face—so much like her mother's, that smooth tan oval framed in fine blond hair—and thinking, You're set, my angel. Set for life.

Keith spent twenty minutes at the Royal Bank, waiting while the teller cleaned out his savings account—six-thousand-eight-hundred dollars and change—and handed it to him in a neat stack of hundreds. With his credit card, always up to date, that gave him eleven-thousand-eight-hundred dollars' worth of clout. And change. It felt strange stuffing his wallet with all that cash, but he'd never trusted those ATM machines, that whole technological shift where money was concerned. Even the credit card had taken him years to get around to and a couple more to actually use. Old-fashioned maybe, but he still preferred a human face to a machine spitting money out at him.

He caught up to Kate in Zellers, where she was busy choosing the fanciest Christmas tree baubles she could find.

"Okay sweetheart," he said. "let's tear this place up!"

Kate's smile filled his heart. He'd often heard it said that money didn't bring happiness, but goddamn, he sure felt fine today.

Bernie was waiting for them when they came out of the mall at noon, the limo idling next to him at the curb, Bernie hunched against the cold in his navy blue chauffeur's coat and thin leather gloves.

When he spotted them he hustled over and took Kate's load of parcels, the trunk of the big Lincoln popping open behind him as if by magic. Kate liked the little guy: that moustache, hinting at a shady past, the quick, mischievous smile it framed, the way the street slipped into his way of talking when he relaxed. When they were underway again Kate suggested lunch and invited Bernie to join them. They agreed on a nearby Italian spot, Pasta e Vino, ordering salads and pasta from a pared-down lunch menu. The waiter was a plump, cheerful guy in a frilly white shirt and black dress pants who scribbled their selections onto a note pad.

When he was gone Bernie said, "Now that's what I like to see, a waiter who writes down your order," and Kate thought, Uh-oh.

"Exactly," Keith said. "I don't eat out all that often, but when I do I like to get what I ask for."

Bernie said, "And so you should. Irritates the hell out of me, the way some of 'em come up to you, standing there with their hands dangling like, okay shoot, nothing escapes this iron-trap mind."

"I'll give you a classic example," Keith said. "The other day I'm in Jimmy's, I order a cheeseburger, lettuce and ketchup only, and a glass of ice water. The girl nods then goes to a table of six and does the same thing, nodding her head and not writing anything down. Twenty minutes later, by now I'm half starved, she comes back with a glass of Sprite and a burger—no cheese, no lettuce, the whole thing dripping with mustard—plunks it down in front of me and walks away. I hate mustard."

Bernie said, "And I bet you're too polite to say anything."

Keith mumbled something and blushed, the sight of him sitting there red-faced making Kate laugh out loud. The waiter rescued him, bringing their drinks, a Sleeman in the bottle for Keith, white wine for Kate and a diet Pepsi for Bernie. The food came a few minutes later, steamy hot and delicious looking. Bernie dug right in.

"So, if you don't mind me asking," he said around a mouthful of penne a la vodka, "what's up with you folks? You from out of town or what?"

"No," Keith said, "we've lived in Sudbury all our lives."

Bernie rolled his eyes. "Shoot, and I gave you my whole out-of-towner spiel there this morning. Sorry about that. I don't know why I thought you was from out of town."

"That's okay," Kate said. "It was entertaining."

"We've...come into some money," Keith said.

"Say, that's great! What happened, a rich aunt kick it or something?"

Keith said, "No, nothing like that," and glanced at Kate, giving her a mildly dazed look. "We won the lottery."

Bernie clacked his fork against his plate. "Not the six-four-nine."

"The very one."

"Ten million dollars?"

Keith chuckled. "Ain't that a caution?"

"*Je*-sus Christ on a crutch...if you'll pardon my French, ma'am, but that's phenomenal. I feel like gettin' your autograph or something. Ten million, goddam. I had a ticket on that baby myself."

Keith said, "When those numbers matched up I thought I was gonna bust a blood vessel and die. I must've checked 'em a hundred times." He looked at Kate. "Honey, did I check 'em a hundred times?"

"Two hundred," Kate said, recalling their dizzy morning in the mall, Keith stopping every few minutes to compare his numbers to the winners, shaking his head each time. "You made *me* check them a hundred times."

"I was gonna ask you how it feels," Bernie said. "Dopey question."

"Feels great."

"So what's the plan? You're gonna need me a couple days, right? Motor you around in style? I got nothing booked now 'til Christmas: that's five days." Bernie's eyes widened and Kate could almost see the idea crystallizing behind them. He said, "You gotta go to Toronto to cash in your ticket, right?"

Keith said, "Yep. If the weather holds we thought we'd drive down later this afternoon. We usually spend Christmas at my sister's place in Toronto anyway. Lee's the only one with grandkids, nine of 'em, and we all like to be there for the kids. We thought we'd get some more gifts bought, you know, special things, then stay with them the few extra days."

"You're not gonna fly?"

Kate said, "Dad's got this...thing about flying."

"I heard that," Bernie said. "I watch those *Life Against Death* videos, *Caught on Camera*, you seen those?" The Whipples nodded in unison. "I'd sooner walk than get on a plane. Spam in a can." He looked at Keith. "What kind of car you got?"

"I don't drive, but Katie's got a nice little Corolla."

"And you think you're gonna get all that gear you bought to Toronto in a Corolla? Listen, let me take you. On dry pavement it's a four hour drive, why not do it in comfort? It'll be fun. Roll up to that lottery office in style. I'll even cut you a deal." Bernie grinned. "Heck, you guys don't *need* a deal. I'll do it for twice my usual fee. How's that sound?"

Kate looked at her dad and smiled. "Why not?"

Keith raised his Sleeman. "My friend, you've got yourself a deal."

They shopped some more after lunch, mostly for the kids, Keith zipping up and down the aisles at Wal-Mart with a push cart, picking out dolls, Transformers, laser guns and noise makers of every description. By the time they got back to the limo the sky had darkened to an ominous gray, especially in the south. Keith barely noticed, but the sight of it struck a chord of alarm in Kate.

Her father's behavior since lunch had begun to concern her, too. His simple joy at winning had begun to shade over into a kind of low grade mania, a nervous energy that left Kate's face feeling cramped from the continual smile that no longer felt genuine. It was like something was winding him up from the inside, propelling him at a rate completely foreign to his character. Added to this was a growing paranoia about the ticket, about having it on his person.

Suddenly, getting to Toronto was priority one. That's where the lottery office was and he was by-God determined to be standing on their doorstep when they opened for business the next morning at nine. With the frequent weather warnings—and now this threatening sky—Kate thought they should wait. But Keith was beside himself, convinced that if they didn't cash the damned thing in as soon as possible it would spontaneously combust or he'd have a stroke worrying about it or the earth would open up and swallow him whole. Kate had never seen him so keyed-up.

By four-thirty they were set to go, but at the last minute Keith remembered something his older brother Clayton had wanted since they were kids and re-routed Bernie back downtown. "Rodale's," he told him. "That fancy restaurant supplier. You know it?" Bernie said he did, and they wound up spending an hour there choosing an espresso machine.

It was dark before they finally got underway, the trunk stuffed with Christmas gifts—lavishly wrapped by a team of elderly women raising money for an MRI machine—the overflow, including a life-size Big Bird for Kate's favorite niece, ending up stacked around them in the passenger compartment. Though they'd spent a bundle, the wallet inside Keith's spanking new Armani overcoat was still so thick with hundreds he could barely fold it closed. He told Kate at Rodale's he felt like ole Saint Nick himself.

As predicted the storm hit hard, but for the better part of the trip it ran ahead of them, leaving the two-lane blacktop snow-packed and icy in places but otherwise passable. They ran into some weather about two hours out, an intermittent sleet carried on a flaring wind, and further on, an eerie crystalline frost that hung in the low spots like fog. It was the wind that concerned Kate most, bulldozing its way across the highway, side-swiping the limo; but the big Lincoln was sure-footed and solid and before long the tension she'd felt earlier had all but vanished.

To pass the time they played a movie trivia game they'd invented when Kate was in her teens, Kate throwing obscure bits of dialogue at Keith and, as always, failing to stump him. At one point she thought she had him: in a Chinese accent she said, "Boards…don't hit back," and Keith looked puzzled, fingering the cleft in his chin that never got properly shaved, repeating the quote a few times in a thoughtful whisper. Then he grinned that cocky grin of his, said, "Bruce Lee, *Enter The Dragon*, nineteen-seventy-three, Robert Clouse, director," and denied being even remotely perplexed. "Just letting you think you had the hook in me," he said and went back to fiddling with the limo phone.

Kate sipped champagne from the bottle she found in the limo fridge, the fizzy cool of it relaxing her. And in quiet moments, she pictured the future in ways she'd never imagined before. They could live together in California now, maybe even start their own production company. Her father knew more about the movie industry than anyone she'd ever met; it had been a life-long hobby of his, tying neatly into his job as a projectionist. He'd read almost everything written about the film business and still flipped through the trade magazines every morning before breakfast. Kate could even imagine him directing, he had such a good eye. She'd write 'em and he'd direct 'em. They could be partners. She still wanted to go to school, though, take advantage of that opportunity.

She poured herself another glass of bubbly, feeling giddy now, the reality of the change that was coming finally sinking in. She offered some of the champagne to Keith, but he was having too much fun with the phone, spreading the news to everyone he could think of. He'd been trying since they left town to reach Aunt Lee, and had just now gotten through to her. Kate snuggled next to him with her coat off, pressing her ear close to his so she could listen in.

"No, Sis', it's true," Keith said into the handset. "I've got the ticket right here in my hand."

Lee said, "Oh my God, Keith, that's fantastic! How much did you win?"

"Are you sitting down? Ten million big ones. Can you believe it? I've been playing the same damn numbers for years."

Lee said, "God love us, I can't even imagine. Where are you now?"

"In a limo on our way to Toronto. I want to get this thing squared away before I wake up and find out I dreamt it."

Lee chuckled. "Where's Katie?"

Keith gave his daughter a ten million dollar smile. "Right here beside me. We'll be staying at the Royal York tonight—splurge a little—but we'll see you in the morning, soon as we're through at the lottery office."

"Okay, sweetheart. You tell that driver to take his time."

"Ten-four, kid. See you tomorrow."

Keith cradled the receiver, folded the ticket into his wallet and tucked the wallet back inside his new overcoat. "I think your aunt wet her pants," he said to Kate.

"I still can't believe it myself," Kate said. Her expression grew suddenly somber. "I wish Mom. . ."

"Me too, sweetie. Me too."

Before anything more could be said the glass partition hummed open and Bernie adjusted his rearview, allowing eye contact with Keith. "If you don't mind me asking," he said, "but winning the lottery—me and the boys at the garage, that's practically all we talk about, what we'd do with a purse like that. You thought about it yet?"

Keith said, "I haven't been able to think about anything else."

"Any ideas?"

"Well, first thing, I'm going to buy my mother a condo in Florida. Right on the beach. Get her out of that seniors' slum. She's eighty-six, but still sharp as a tack. Then I'm going to look after my gang. I've got two brothers and a sister, worked hard all their lives. There's more than enough for all of us."

Bernie undid his seatbelt and shifted, glancing over his shoulder at Keith. "I hear you, but you're missing my point. I'm talking about you. What are you gonna do for yourself? You know, with the big money?" He looked back at the road, easing the limo into a long curve.

Keith said, "Well, after Christmas, I thought I'd take my little girl here on a trip," and winked at Kate. "Someplace warm."

Kate gave a little squeal. "Oh, Dad, could we? I know just the place. I saw it on *Lifestyles* the other night. Harbor Island in the Bahamas. Tom Hanks vacations there sometimes. It's a tiny island with a mile-long beach of pink sand, and a hotel—Tingum Village, I think it's called—where a neat old gal named Ma Ruby makes the best cheeseburgers in the world. According to Hanks. They showed him taking a huge bite out of one."

Bernie said, "She write his order down?" and Keith laughed.

"Harbor Island it is, then," Keith said.

Bernie said, "Okay, that's short term, but I'm talking about the long haul." He glanced back at them again. "What are you gonna do?"

Keith looked at Kate, and when he spoke it was more to her than to the driver. "My wife and I honeymooned in the South Pacific. We both loved to fish, so we chartered a nice forty-footer and spent the entire two weeks on the water." He gave Kate a warm smile. "It was heaven. So I think that's what I'd like to do. Get a boat, maybe a cozy little beach house someplace—"

Kate's shrieking voice cut off Keith's words.

"Oh God—*look out!*"

An oncoming tandem oil tanker rose out of the December mist like a chrome behemoth, its star-sharp running lights seeming to fade back into the infinite enormity of the thing. In that first instant, as Keith's eyes fixed on the rig, he failed to comprehend Kate's alarm. But with his next frantic eyeblink he saw what was coming.

The trailing tank materialized out of the swirling fog, jackknifing into the limo's lane as it surged inevitably forward, propelling the tonnage ahead of it. The limo was close enough now for its occupants to make out the driver's arms, frantically jockeying the wheel. Kate saw the glowing ember of a cigarette wobble at mouth-level for a beat, then shear away in a cascade of sparks.

"Black ice," Bernie said, his voice as dead as he soon would be.

In his panic he tramped too hard on the brake pedal and the limo became weightless, spinning to its doom in a series of wild donuts. Kate heard her father scream, a sound somehow more chilling than the impending collision, and she reached out for him in the strobing dark. Then a neatly wrapped gift—a steam iron for her aunt Lee—struck her on the forehead, mercifully stunning her.

The limo entered the closing jaws of the tanker trunk-first and bounced off one of its tires. It twirled once, went momentarily airborne, then plowed down the long slope of the ditch into a rock cut, staving in the front end and popping the trunk. Festive packages flew out and littered the ditch. Steam hissed from the crumpled radiator; it also issued from Bernie's skull where he lay on the buckled hood.

The rig left the road on the opposite side and surged up the embankment, the cab turning turtle onto the tanker and becoming an instant inferno. The driver managed to open his door, but the liquid flames found him instantly, transforming him into a human torch. He hit the ditch on his back, rose briefly to his knees then tumbled face-first into the snow, which in the heat of the conflagration above him began to melt so quickly it boiled.

The night resumed its glacial stillness, marred only by the crackle of flames.

2

HEADING SOUTH ON HIGHWAY 69, trailing the Whipples by a bare three minutes, Marty Small grumbled to himself in the drafty cab of his van. The goddam thing was so rust-eaten his ankles sometimes got wet from the roadshit that splashed up through the floor boards. He'd pinched a nice set of rubber mats from a 4-Runner the week before, but some other son of a bitch had stolen them from *him* not two days later.

His trip north had been a total washout. Not only had he picked up barely enough fenceable merchandise to cover his rent—a couple well-used VCRs, a plastic grocery bag full of pennies so goddam heavy it had sprung a leak, leaving a Hansel and Gretel trail of coppers all the way to his van, a couple handfuls of cheap costume jewelry—he'd almost got himself shot in the process. Sonofawhore comes out of nowhere in his Blue Jays pajama bottoms, plinking away at Marty with what sounded like a .22 target pistol. One of the slugs grazed his right ear, frying out a neat little trough, and Marty guessed he'd hear the whine of that hot little sucker 'til he was sixty. The place had been a honey, too. Set out all by itself on a rural road, no vehicles in the driveway and—even more promising at the time—no response to the five minutes Marty spent leaning on the doorbell, practicing the line he'd use should someone appear: "I hope you'll excuse the late hour, friend, but did a little guy about this tall come by here earlier selling chocolate-coated almonds for a school trip? See, he's my son and he hasn't come home yet..." He'd gone in through a basement window—unlocked—and started stuffing a pillowcase full of quality shit that would have made the whole fucked-over trip worthwhile. He'd been working with the crowbar on a fancy set of locked cabinets when the tubby prick came around the corner from the staircase howling, "My records!" and started blasting away with the .22.

Fucking records. Marty caught a glimpse of them before hauling his empty-handed ass back out through the window into the hip-deep snow of the nearby woods: precise rows of individually sleeved 78s. Good for nothing but maybe skeet shooting for the legally blind.

Marty cursed. His ear ached, his feet were frozen stiff, and when he caught up to Ziggy, the numbnuts who'd convinced him to head north in the first place—"Go up to Sudbury, man. I was there two weeks ago and scored big. Half of 'em don't lock shit and they're so fuckin' country a guy's neighbor helped me load the guy's entire rec-room into my truck"—he was gonna kill the bum.

Orange light flared in the near distance, a high pulsing corona that lit up the low cloud cover.

"What the...?"

Marty rounded a curve and was confronted by a glimpse of hell, black smoke roiling out of spiraling flames, reminding him of an IMAX film he'd seen called *The Fires of Kuwait*. Looked like a goddam double-decker oil tanker. The heat was so intense that as he rolled up on it, even through the closed window, he started to sweat. He let out a gasp when he spotted the driver's cremated remains lying face-down in the ditch, which had begun to run with snow-melt.

Marty accelerated past the holocaust and saw the limo marooned in the ditch, rear deck canted up, chrome flashing back in the glare of the van's single headlight. He pulled onto the shoulder and got out, following the beam of a balky flashlight he'd boosted from an usher at a Toronto multiplex. After checking for oncoming vehicles and seeing none, he started down the slope, following the deep ruts left by the limo.

The first thing he noticed was the sprung trunk and the litter of gifts. Premium stuff, judging by the wrapping paper. When he reached the limo itself, he tried without success to peer in through the tinted windows. He moved next to the driver's door and gave the handle a tug—jammed—then in the jittery flashbeam saw the driver out on the hood, obviously dead.

"Seat belt, Gulliver," Marty said, transfixed by the spectacle of the guy's split skull. In the bob of the flashbeam something glistened whitely in there. The guy's brains, Marty guessed, swallowing dryly. One thing for sure, he'd never eat oatmeal again.

He backtracked to the rear passenger door and yanked it open. An old guy flopped out backwards into the churned-up snow, face a mask of blood, and Marty took a quick step back from him. He aimed the flashlight into the car's interior, but the cheap thing chose that moment to quit on him. Marty whacked it with the side of his fist, producing only a brief, fading flicker.

"Piece of shit."

He gave his eyes a moment to adjust—the pig roast up the road was throwing off a pretty fair glow—then set the flashlight on the roof and started to drag the old guy out by the lapels. As the man's body cleared the limo his wallet slid out of his overcoat and came to rest under his chin. Marty snapped it up, leaning it toward the firelight, thumbing through the thick sheath of C-notes. He grinned and made the wallet disappear.

From inside the limo came a moan of pain and Marty turned to run, his balls springing up inside him like startled squirrels. Then he caught himself and crept closer, trying to get a look inside. It sounded like a girl.

"You okay in there?"

No answer.

He picked up the flashlight, gave it another swat and was rewarded with a steady beam. He aimed it into the car and saw the girl's face, pale with shock, a single runner of blood coursing from an inch-long gash near the hairline. She was jammed in there pretty good, trapped between her seat and the one in front on her, with what looked like a jeezly-big yellow bird squashed up against her chest.

"Please..." the girl said.

Marty scanned the interior with the flashlight, picking out the scattered heaps of Christmas loot, then returned the beam to the girl's face.

"Okay, sweetheart, listen," he said in his most sincere tone. He started digging the gifts out of the car, stacking them on the snow drift behind him. "I'll just get all this shit off you, then call for help. This baby's got a cell phone, right?"

"My father..."

Marty said, "Hang on," and left her, trekking back to the trunk, gathering up whatever he could find that wasn't obviously ruined. It took about five minutes and as many trips to load all the stuff in the van, Marty's instincts tingling with every plodding step. He'd been lucky so far, the storm keeping traffic off the road, but man, it was time to book.

He made one last run to the limo, turning the light on the girl again, but she was either passed out now or dead. He couldn't see a purse, and after a quick look for a cell phone he tramped around to the hood and rolled the driver onto his side, trying not to focus on that split-cantaloupe head. He found the man's wallet in his hip pocket, forty bucks in there and a couple credit cards. Marty couldn't believe how heavy the guy was for the size of him. Dead weight.

On his way back to the van he wrestled the old guy out of his overcoat and draped it over his own shoulders like a lord. He climbed into the van that way and got the hell out of there.

Marty Small floored it leaving the scene of the accident, a peeling whine coming from the rear tires as the van roared away. The harsh combination of sounds roused Kate from unconsciousness into a haze of disorientation and pain. She reached out in the dark, a grunt coming from deep in her chest as she tried to move and found she couldn't. There was a dense, oily smell of something burning, and for a panicky instant Kate believed she was trapped in a fire. But there were no flames; only the smell and the dark and the brutal cold, snow whipping in through the open door. Every inch of her shivered.

She tried to take stock. Her head hurt where the package struck her, a dull concussive throb, and her chest was painfully constricted, making it difficult to take even a shallow breath. Her right wrist joined the chorus of misery, its voice the clearest, and when Kate held it up in the dark she could just make out its unnatural angle. *Broken.* She put it back down, afraid her sudden nausea at the sight of it would end in vomiting. And the way she was trapped in here—Big Bird's feathery head wedged under her chin, forcing her head back—it was a fair bet that if she started throwing up she would choke to death.

She turned her head as much as she could, trying to find her father. At first she couldn't see him at all, only the gaping door and the snow beyond it, a blanket of dull luminescence out there against the black of the night; then she craned a little more and saw him, just his shoulders and head, lit faintly by the blazing rig. His coat was gone and the falling snow had begun to cover his face.

"Dad?" Kate said, surprised at how weak her voice sounded; she'd intended to shout. "Dad," she said again, more forcefully this time. But Keith didn't move. She looked in the front seat and saw Bernie's legs dangling in through the shattered windshield.

Panic reared like a dark stallion. She turned to her father again, calling his name, getting no response. She'd never seen him so still, even in sleep, and where was his coat? He was going to freeze to death out there…if he wasn't already dead.

Kate began to struggle against the mangled seats, grunting and heaving, trying to collect enough breath to scream her father's name. But it was pointless, and when a flock of red dots swarmed through her vision, signaling a blackout, she stopped. Her breath came in painful little jabs now, her racing heart seeming lodged in her throat.

A fleeting hope came to her then. Hadn't someone just been here? Talking to her? Yes, she was sure of it.

But her head was so foggy…

She held her breath and listened, five seconds, ten, hearing only the low moan of the wind and more faintly, the roar and crackle of flames.

Maybe he's gone for help, she thought. If he lived around here he'd know exactly where they were. He must have gone for help.

Kate's mind reeled. Her father was alone out there and she couldn't remember...

The phone!

The idea struck her with an almost physical force. Her left arm was free and she sent it out blindly across the plush upholstery, numb fingers picking over jewels of glass, one of her dad's new Isotoner gloves—and there it was, dangling from its cord at the limit of her reach. She hooked her baby finger around the last coil before the handset, fished it in close enough to grab and raised it to the level of her eyes. In the dark she couldn't make out the details of the keypad, but with a little trial and error she found the power button, pressed it and the keys lit up dully. Kate thought she'd never seen a more beautiful sight.

Clumsily, using her thumb, she punched in 911.

It rang. Kate pressed it to her ear, already stinging from the cold.

"Nine-one-one emergency," the dispatcher's voice said.

Tears welled in Kate's eyes. "We've had an accident..."

"Is anyone seriously hurt?"

"Yes..." She could feel herself fading and bit down hard on her lip.

"Ma'am, what is your location?"

"I'm not sure. We were on our way to Toronto..."

"Can you think of any landmarks you might have passed?"

"A restaurant...five or ten minutes back. There was a neon sign. A pig, I think...a big pink pig..."

"Porky's," the dispatcher said. "I know it. Hold tight..."

The dispatcher's voice broke up and disappeared. Kate looked at the handset, the keypad black again. She found the power button and pressed it; the keys flickered with green light and then died. She tried it again and got nothing.

Shivering, she set the phone on the seat beside her and huddled into Big Bird's feathery breast, wishing she'd left her coat on. She was afraid they were both going to die out here.

There was a voice then, a ghostly whisper...

"Katie?"

"Dad? Are you all right?"

"I dreamt I was with your mom..." Kate had to strain to hear him. "Are you okay, sweetheart?"

"Yeah, I think so, but I'm stuck. Can you move?"

She heard him grunt softly, then sigh. "Nope. Old legs don't want to work."

"That's okay," Kate said, flashing on an image of him strapped in a wheelchair. She shook it off, saying, "I called nine-one-one, the lady said she knows where we are. She's sending help; it shouldn't be long now. Are you in pain?"

"Not so bad..." His voice fading. "Just...cold..."

"Tell me about the dream," Kate said, wanting to keep him talking.

"It was about when we met...your mom and I. Nothing really. Stuff you already know."

"Tell me anyway. To pass the time. Pretend I don't know."

There was a silence, Kate ready to break it, when Keith said, "Pretend you don't know?"

"Sure, it'll be fun."

Keith said, "Okay," and Kate craned her neck to see him, lying motionless out there in the snow, his words coming out on faint puffs of frost. "I was nineteen that year, summer of fifty-seven...fresh out of Garson High and I was gonna be a star." He gave a pained little chuckle. "There were five of us: Dave Danylchuk, Pete Aube—you met Pete once, remember?"—Kate said she did—"Mike O'Connor, Dan Ring and I. Called ourselves the Eighty-Eights, after Dan's old Rocket Eighty-Eight. Dan sang bass, which was funny, considering he weighed about ninety pounds, that big voice coming out of him. We'd worked up a real sizzler, 'I Wonder Why' by Dion and the Belmonts, and we were nervous as hell. So far we'd only sung in the stairwells at school. Sounded great in there with the echo..."

"Dad?"

"Yeah, I'm here, sweetie. Just remembering. We had that whole J.D. look going. Pompadours slick with Brylcreem, white T-shirts with the deck of smokes rolled into the sleeve, you know. Black jeans, those big old engineer boots. We came on after the pig calling contest at the Saint Michael's church social. Talk about a tough act to follow."

Kate snickered. Her father could always make her laugh.

"Your mom confessed to me later she'd had her eye on me the whole evening. Thank God we didn't meet 'til after the song or I'd've never got through it, knowing she was watching...so beautiful..."

He groaned then, a sound of deep pain, and when he spoke again his voice was dead serious, a tone Kate had never heard him use before.

"Kate, I want you to know how much I love you. What a privilege it's been to be your father."

"Dad, please, you're scaring me."

"I've thanked God every day since you were born for giving me the job. I only wish I could've done better. Given you more..."

Kate's eyes stung with tears that ran cold on her face. "Dad, I love you too, but why don't we talk about this later, okay? Tell me more about mom. Dad?

"Dad!"

Kate's 911 call was dispatched to Ontario Provincial Police cruiser 301, the closest unit to the presumed scene. The senior officer in the cruiser, O.P.P. Sergeant Mitch Buchanan, took the call from the driver's seat. The dispatcher played back the garbled message for him and after hearing it, Mitch agreed with her estimation of the caller's location.

Mitch's partner and trainee, Constable Steve Seger, shrank inside when he heard the dispatch. He'd been hoping they were done for the night. They were already three hours into overtime and he was exhausted. They'd just left the scene of the young rookie's first fatal accident, and Steve had performed miserably. It left him wondering whether he was cut out for the job, despite his life-long ambition to take the oath.

Mitch replaced the radio handset, switched on the roof lights and pulled a U-ie. Glancing at Steve, he said, "That's about a ten minute ride from here, chum. This might be a good time to talk about it."

"There's not much to say," Steve said. "I lost it."

"Well, if it's any consolation, I know how you feel."

Steve said nothing. Mitch was a twenty-year veteran of the force and Steve's supervising officer during his probationary year, now almost half over. Steve felt about two inches tall sitting next to the man.

"Look," Mitch said, "all I'm saying is, go easy on yourself. After tonight you've got what, two weeks off? So go home, get drunk a few times. Let it go."

"I appreciate what you're saying, Mitch, and it makes sense. I just don't feel up to talking about it right now."

"That's fine. And if you decide you want to sit this one out..."

"I'm not sitting anything out."

"Fair enough," Mitch said.

They drove in silence for a while after that, Steve grateful to Mitch for not pushing it. It'd be a brief reprieve at best, he knew, only a matter of time before the customary ribbing began. He'd seen it around the locker rooms already, the more experienced guys riding the rookies—and God help him when his mother, a decorated eighteen-year veteran of the Toronto Metro force, got wind of it. He knew he could take it when the time came...but right now he needed a breather.

He hunched forward in his seat and covered his eyes with his hands, trying to erase images he knew were indelible. Three hours earlier those images had not existed. Three hours earlier they'd been sitting in the Taco Bell in Barrie, arguing hockey, when a call came in on Mitch's repeater: a major accident on Route 7, a rural road twenty minutes north of their location. Somehow in the five months Steve had been partnered with Mitch they'd managed to miss all the really bad ones, either off duty at the time or involved in something else and unable to respond. Steve had heard some of the horror stories, though, told in hushed tones over coffee in the common room, and at the back of his mind that whole time had been the nagging question: When the time comes, am I gonna be able to hack it? Tonight he had found out.

Mitch had taken the call, responding with a coolness Steve now wondered if he'd ever possess, and a minute later they were in the game, Mitch pushing the beefed-up Caprice as hard as the road conditions would allow.

"Relax, chum," Mitch had told him. "We've talked about this a dozen times, both knew it was coming. I've done a hundred of these. Nobody likes 'em, but when you're in the middle of it the training kicks in. You'll do what needs to be done."

"I just wish I hadn't eaten that burrito," Steve said, pressing a thumb into his solar plexus. "It's sitting in there like a hot coal."

Mitch chuckled. "Told you to go with the clubhouse."

They sped east along Route 7 through farm country, coming onto the scene at the crest of a steep grade, the cruiser's high beams illuminating a scene of awesome destruction. Multiple vehicles—three cars, the shredded remains of a minivan and what looked like a five-ton Rider moving truck—tangled and strung across the highway, one of the cars lying on its roof in a nearby field, another leaning half in and half out of the five-ton's ruptured box, the third buried deep in the minivan's rear end.

"First thing," Mitch said, slowing the cruiser to a crawl, "we gotta get some flares planted around here." Then he hit the brakes hard, a coatless woman stumbling onto the road in front of them. She glanced at them zombie-like, eyes shock-white through a mask of blood, before wading into the ditch on the opposite side of the road. Mitch slammed the cruiser into PARK and went after her, shouting back to Steve, telling him to get busy with the flares.

Steve got out and did as he was told, a shudder running through him as he lit the first flare and drove it into the snow. He did not want to see what was inside those twisted vehicles.

"My baby!"

Steve spun toward the woman's cry and saw Mitch stamping toward her through hip-deep snow. In the twitch of Mitch's flashbeam Steve saw her reach for something in the snow...a rattle, a pink baby rattle clutched in her fist—

"MY BABY!" she shrieked again and now Mitch was there, bearing her up like a groom about to carry his bride across the threshold. The rattle fell from the woman's hand and Steve began to shiver. He couldn't stop himself.

"Steve," Mitch shouted, already winded. "Check the vehicles for survivors!"

Steve sparked another flare and held it out in front of him, rushing red light casting ragged shadows over the wreckage. He ran to the nearest vehicle, the minivan, ruptured like a party favor from its impact with the five-ton, and peered inside. A beer-bellied man sat draped over the wheel, a CB radio handset in his lap. Steve thought: Must be the guy who called it in. His face was turned away and at first glance Steve thought he didn't look all that bad. Then he realized the steering wheel and the driver's seat were maybe eight inches apart, the man's chest compressed to a third its normal thickness. He looked in back and saw a blond woman impaled on a jag of hard plastic from the front end of the Honda that had plowed through the rear door and come to rest against the back of her seat.

Steve said, "Jesus," and the blond woman opened her eyes and screamed. Steve backed away from the vehicle and stumbled over something in the snow; in the light of the flare he saw what it was, a boy of no more than six, ready for bed in his Spiderman pjs...

Steve's stomach bucked and he shrank away from the child, dropping the flare, the burrito coming up his throat in a gagging bolus. He damned himself in the vilest terms, hunched there in his sickness, cursing his cowardice in the face of duty, vowing to turn in his badge that very night.

Then Mitch was there, leading him away. A team of paramedics rushed past them and Steve thought he'd never been more relieved to see anyone in his life. He hadn't even heard them arrive.

"It's okay, partner," Mitch said, clapping him on the back. "I barfed on my first bad one, too." He led Steve to the cruiser and helped him inside. "You sit tight. Five minutes there'll be more cops around here'n you can shake a stick at. I'll get 'er wrapped up, then we'll go get some coffee."

Trembling like a child, Steve huddled in the cruiser and watched as other teams arrived and the survivors were extracted from the wreckage.

He'd never felt more ashamed...

But now, heading out on this new dispatch, feeling the adrenaline surge, the knee-jerk notion of giving up his badge was already fading. He'd wanted to be a cop for as long as he could remember. The day the call had come from the academy had been the proudest day of his life. Even now, almost a year later, each time he put on the uniform it felt like that first time, alone in the eight-by-ten dorm room they called a pod, slipping the dark blue shirt with the gold shoulder insignias out of the tailor's bag, and the matching cargo pants with the pockets for his gear, pulling them on next to his skin. Sinking his feet into those big insulated Prospector work boots, spit shined and snug, making him feel a foot taller than he was. Then the nylon web belt that held his hardware, a working cop's tools. The repeater radio, a heavy job with a mouthpiece that clipped to his lapel, a big Maglite flashlight that doubled as a club, a twenty-three inch expandable baton and a canister of pepper spray, nasty stuff. And the real deal, a .40 caliber Sig Sauer semi-auto, twelve in the clip, one in the pipe, two extra mags for a total of thirty-seven rounds. What a feeling, like being a kid again but with a clear sense of the responsibility he now carried. And the training, not like work at all, but day after day of challenge and personal enrichment. He'd excelled beyond his expectations, discovering natural talents in marksmanship, pursuit driving and use of force. He'd finished with honors near the top of his class and made friends he believed he'd have for the rest of his life.

Yeah, it might take a while, but he would take what happened tonight in stride.

Breaking the silence, Mitch said, "Oh, shit," and pointed across a field bordered by a forested rise. There, just visible above the tree line, orange light flickered against the night sky.

Steve said, "What is it?"

"Looks like a fire," Mitch said. "A big one." He flicked on the siren. "Better call it in."

Steve did as he was told.

Kate was in her mother's arms, shivery with fear, a high crowing sound coming from her throat, and over it, her mother's voice in her four-year-old ear. "It's okay, honey, everything's going to be fine. Just breathe in the steam." They were in the bathroom, the hot taps roaring in the sink and tub, her mother's cool skin pressed against her own and they were rocking, rocking, and the steam was reaching inside, coaxing open the hole, allowing her to breathe...

"Mom," Kate moaned. "Oh, Mom..."

Now she was standing in the sunlight in her Sunday best, a pretty blond girl of six-and-a-half, the weight of her father's hand on one slender shoulder, the bony curve of her aunt Lee's hip against the other. There was a carpet of grass, fake grass humped over a mound of raw earth, and a shiny wooden box sinking into a hole with neatly-squared walls. Her mother was in that box, and when Kate leaned forward to see how deep the hole was she saw her own small face reflected down there in a puddle of standing water. As the box sank deeper and the priest's voice chanted incomprehensibly, Kate felt something slam shut inside her...

Kate gasped, catching her head as it drifted back, trying to shake off the almost euphoric numbness that had come over her, this seductive detachment that had the scent of death to it. It was like dreaming only more vivid, an eerie, image-filled calm that seemed to free her, the cold no longer reaching her, fear melting away. Even now, fighting it, it seemed easier to just let it come...

Kate shook her head, filling her lungs with winter air, inducing a brief spasm of coughing that brought water to her eyes. She called out to her father again, wondering in the damnable silence how much time had gone by, if the ambulance was on its way or had she dreamt that, too? Imagined it in this strange, enveloping fog? She picked up the phone again, stabbed the power button, but the thing was dead.

Death. She'd been thinking of Aunt Lee—the memory so vivid—feeling the slickness of her aunt's funeral dress against her bare arm, smelling her sachet over the damp aroma of cut grass and freshly spaded earth. Seeing the sun reflected in the polished mahogany of her mother's casket, an intense smudge of light, painful to look at.

She raised her uninjured hand to probe the gash at her hairline, the hard crust of blood, frozen before it got a chance to congeal. She pressed her thumb into it, hoping for a bright flare of pain, anything to snap her out of it. But there was only numbness followed by a faint trickle of warmth, the wound starting to bleed again.

Aunt Lee had been a rock during those trying days, leaving her own family to fend for themselves while Kate and her dad made those first reluctant adjustments to her mother's death. Soaking Kate's tears into her blouse, sitting with her in silence, cramped into Kate's tree house in the oak tree behind the house, where she chose to do her grieving, surrounded by artifacts of a life that had included her mother: a stack of her favorite photographs bound with elastics; one of her mother's cameras, an old Leica she'd once told Kate was magic; a tiny phial of perfume; the lacy garter with the single stitched rose Keith had peeled from her thigh on their wedding night. Lee telling her to hold her mother inside now, laying her palm against Kate's thin chest: "In here, sweetheart. Forever." And for a long time, years, she'd managed to do that, hold her mother inside, conjuring her image easily, her memory. But in time this ability faded, until one morning in her early teens, after skinning her back on the door to the tree house that had once fit her so well, she found that when she closed her eyes she saw only darkness. And from that day on, despite a vivid imagination, to summon her mother's image she had to look at a photograph.

Not now, though. Now, she could see everything so clearly...

Gord, the first boy she'd ever slept with, saying the words he'd spoken to her five years before with tears in his eyes, and as she heard them now she finally understood what had slammed shut inside her as she stood by her mother's grave.

"You won't let me in, Kate. You want to, I know you do, but then you run to your stories and I'm left out in the cold..."

Cold...so cold...

"Dad?" Kate murmured, head drifting back again. "Dad?"

The reels for the movie *Aliens 3* arrived at the Grande Theater three days ahead of its release date and when her father mentioned it to her that night Kate begged him for a private screening. They'd done it before, just the two of them, munching leftover popcorn from the concession machines and sipping canned cokes, watching movies 'til sun up. It was her fourteenth birthday and she could think of no better gift. Without much coaxing Keith agreed, smuggling Kate and three of her friends in after hours. Kate screamed when the first alien appeared, and when they got home that night she began her first screenplay, *It Came From The Planet Zemuron*, a wild epic she finished a month later, a hundred pages of gore and cheesy dialogue. It was the proudest accomplishment of her young life.

She flashed again on Gord, her high school sweetheart, the reluctant tears in his eyes, then saw Jamie, the only other man she'd slept with, walking away from her for the last time two years ago, his disenchanted words ringing in her ears. "You don't love me, Kate. You don't know how..."

Tears rolled down Kate's cheeks as a strange, ululating cry intruded on the spell, dragging her back to the dark and the cold and the fear. She was going to die out here with her father and an awful wave of regret swept over her at the realization. She had squandered her passion on words, closed off her heart to everyone but her father, and now...

Kate's ears sharpened. *That sound—*

It was a siren.

Ten miles down the road Marty Small pulled the van onto the shoulder and put it in PARK, his head starting to ache from squinting into the storm. He shrugged out of Keith's overcoat, climbed into the back and started opening packages—carefully, peeling back the tape on the folded ends, trying to figure out what each one contained without messing up the flashy wrapping paper. If all went as planned, he wanted Earlene to have that pleasure.

He opened the biggest one first and found a shiny new espresso machine. In the dull glow of the ceiling light it looked like the real thing, one of those snappy restaurant models with the hood ornament on top. That was great. Earlene loved shit like that. The next one turned out to be a steam iron. Bummer. And there was blood on the wrapping paper. Marty tucked this one aside. He'd give it to his mother. The next five or six were toys. Maybe he'd drop them by his old church, get a novena or something. There was a bunch of stuff in clothing boxes with names like Satin 'n Lace, Sears and The Gap. With any luck some of it'd fit Earlene. Not that it mattered. There was a slew of other great merchandise—gold chains, watches, diamond earrings, perfumes, some nifty kitchen appliances, a stereo amplifier and a fourteen-inch Sony color TV. He found a CD Walkman with a bunch of fairly cool CDs—Eric Clapton, Smashing Pumpkins, Blues Travelers, a collection of Christmas Favorites—and decided to keep these for himself, struggling a good five minutes to get the batteries in right. There were a dozen or so other things, but he didn't have to open all of them to know he'd struck it rich. If this didn't get Earlene on her back, nothing would.

Problem was, the girl could be a bitch. Marty had bedded her only the once, three months ago—on the couch in her living room, against the fridge, in the shower, you name it—Earlene in complete control, finally making him come with his ass against the cold hardwood floor in the hallway. Man, he still couldn't get that night out of his head. Earlene knew tricks Marty'd never even seen in the triple-X features he sometimes rented from the adult video outlet down the block from his Spadina Avenue apartment. He'd enticed her that night with a combination of pharmaceutical-grade cocaine he'd ripped off from a dental surgeon's office and three bottles of vintage wine he'd scoffed from some fat cat's wine cellar. Earlene'd had a glow on already, and once Marty got a few lines of blow into her she'd softened right up. Jesus, what a night. What a *fucking* night. But when Marty turned up a few days later looking for more, Earlene had cut him off at the ankles. "Think of it as a charity fuck, Marty. I don't think I could get that stoned again."

That had stung, but after a while Marty believed he understood. It was just her way. Earlene was tough, hardcore, just trying to protect herself. The kind of work she did, it didn't make sense to get close to anyone.

But Marty wanted her. He just needed to show her he could provide, and that what she did for a living, should she choose to continue, was entirely up to her. Cum washed off.

He climbed into the driver's seat and got underway, his conscience nagging him now, spoiling his fantasies of Earlene. He couldn't help wondering if the girl in the limo was still alive. Ripping them off was one thing—it was what he did—but walking away and letting one of them die...well, he was a thief, not a killer. True, he'd had a look for a phone, but not a very good one. Must've been the adrenaline clouding his judgment. He'd always resented rich bitches like them, born with a silver spoon up their ass while his own life was a steady grind, worrying where his next score was coming from, whether or not he was going to get his balls shot off—like last night—trying to make it and, on the few occasions he'd done time, sweating over how long it'd be before the yard-ape he was celled with tried to cop his cherry. Robbing the rich had always made him feel like a kind of folk hero, a modern day Robin

Hood hip enough to say, fuck the poor, man, I'm keepin' this shit for myself.

But he was no killer.

Marty decided the next joint he saw, he'd stop and call it in. Dial 911. He just wanted to put a little more distance between himself and the limo. That's all.

The first place he saw—

A circus of flashing lights appeared in the near distance, bearing down on him fast. *Cops!* Marty's first instinct was to flee, but he was locked in. Best to just play it cool.

He drove on, hunched low in his seat, the cruiser closing the distance fast and then blowing by, trailing a parachute of snow. Marty tracked it in his sideview until it disappeared. Two minutes later another light show materialized into an ambulance.

So somebody'd called it in already. Good. One less thing to worry about.

At ease now, Marty strapped on the Walkman headphones, slipped in the Christmas Favorites CD and began to sing along with the first selection, his raspy smoker's voice so far off key old Bing was probably rolling over in his grave.

"Here comes Santa Claus, here comes Santa Claus, right up Earlene's lane..."

They saw it as they rounded the curve where the rig lost control, the blaze reaching up from the ruptured tanker to the branches of overarching trees, igniting them into torches of yellow flame.

"Jesus," Mitch said, touching the brakes. The rear deck slewed on the ice and Mitch corrected for the skid, slowing the cruiser to a crawl. He came abreast of the limo and stopped, leaving the cruiser in gear.

"Check the limo," he said to Steve. "I'll take the rig."

Steve got out and strode to the trunk, determined to stay cool this time. At the last scene he'd gotten out of the cruiser after a while to lend a hand, cold and weak as a baby, but by then the important stuff had been done, nothing left but the clean up. No one said anything to him about it, but he felt their eyes on him, saw a few stifled smirks. He never wanted to feel that way again.

He dug out some foil shock blankets and flares and slammed the trunk shut, watching as the cruiser took off toward the tanker, five hundred yards further on. He paused a moment, the stench of burning oil sharp in his nostrils, then triggered a flare and drove it into the drift at the side of the road.

He approached the limo from its front end, following his flashbeam into the ditch. He checked the driver first, sprawled face down on the hood, but the guy was obviously deceased; frost had begun to crystallize on the exposed contents of his skull. Steve looked away quickly, his stomach doing a threatening little flip-flop, but then he made himself look until the shock of it subsided. He noticed Marty's footprints in the snow and assumed the silver-haired man lying on the ground had wandered around stunned for a while before keeling over dead or unconscious. Steve bent over the body and checked for a pulse, surprised to find it palpable, faint and irregular. The man's skin felt like refrigerated meat. Steve threw a couple of blankets over him then aimed his flashlight into the limo.

He saw a girl in there, pale and motionless in the flashbeam, and he leaned inside, knocking his cap off on the doorjamb. He pressed a finger to her neck and she opened her eyes. Startled, Steve shrank back from her, bumping his head on the plush ceiling. The girl blinked up at him, semi-conscious, her voice a dreamy whisper:

"Am I dead...? Are you an angel?"

"You're not dead," Steve said with a nervous chuckle. He snugged the remaining blankets around her, glad to have something to do. "And I'm no angel. I'm a police officer."

The girl managed a wan smile. In the same instant she reached up and touched Steve's face, as if to verify his reality. Her touch sent a chill through him and Steve found himself absurdly embarrassed, unable to meet her gaze.

She took her hand away, trying to look past him now at the man in the snow. "What about my dad?" she said.

"He's alive," Steve said, "and there's an ambulance on its way."

"Thank God," the girl said, her eyes drifting out of focus. "Thank God..."

Mitch stuck his head in next to Steve's. "Rig jockey's dead."

Steve said, "The limo driver, too."

The ambulance could be heard in the distance now, a dismal wail, approaching fast.

"Here we go," Mitch said, leaving to greet the paramedics.

"It's the ambulance," Steve said to the girl. "It's almost over now." He started to back away but she caught him by the sleeve, cold fingers finding his hand, holding on tight.

"Don't leave..."

"Okay," Steve said, feeling strangely at peace. He began stroking her forehead, calming her. "I'll wait here with you."

They got the girl organized first, freeing her from the wreckage, then loading her into the ambulance in a cocoon of blankets, a sling on her fractured arm and a collar around her neck. Steve found her ski jacket and leather handbag in the limo and brought them to her in the ambulance, sitting with her while the paramedics readied her father for transport: starting IVs, applying a cervical collar and splints to his broken legs. In spite of the morphine they'd given her, she didn't seem to want to let go of his hand. Steve didn't mind. His heart went out to her. She must have been terrified out here in the cold, wondering if her dad was dead and whether she was going to end up the same way. It was a good thing she'd managed to call it in herself because the highway had been closed for the past hour. The tanker and the limo must have been the last vehicles to make it through before the barricades went up.

And that van with the bum headlight, Steve thought.

One of the paramedics climbed into the front seat, startling Steve. She got something out of the glovebox, then simply sat there, blowing warm air into her cupped hands. In the stark light of the cab Steve thought she looked a little anemic. He asked her how long she'd been doing the job.

"That obvious, huh? I'm a second year student."

Steve said, "Rough night?" and the girl nodded. He said, "I know how you feel."

She unwrapped the bar of chocolate she'd taken from the glovebox and took a big bite. "We haven't had time to eat, I got dizzy..."

"Take it from me," Steve said, "you're better off with an empty stomach." He glanced at the girl on the stretcher, sleeping soundly now. He said, "So what's the plan for these folks?"

"We're gonna meet the air ambulance in Barrie. From there they're gonna airlift them to Toronto."

"Whereabouts in Toronto?"

The paramedic said, "North York Trauma," and Steve said, "Yeah? I live about ten minutes from there," but the girl was gone.

He looked out the rear doors and saw her run to help the other two hoist the stretcher out of the ditch. Gently, he disengaged his hand from the girl's. It was time to get out of the way. He started for the open doors.

"Thanks..." the girl said, the word almost inaudible.

Steve hopped to the ground and looked back at her, giving her a boyish grin. "Good luck, ma'am," was all he could think of to say.

The paramedics slid her father's stretcher in next to hers and hopped aboard.

She said, "It's Kate—" but the big doors closed on her words.

Steve thought, *Kate*, then stood watching as the ambulance rolled away, dome lights flashing in the freshening squall.

3

FOR KATE THE TRIP to the trauma center was a surreal blur. Superimposed on a mild concussion, the morphine they'd given her tipped her into a restless twilight, punctuated at intervals by hallucinations. During the transfer from the ambulance to the waiting helicopter she roused briefly in the scouring wind and thought one of the paramedics was the police officer who'd held her hand in the limo; Kate grinned at him shamelessly and told him he should call her sometime, even recited her phone number. Later in the air, she became convinced Tom Cruise had optioned one of her screenplays and began to fret over what she'd serve him when he came over that night for dinner. During one giddy episode she got the crazy idea that she and her dad were millionaires, but the notion was shattered by a sudden flurry of activity around her father, whom she caught only glimpses of stretched out beside her, looking so still under a green oxygen mask. "Where are we?" she said, and heard a strange voice bark in alarm, "Hand me an airway!" People in orange jumpsuits surrounded her father then, obscuring her view, and her last awareness before a curtain was drawn and she slipped into the twilight again was of that same frantic voice: "Get me some atropine over here!" Twenty minutes before the chopper touched down on the trauma center helipad she thrust herself against her restraints and began sobbing in a child's voice, "The Grinch stole all our gifts..."

Later, as the morphine began to wear off and the pain reawakened, Kate's impressions became more solid. They'd had an accident, she remembered that, and her father had been badly hurt. She tried to ask someone about him but things were happening so quickly now, silent men whisking her out of the helicopter in a tight bundle of blankets, the brisk stretcher ride to the ER, someone asking her about drug allergies then a doctor saying, "Let me know if this hurts too much."

Then her own voice screaming, the sound seeming to rip itself from her throat as the doctor yanked on her broken arm.

"Better sedate her..." were the last words she heard.

Marty Small crawled into the city at midnight. By that time the storm had reached full throttle, a drop in temperature turning the wet flakes into icy shrapnel, high winds buffing the roads into skating rinks. Driving was a nightmare, every asshole and his cousin out on the roads, and for the hundredth time Marty cursed his piece-of-shit van. The defroster couldn't keep up, so he had to lean out at every stoplight and scrape a peephole in the rippled sheet of ice that crusted the windshield. When he finally pulled up in front of the Fantasia Club, he was fried.

There were a couple of creeps Marty recognized standing in the club's recessed doorway. He'd seen them around the strip before, a pair of dreadlocks-wearing white boys, smoking reefer and freezing their asses off with style, shifting from foot to foot with a kind of fogged-out reggae rhythm. They were thieves, Marty knew, and before leaving the van he threw a blanket over his loot. They were probably the dinks who jacked his floor mats.

He got out, locked the van and headed inside, trying to look as bad as he could for the criminals in the doorway.

As usual the Fantasia was hoppin'. The place was classic sleaze: blaring, ass-grinding music; a haze of smoke so thick you needed a seeing-eye dog to find the shitter; a stable of lap dancers making the rounds, half of them green enough for the senior prom; a red-carpeted runway featuring a smeared brass fuck-pole that saw more snatch in a week than Marty'd seen in his entire life; and completing the picture, row upon row of gawking shitfaces, sucking back beers and adjusting their hard-ons. No shortage of degenerates in the big city.

Though Marty was a regular, he didn't see himself in that light. Earlene worked here, and as soon as he managed to convince her to come crib with him, he could give a shit if the place burned to the ground. Except for Dane, of course. Dane was the bartender and Marty had a special relationship with him. The supply and demand kind.

Before straying from the doorway Marty scanned the crowd. There were a couple of hardcases he owed money to and there was no way he wanted to run into one of them tonight. Not that the shitbirds scared him or backed him down. If push came to shove Marty could be pretty handy with his fists, and he always carried a switchblade, six inches of Brazilian steel he was ready to use. He just didn't feel like parting with any of this score. Not that way. It was lucky money, and he didn't want anything throwing a hex on it before he had a chance to take a run at Earlene.

Satisfied the coast was clear, Marty made his way to the bar.

"Marty Small," Dane said when he spotted him. "The usual?"

"Tonight, my man," Marty said, "make it a triple." He unzipped his jacket and slid onto a stool, glad to be someplace warm.

"My, my," Dane said, dipping two big fingers into a pocket on his red silk vest. Dane was a South African giant, six-foot-six-inches of burnished ebony and a smile that dazzled the eyes. "Did Martini finally score?"

Marty smiled. "That he did, Dane. That he did." He watched Dane's hands, trying to see how the man pulled off this next little trick.

Dane drew a draft in a frosted mug and slid it across the bar. Marty paid him with three crisp hundreds from Keith's wallet. Concealing the action with his body, he raised the mug off the bar and palmed the three flat pouches of cocaine tucked underneath.

"Damn, man," he said. "How do you *do* that?"

Dane gave him that smile, all pink gums and polished ivory. "Magic," he said and moved off down the bar.

Sipping his brew, Marty turned to face the room. It took a few moments, but then he spotted her by the far wall, pantomiming a blowjob for a sweaty bald guy having a stag party.

Earlene.

Six blocks south of the Fantasia Club, Detective Sergeant Alister Raybould cruised Yonge Street in an unmarked car, wipers working hard against the weather. He pulled up to the curb next to a bus kiosk, a pair of hookers in there huddled in cheap furs, and powered down his curb-side window. The ladies stepped into view, open for business, their stock fuck-me expressions vanishing the instant they saw who it was in the salt-bleached sedan.

Trisha, a tall black girl in a red wig, stuck her head through the window and did her best to smile. "'Evenin', detective. Just lookin' tonight or buyin'?"

"Keep your trash-mouth shut 'til I tell you to open it," Raybould said. "Where's that cocksucker, Swain?"

"I seen him outside the Strand 'bout an hour ago."

Raybould accelerated away from the curb, almost taking Trisha's head off. "Bitch motherfucker!" she yelled after him, then prayed he hadn't heard.

Swain stood in front of the Strand Hotel, coat hanging open to show a little skin, propositioning a pair of teenage boys who looked like they'd rather beat him to death than sample his favors. He was walking a fine line with these two—a couple of mean looking shave-heads, not sure which way they wanted to go yet—but his last fix was hours behind him. If he didn't score soon he was going to be one sick little puppy.

"I'll give you the kind of blowjob you'll never get from the prom queen," he told them, teeth chattering in the cold. He didn't notice Raybould's car rolling up to the curb behind him or he'd've shut his trap. "How 'bout it, boys?"

"I wouldn't let you suck my dog's dick," one of the kids said, then high-fived his friend.

Raybould gave a short blast on the siren and the teenagers pulled a quick fade. Knowing better, Swain buttoned his coat and waited, trying not to betray his fear. The last time this psycho hassled him he ended up with three broken ribs.

Raybould got out of the car fast, put Swain in a wrist lock and slammed him face-down across the hood.

"What's wrong?" Swain said. "What did I do?" Blood leaked from his nose, salty and hot on his lips.

Raybould cuffed him in silence, ratcheting the cuffs on tight around Swain's slender wrists. He pulled Swain up by the scruff of the neck and shoved him into the front seat, then got in behind the wheel and sped away from the hotel.

"What did I do?" Swain said again and Raybould slapped him in the mouth.

"You speak when you're spoken to, Swain. You know the rules. You fucked up this time, boy, so don't gimme any of that 'What did I do?' horseshit. I'm tired of carrying your faggot ass. This time you're going down."

"Please, Detective Raybould," Swain said, tears spoiling his mascara, pulling it down his gaunt face in runny smears. "I can't go to jail. Was it that bitch, Ernesto? I'll never buy smack from him again, I swear—"

Raybould slapped him again. "Speak when you're spoken to. Don't make me tell you again. And quit that weepy shit. You're fucking up my concentration."

Swain did as he was told and within seconds Raybould seemed oblivious of his presence. It didn't take long to figure out they weren't headed for police headquarters, at least not right away, and Swain thought maybe he could squirm out of this yet, with only a few bruises and maybe a quick back-alley favor. He became almost convinced of this when they pulled into the underground lot of a Regent Park apartment complex. The detective just wanted his rocks off.

Raybould wound deep into the multi-level lot, giving Swain the impression he knew exactly where he was headed. He backed into a shadowy corner slot across from an elevator and switched off the ignition. His gaze touched on a sporty champagne-colored Mercedes, parked near the elevator, then shifted to Swain.

"Okay, Swainy, look," he said. "Maybe I was a bit harsh." He motioned for Swain to show him his hands. Swain complied and the cuffs came off. Raybould slipped them into his overcoat pocket. "It's been a long day, and when I saw you hitting on those kids—"

"The little shits were trying to sell me a hot stereo."

Anger flared in Raybould's eyes and Swain shrank against the passenger door, but the detective restrained himself. Swain was certain now he'd have to suck this bully off.

"Like I was saying," Raybould said, "it's been a long day. I'm sorry, okay?"

Swain nodded noncommittally.

"The real reason I looked you up..." He reached into his pocket and came out with a ziplock Baggie of heroin. To Swain it looked pure, at least a half G's worth. His mouth flooded with saliva. "I've got a job for you."

"What kind of job?"

Grinning, Raybould said, "Not what you're thinking." He pressed a finger to Swain's painted lips, smearing them. "Though that is one pretty pie-hole you've got there, Swainy." He tucked the heroin into Swain's clammy palm. "I need you to eyeball somebody for me. Tell me if you've seen him around the clubs. Two minute job, then you walk. And I don't bust your skinny ass. Agreed?"

"I can do that."

Raybould said, "I knew you could," and smiled, a warm smile that made it all the way to those black eyes. Swain even found himself relaxing a little.

He said, "So what do we do now?"

"We wait."

"I have a taste in the meantime? Take the edge off?"

"If it'll keep you sharp."

"As a tack," Swain said, opening the Baggie. He fished his works out of an inside pocket and got busy, cooking up a batch in a well-used spoon, then drawing it up into an insulin syringe through a tiny wad of cotton. Not bothering with a tourniquet, he injected the hit into a track-marked vein at his wrist.

His head drifted back and he sighed.

Raybould said, "You nod on me, Swain, I'll break every bone in your body."

Swain grinned. "I'm fine. Just point the man out."

"He'll be along. Just sit tight."

Swain reached for the radio, saying, "How 'bout some tunes while we're waiting?" and Raybould slapped his hand away.

"Just...sit tight."

They sat in silence for a while, a tense silence, spoiling Swain's buzz. It was like sitting next to a caged animal, the man's gaze fixed on the elevator doors, the air going in and out of him in slow tides, all Swain could hear in the close quarters of the car. The windows were starting to steam up and Swain became aware of his heart, a startled sparrow in his chest. He could hardly breathe. He wanted out of this car, away from this man.

Breaking the silence, Raybould said, "Fucking politics," giving Swain a sideways glance before looking back at the elevator. "It's getting so a cop can't do his job without being treated like a criminal himself. Ten years ago, even five, a clean shoot was a clean shoot. The whole deal was handled internally; we did our own dirty laundry. You showed up at the Coroner's inquest in a suit and tie, you said your piece, next day you were back on the street. Now, fuck, fire your weapon on duty, you've got the Special Investigations Unit all over you, so fast, you're spending the next two years of your life being raked over the coals."

Raybould looked at him again and Swain tried to show some level of interest, some degree of understanding. Raybould shook his head, saying, "What am I talking to you for? Fucking SIU. So far up my ass right now I can hardly breathe. Eight months on light duty, doing call backs, waiting for the ax to fall. Government pricks, sticking their nose in everybody's business. They're all ex-cops, too, if you can believe that. Whatever happened to the fucking code?"

Raybould staring at him now, nostrils flaring, hard eyes searching Swain's like he believed Swain had an answer. Swain just shrugged, praying for whatever this was to end. Why was the man telling him this shit anyway? Swain had no idea what he was talking about.

The elevator opened and a balding guy in an ankle-length coat stepped out carrying a trim leather attaché case.

Raybould said, "There's our mark," no trace of agitation now, totally cool. Like a switch had been thrown. He opened his door to get out. "You're up, Swainy. Move it."

Swain could tell from here he'd never seen the guy, but he decided to play along. The cop had given him quality scag, the least he could do was put on a show.

He got out and followed Raybould, who was intercepting the guy now, showing his badge.

"Nelson Flexner?"

The guy said, "Yes," openly annoyed. "What's this about?" He checked his watch. "I'm on my way to a law review—"

Raybould said, "Look at him, Swain. You ever suck his cock?"

Swain said, "I—" and snapped his mouth shut. Flexner's gray eyes flashed on Swain, then shifted back to Raybould, already narrowed with outrage. An instant before they fixed on the detective, Swain saw Raybould wrap a gloved hand around the man's neck and with the other drive something into his belly, drive it in hard, something that gleamed in the overhead fluorescents. He saw the man fold over Raybould's arm, heard the air go out of him in a brisk expulsion, then saw Raybould lift the man off his feet, the whole time looking into his eyes, foreheads touching, murmuring something to him.

Swain saw blood—a shocking plume of it, soaking Flexner's shirt—and let out a womanly squeal. Flexner slid off the Bowie knife Raybould had filleted him with and sagged to the damp pavement.

"Hold this," Raybould said, holding the knife out to Swain.

Frozen with shock, Swain only whimpered.

"Hold this!" Raybould said again and Swain reached out with a trembling hand and took the knife.

"Why'd you do that?"

Raybould sank to one knee next to the body. Unseen by Swain, he palmed an untraceable .380 Colt semi-auto from an ankle holster and with a sleight-of-hand as slick as any stage magician's produced the gun from inside the dead man's coat. He showed it to Swain.

"This a good enough reason for you? The prick was going to shoot us."

"Who is he?" Swain said.

"That's none of your concern. But listen, sweetheart, maybe you should make yourself scarce. Anybody sees this scene, they're gonna think you killed the man."

"Me...?"

"Yeah, you. Now go. And get rid of that knife. Toss it down a sewer or something. It's got your fingerprints all over it."

Swain hesitated, mincing from foot to foot, holding the murder weapon at arm's length.

"Go!" Raybould said. "I'll try to keep you out of it."

With a last glance at the body, Swain stumbled away.

Raybould lifted the dead man's hand and put the gun into it, poking the index finger into the trigger guard, holding it in place with his own. Hunkering down further, he raised Flexner's arm and sighted the semi-auto on Swain's back.

"Oh, and Swain."

Twenty feet away, Swain stopped and turned.

"You're under arrest."

Raybould put three rounds into Swain's chest, the reports clapping flatly through the underground lot. Swain toppled over, the knife spinning from his grasp.

Raybould lowered Flexner's arm to the wet pavement, leaving the pistol in his hand, then took the lawyer's wallet and attaché case and planted them on Swain. He fished the Baggie of dope out of Swain's pocket and tucked it into his own.

Ninety seconds later he was back on the street, squinting through a fresh snow squall for a corner store. He was out of smokes.

Seated in a chair by the runway, Marty Small tucked a ten into Earlene's outstretched hand and waited for the next song to begin. He hoped it'd be a grinder. Earlene stood between his spread legs and chewed her gum, gaze clicking idly around the bar. If she weren't almost naked, she could be waiting for a bus.

Marty was unfazed. He was biding his time.

The song began and Earlene went into her act, cool and mechanical, dipping her hair into Marty's upturned face, straddling his lap to rub her crotch hard against his, lithe body glistening in the club lights. Marty's cock was already painfully stiff. The rule was no touching the girls and it was all he could do to comply.

Halfway through the song he plunged. "Wanna party later?"

"You bore me, Marty," Earlene said. "Marty Small-time."

She sank to her haunches and began bobbing her head up and down in his lap. Marty looked around to see if anyone was watching. He should've sprung the twenty for a private booth. He could afford it.

When she glanced up at him, teasing, he tucked a folded hundred between her teeth and flashed the coke. "And this ain't the half of it."

Showing some interest now, Earlene slid up his legs into his lap, folding the hundred into her palm.

Marty said, "Know who's lap you're sittin' in?"

"Tell me."

"Santa's. That's Santa's stiff dick you're sittin' on. And I got a van full of Christmas booty with your name on every box."

He let his hand slide to one of her breasts. Earlene slapped it away. But playfully.

The song ended. Earlene hopped off. Considered.

"My place," she said at last. "Two A.M. And if you're jerking my chain, Marty..."

Marty just smiled.

Steve Seger and his partner stood in front of their lockers, Barrie O.P.P. Headquarters, changing into their civvies. The clean up on the limo-tanker accident had drawn them deeper into overtime, four more frozen hours' worth, and Steve had never been so beat.

"Well, Maggie Muggins," Mitch said, "I'd say you had quite a day."

"And then some," Steve said. Lowering his voice he added, "Uh, Mitch, about that burrito..."

Mitch chuckled. "It never happened, okay? You want to come over to the house for a nightcap? I won't be seeing you again for a while."

"If you don't mind I'll take a rain check," Steve said. He cut his eyes away. "I thought I might head down to Toronto tonight, you know..."

Mitch said, "You're gonna drive another hour in this shit?" Then: "Whoa. Hold the phone a minute. The girl, right?" Steve didn't even try to play dumb; he was too tired. Mitch said, "I thought so," and shook his head. "A word to the wise here, okay? Even if she's available, you're only begging for grief. Intense circumstances like these, people start thinking they've got feelings that aren't really there. I've seen it before. If I was you, I'd head back to the dorm tonight. Sleep on it."

Steve said, "I hear you," shooting for casual and failing. "But it's nothing like that. I just want to see how she's doing."

Mitch slammed his locker and shrugged. "It's your ass," he said, starting away. Then he was back, shaking Steve's hand. "Have a nice holiday, chum."

"You, too. And thanks for all your help."

Mitch smiled. "You're all right, kid. If you're looking for a partner when you're done, I'd be proud to team up with you."

Steve felt himself blushing. "Thanks, Mitch."

Mitch nodded and walked away.

Steve stood in the abandoned locker room a few minutes longer, mulling over Mitch's words. Deciding. Then he closed his locker and left.

The bodies of Thomas Swain and Nelson Flexner were found by a member of the building's security staff shortly following the incident. From the available evidence it was assumed by police that Flexner was slain during a botched mugging attempt by Swain, a junkie street fag with a long list of minor drug- and prostitution-related offenses. That Flexner was able to put three slugs into his assailant before dying of his horrendous wound was further testament to the man's toughness. Flexner was a criminal prosecutor and as such, well known to the officers investigating his murder. He showed the same kind of balls in court, going toe to toe with some of the nation's most notorious criminals.

Flexner's wife, Abigail, insisted on seeing his body. A slender, poised woman of forty-six, Abigail flinched visibly at the sight of the knife wound, which she also insisted on observing. When asked, she told the investigating officers that if her husband owned a gun she had no prior knowledge of it. It was assumed, therefore, that

Flexner had somehow gotten the gun away from his assailant, probably during the struggle that must have preceded his stabbing, and killed the wild flake with his own piece.

Exhibiting some of her husband's grit, Abigail proceeded dry-eyed through the entire ordeal and afterward, saw herself out to her car. She'd be fine, she told the female officer who offered to drive her home. She could take care of herself. She left Metro headquarters at one in the morning, wrapped in fur, heels clocking briskly against the damp cement surface of the underground lot. She climbed into her car, a snappy champagne-colored Mercedes, an exact duplicate of her husband's, and at last allowed herself a shudder. Though she was glad it was done, the brutality of it had startled her. She had thought the job would be...cleaner.

She started the car and felt something cold touch her neck.

"Nice wheels," Raybould said, breathing the words into her ear.

He was hunched behind her in the backseat; Abigail could see his image in the rearview mirror. The cold thing against her neck was a Bowie knife—an exact duplicate of the one that had taken her husband's life.

Without moving, Abigail said, "What do you want?"

"I just wanted to know if you were satisfied with the work."

"Did it have to be so...monstrous?"

"Didn't you tell me with your own sweet lips that he was a monster? That he humiliated you? Made you...do things? Threatened to cut you off from the mon-ey?"

"Yes, but..."

Raybould showed her the knife, rotating it slowly before her eyes. "So I gutted the pig coming out of his girlfriend's apartment. The one you said he pays for. I thought you'd be pleased."

"I'm glad it's over," Abigail said. "And you'll get your money, you needn't worry about that. Mister Corsino told me he'd work out the details with you—"

The knife went back to her throat, the cutting edge stinging her skin.

"Don't confuse the issue, Abby. Corsino may have set this up with me on your behalf, but you're dealing with me now. You understand?"

"Yes...I understand."

"Good girl."

The knife was withdrawn. Abigail heard Raybould slide across the seat behind her and get out on the opposite side. Badly rattled, she put the car in reverse, shifting in her seat to back out. In the same instant the front passenger door opened and Raybould got back inside. He closed the door and smiled at her.

"I was thinking, Abby," he said, opening his zipper, "about a little advance."

"You've got to be kidding."

He pulled out his penis. It was rock hard. "I look like I'm kidding?"

"Here? In the police station?"

"Works for me."

Numbly realizing what kind of animal she'd invited into her life, the widow Abigail lowered her head into Raybould's lap and took him in her mouth. She'd had plenty of practice with her husband and his friends.

"Jesus," Raybould said, "I love my work."

This time Marty came into the game with a strategy. He started her off with the coke—nothing put a happy in Earlene's ass like cocaine, especially when those lovely white lines made the trip to her nose through a rolled up C-note—then gave her the espresso machine. The girl nearly freaked. After that he coaxed her into a kind of prefuck party game, a hybrid of strip poker and spin the bottle—spin the gift—the only rule being that whoever was closest to the bow when the box stopped spinning lost an item of clothing. And by nature, Earlene dressed light. He let her rip through about a third of the goodies—the rest he kept locked in the van, planning to dole it out a little at a time—but there was no way he could keep her out of the dope. Earlene loved her nose candy and she knew exactly how much he'd scored. He'd blown that carrot going in. And at the rate she was going, he'd be cleaned out before sunrise.

No problem, Marty thought. Plenty more where that came from.

The final round took place in the bedroom, Earlene so toasted on coke and white wine Marty figured there was no way now he could miss. But with Earlene, you never could tell.

"You got protection?"

"What?"

"Rubbers. Protection."

"Aw, come on, Earlene, I hate 'em. It's like wearin' a raincoat in the shower."

Earlene snaked a hand under her pillow and came up with a cherry-flavored Trojan, ribbed for pleasure. She tossed it at him and it stuck to his chest. Marty peeled it off like it was a leech. "Put a hat on it, *Small*," she said, "or tell your story walking."

Marty grumbled but obeyed. And at last, Earlene was his.

He went at the task with real heart, the coke conspiring with the sensation-dulling rubber to turn him into a tireless stud. And when he finally came, the lights shivered on the miniature Christmas tree that stood on the bedside table.

"Jeez," Earlene said as Marty rolled off her, breathing hard. "That was great." She got up and went into the can, not bothering to shut the door. Marty could hear her tinkling in there.

"You off for a while now?" he said, testing the water. "Holidays and all?"

Earlene flushed the john, raising her voice to say, "I'm on at the club tomorrow night. And I got some appointments, next few days." She was brushing her teeth now, the water in the sink running full blast.

Marty said, "What would it take for you to call in sick and cancel the appointments?"

Earlene appeared in the doorway, still nude and so cool about it, leaning against the jamb with that trimmed bush staring straight at him, a red toothbrush in her hand, toothpaste foam on her lips. She flashed him a smart-ass grin.

"More than you can afford, Small."

"Try me." He wished she'd call him by his first name.

"Five hundred a day, cash money."

Marty did the math in his head. It took a minute. He said, "Four days, okay? Plus blow, plus Christmas every day for four days, plus a partridge in pair of BVDs."

That got a laugh out of her.

Call me Marty, Marty thought, willing it.

Smiling, shaking her head, Earlene said, "I don't mind the easy money, Marty, if that's how you wanna spend it."

Marty grinned and flipped back the covers. "Look who's awake already."

Feeling playful, Earlene climbed aboard.

Later, while she slept, Marty lit a smoke and leaned against the headboard, feeling like the luckiest man alive. Had he any idea what was tucked inside the stolen wallet in his jeans, he might have realized just how close to the truth this was.

When his smoke was done he switched off the lamp and snuggled into Earlene's back, one arm around her waist, breathing her scent. He fell asleep that way, dreaming about the days ahead.

Following a brisk assessment in the ER and a barrage of X-rays and Cat scans, Keith Whipple was rushed to the waiting OR. Apart from a nasty scalp laceration, which was sewn up in the ER, all of his serious injuries were orthopedic. Under normal circumstances, his right femur alone would have been enough to finish him. The mid-shaft fracture was compound, the shattered ends protruding from the flesh like roots spaded from the earth, and Keith would have bled out in under an hour had it not been for the numbing cold. As the surgeons worked to repair his fractures—his left leg was broken, too, as were his pelvis and three of the fingers on his left hand—the anesthesiologist warmed him gradually, using a combination of heating blankets and warm intravenous fluids. Keith had also sustained a non-depressed skull fracture, but since the Cat scan indicated only a moderately severe concussion, it was elected to leave the fracture alone.

He spent five hours under anesthesia before his transfer to ICU, where he was placed on a mechanical ventilator and attached to a bank of sophisticated monitors.

Once her fractured wrist had been set and a short-arm cast applied, Kate was transferred to a private room and left to sleep off the sedation. Her sleep was restless and rife with dreams, grinding, slow motion replays of those few weightless moments in the limo before it slammed into the rock cut. Though Kate would not remember it, a nurse came in every hour to waken her and check her vital signs. During one of those visits a warm hand linked with hers and she opened her eyes. It was the policeman again, the one who had saved her life, and she smiled at him, saying, "It's my angel...."

She had no further dreams after that and no clear awarenesses, until the morning light stung her eyes and the worst headache she'd ever experienced took hold of her consciousness and squeezed.

Three-forty AM, Detective Raybould put his feet up on the coffee table in his third floor apartment and lit a smoke. There was a late-night documentary on the tube, grainy black and white footage of Nazi Germany, and not for the first time he wondered what it must have been like to live and operate in those days. Too easy, he imagined, at least when the Krauts were on top. It would've been a kick for a while, that kind of unchecked power, but he could see himself loosing his edge in a system like that. Getting lazy.

Hitler appeared on the screen, addressing a sea of cheering humanity, and Raybould shut the thing off. Unless he'd been the head Kraut himself, he never would have been able to tolerate all the goose stepping and ass kissing that went with the territory. Pretty much the way police work was headed these days when you thought about it. The past ten years. Fucking SIU, police watchdogs, trying to turn good cops, effective cops like himself into common criminals, and for what? For doing their jobs. It infuriated him every time he thought about it. Cap a crackhead coming at you with a hunting knife, a justifiable use of deadly force in the old days, an hour later you're off the street and under the microscope, dirty until proven otherwise. Four clean shoots back in his Holdup days, they're handing him commendations. Now, one doper punk, the knife in his *hand*, and they're trying to put him away. Calling it manslaughter. The prosecutor calling him a gunslinger, a dinosaur, a fucking menace. It had occurred to him more than once since this pony show began to pay that loud mouth a visit, get him sucking on six inches of stainless Smith & Wesson and see how randy he feels.

The hell of it was, they might actually nail him this time. The hearings weren't going that well, the prosecutor goading him on the stand, making him angry in front of the jury. Bad form. He'd have to watch that.

Jesus, wouldn't that be a cunt? Actually doing time?

"No way," Raybould said into the silence.

He got up and poured himself a bourbon, then settled back on the couch, lighting a fresh cigarette, the butts from the half-dozen others he'd already smoked ranked around the inside curve of the ashtray in his lap, a souvenir from a hotel in Vegas.

He sipped his drink and thought of Constantine "Connie" Corsino. Another thorn in his side. It fascinated him how these old wops operated, that whole mindset. All that shit about honor and respect, meanwhile they're knocking each other off like flies. The way they figured they owned you once you entered their circle, expected you to subscribe to that same almost childlike code. Charming fuckers when they were courting you, though. It still amused him when he thought about it, how easy it had been. Just another line to cross.

The first kiss had come during the Coroner's inquest on his last clean shoot working Holdup, eleven years ago now. A mob under boss he'd capped, the twitchy asshole taking a shot at him during a routine gaming house raid. Raybould had dropped him without hesitation, double-tapping him through the heart, finding out only later the man had been a heavyweight in one of the Hamilton families, looking to get a turf war going with the Corsino clan. Raybould had been sitting near the back of the courtroom that day, his part of it over, when a guy in a dark suit squeezed past him into the aisle, handing him a thick envelope as he passed. "From an associate of mine," the guy said, "in gratitude," and walked away.

Fifty grand' worth of gratitude. Over a year's salary in those days.

A month later on a cold night in February, Raybould off-duty coming out of a favorite steak house, a black Mercedes pulls up to the curb beside him and a goon in an oilskin coat pops out, holding the door open for him. Corsino sitting alone in there, saying, "Get inside, detective, and close the door. It's cold outside."

That easy.

The old man handing him a glass of vermouth as the Mercedes pulled away from the curb, saying, "You got what I gave you?"

Raybould saying, "Yeah, I got it," his mind already made up.

"You keep it?"

"It was a gift, right?"

"Yeah. A gift."

"So I kept it."

Corsino smiling, showing his dentures. "You had enough time to think about it?"

"I thought about it."

"And?"

"It's do-able. Long as you don't expect me to work for that kind of money."

Corsino laughing then, touching Raybould's face with a bony hand, saying to his driver, "I knew I was gonna like this guy."

And it was done.

Nearly a year had gone by before he heard from the old man again, always through a messenger after that first brief meeting, the night he lost his cherry. And until the last couple of years the arrangement had been a good one, Corsino using him for targets he could get close to where others could not, simply by virtue of his badge. The money was good, the wire transfers prompt, the jobs spaced widely enough to deflect suspicion.

But recently the old man's attitude had begun to deteriorate, Corsino treating him like an underling now, using tactless messengers to assign shitty jobs with even shittier pay days, refusing to meet or speak with him, making it known that as far as he was concerned he owned Raybould outright. No more charades. No more pretense of a gentlemen's agreement.

Another fucker that needed a wake-up call, Raybould thought, finishing his drink. Maybe it was time to clean house. Pay the old guinea a visit—the prosecutor, too, what the hell—then retire. He didn't have the kind of money he'd hoped for, but he had the place in Switzerland, and surely in Europe he could find employment. Something specialized. Keep his hand in. It was a soothing thought...

He leaned back on the couch and took a drag off his smoke, his mood reflective. Using the remote, he turned the TV back on and half-watched the documentary, letting his considerable imagination roam free. When his cigarette was finished he tamped it out in the ashtray and lined it up with the others. He placed the ashtray on the coffee table, unholstered his sidearm and lay it in his lap, cocked and locked, where the ashtray had been.

His head drifted back, his eyelids heavy. He would sleep an hour, maybe two, dreamlessly but close to the surface, like a shark cruising for prey. Then he would return to the street.

4

STEVE OPENED HIS EYES, surprised to find the room filled with morning light. He must've nodded off, because when he closed his eyes with the intention of only resting them a minute it had still been dark. It surprised him too that he'd fallen asleep, the tension he'd been feeling, the horrors of the road still fresh in his mind. Then this new madness, sitting in the dark with a sleeping stranger, trying to dream up some excuse for being here that wouldn't give away the obvious. Professionalism? Forget about it. He'd checked that in the hospital lobby along with his brain. For all he knew he could be kicked off the force for a boneheaded move like this. He should've listened to Mitch.

His hand was still linked with Kate's and now he gently withdrew it, feeling adolescent in the light of day. He looked at Kate's sleeping face and felt the same half-startled and wholly inappropriate pleasure he had the night before when he first laid eyes on her in the limo. It was crazy, his being here, about as far out of line as he cared to get, but jesus, there was something...

He shook his head and said it out loud, "Crazy." Crazy to read so much into a glance, a simple touch, especially given the circumstances. And yet... it was as if he'd known her, a gleam of recognition shared for just that instant in their eyes; but the details, the true shape of it lingering just beyond memory's reach.

Crazy all right. The girl was a complete stranger and he'd do well to remember that.

He got to his feet and stretched, his back kinked from the hard contour chair he'd been slouched in. His boot heel bumped the chair leg, making a racket, and Kate stirred, shifting onto her side on the bed. Steve turned away, feeling like a voyeur. He left the room on tiptoes, rubbing the sleep from his eyes. There was a doctor at the nursing station down the hall, chatting with the nurses, and Steve approached him now, introducing himself, showing his badge.

Kate awoke a few minutes later with a blinding headache. She raised her right hand to her forehead and bonked herself with the cast. She blinked at it a moment, disoriented, until the events of the previous night came rushing back at her.

Dad...

She sat up by increments, wanting to get to her father but feeling a hundred years old, the effort doubling the throb in her skull. Once she was upright, the walls swapped places a few times and she had to lie back down. After a little trial and error she figured out how to raise the head of the bed with the control buttons.

Steve came in at that point and said hello. Kate stared at him a moment, then said, "You were here last night," and Steve nodded. "So I wasn't dreaming."

He said, "How do you feel?" and Kate remembered how soothing his voice had sounded in the cold tomb of the limo, the strangely intimate feeling she'd gotten looking into his eyes in the chancy glow of his flashlight.

She said, "Sore. Flaky. I'll be fine once I'm up and about."

He sat in the chair he'd slept in, rumpled looking in faded blue jeans and a white crew-neck sweatshirt with the O.P.P. crest on the arm.

Kate said, "Did I thank you?"

"Sure you did. You thought I was an angel."

"Honest mistake," Kate said, smiling now, color coming into her cheeks. She glanced past him into the hall. "Would you...? I'm sorry, I don't even know your name."

"Steve. Seger. Steve Seger."

"Steve. Would you mind getting me a nurse? I'd like to find out how my father's doing."

"I, uh, took the liberty of talking to your doctor. I hope you don't mind. You've got a broken wrist and a mild concussion...but you probably figured that out for yourself already. He said he'd be discharging you later today, all things being equal. It looks like Big Bird saved you some skin. Your dad's in ICU. He was in surgery half the night, fractures mostly. Pelvis, femur, a few fingers. The rest was pretty much just cuts and scrapes. The doctor said you can see him when you're feeling up to it."

Kate said, "I'm feeling up to it," and sat up, swinging her legs over the side. She got her feet to the floor, pushed off too quickly and her knees gave out. Steve was up in a flash, taking her weight, helping her back into bed.

"Let's give it a minute," he said, sitting down again.

There was an awkward silence then, Steve staring at his shoes, Kate lying with her forearm across her eyes, waiting for the room to stop spinning. Somewhere down the hall a woman moaned, the sound low and mournful, and from the street the first wave of morning traffic could be heard, revving engines and impatient horns.

It was Kate who broke the silence, saying, "I don't think I could bear to lose him," and Steve looked up to meet her gaze. "My mother died when I was six and my dad never remarried. He's a romantic. I've tried to get him past just dating, but he always says, 'Your mom's the only gal for me.' She spilled a cherry coke on him at a church social and they were married a month later. I've always wanted to ask her if she did that on purpose." She smiled, thinking, Why am I telling him all this? "Anyways, we're great pals. A couple of movie nuts."

"Really? I love movies."

"That's practically all we do. Watch movies, talk movies. We've even thought about putting together a board game and trying to market it. You know, a sort of cinematic trivial pursuit? My dad's a champ. He worked as a projectionist for almost forty years in a great old theater back home called the Grande. He's seen 'em all. I've been trying to stump him for years—it's like a personal vendetta by now—but I can't. Ask him anything. Quotes, directors, stars. He's amazing... God, I'm rambling."

"Sounds like a great guy."

"The best," Kate said. She plucked a tissue from the bedside dispenser and gave her nose a brisk honk. Then she sat up. "Would you mind tracking down a nurse for me, Steve? I'd like to go see him now."

"I'll do you one better," Steve said, hopping to his feet. "Hang on a sec." He ducked out of the room, back a few seconds later with a wheelchair. He smiled—a winning smile, Kate thought—and said, "All just part of the service, ma'am."

She let him help her into the wheelchair, feeling the muscled hardness of him through his sweatshirt. He flipped the foot rests into position for her, then wheeled her through the open door, bearing left toward ICU.

They'd made it as far as the unit's automatic doors when Kate said, "Steve, wait," and Steve stopped the wheelchair, turning it to face him. Kate's eyes were round with shock, the eyes of a woman who has just realized her child has gone missing in a crowded department store.

Steve said, "What's wrong?"

"Last night," Kate said, "we were on our way to the city to cash in a lottery ticket. Ten million dollars."

"Jesus..."

"Yeah." She looked into his eyes. "But somebody stole it. Somebody stopped and stole all our stuff. We had a ton of Christmas gifts for our family. Until just this minute, I thought I'd dreamt it. I watched him take my father's wallet."

"Did you get a good look at him?"

"Not really," Kate said, a terrible sinking feeling in her stomach. "It was dark and I was in and out... This is going to break my father's heart."

Steve took a notepad and pen from his hip pocket, flipping the pad open. "Before we go inside, can you give me a list of the items you had in the car?"

"I think so." She'd almost forgotten he was a cop.

"Okay, let's do it."

She rhymed off what she could remember of the whirlwind of purchases they'd made the day before, Steve recording each item. When they were done he said, "I have to go to Metro headquarters today anyway. Let me see if I can get this out on the computer. My mother works there—she's a detective—maybe she'll have some ideas."

"Thanks," Kate said, scarcely aware she'd said it, a lifetime of dreams, so easily within reach only hours ago, crashing down around her. How was she going to tell her dad?

Steve pocketed the notepad and wheeled her into ICU. A nurse met them at the main desk and Kate forgot about the money, her senses suddenly bombarded: the rank odors of sickness masked thinly by disinfectant: the backbeat of monitors and alarms; glimpses of bodies in high-railed beds, still as statues; wires and tubes and drains. Her mother died in a place like this.

The nurse escorted them to a corner cubicle, giving a running commentary as she walked. "Don't expect too much right now. He was on a ventilator over night so he's still heavily sedated. I'll have to ask you to keep it short."

Kate pushed herself out of the wheelchair, her legs steady beneath her now. She started into the cubicle, hesitating in the doorway. She looked at Steve with fear in her eyes.

He said, "Would you like me to go in with you?"

"No. Thanks," Kate said, "I'll be fine." She paused, adding, "I hate to just dump you like this."

"I've got a full day anyway. Errands to run. Groceries, Christmas shopping, stuff like that."

Kate felt herself blushing. "Will I see you again?"

"Why don't I drop by tomorrow, see how you're doing."

"Okay." She glanced into the cubicle, then touched his arm. "Thanks again, Steve. For everything."

"Glad to do it," he said, starting away. "'Bye, Kate."

"'Bye," Kate said.

She watched him leave, then took a deep breath and went inside.

Internal Affairs detectives Rodney Hicks and Bryan Mayer sat in the office of their immediate superior, Stan Howson, waiting for him to finish a tense-sounding telephone conversation with one of his four teenage daughters. Hicks, a lanky man of thirty-nine with a heavily pock-marked face, was on edge this morning, more so than usual. Mayer, his partner of four years, sat in a chair next to him, doing a sloppy job of eating a meatball sandwich over a collapsing paper plate. His ever present coffee, doused with Coffee-mate, sat on the edge of Howson's desk. Mayer was thirty pounds overweight, but a genius at surveillance.

"Look," Howson said into the phone, "we'll talk about this when I get home," and hung up, his daughter's voice squawking from the handset all the way down to its cradle. He looked at the men with a weary shake of his head. "Jesus Christ, I need a used car lot with that bunch."

Mayer snorted. "Teenagers."

Howson said, "So what can I do for you guys?"

Hicks popped out of his chair, leaning over Howson's desk on fisted hands. "It's about the Flexner murder—"

Howson said, "That's Buzz Caldwell's case, am I right?"

"Yeah, but—"

"Rodney, do me a favor and sit down. You make me nervous."

Hicks complied, but on the edge of his seat, still managing to lean over Howson's desk. "It's Caldwell's case, yeah, but he's way off track, don't you think?"

Howson rolled his eyes at Mayer, who currently resembled Dizzie Gillespie, his ample cheeks stuffed with hoagie. "Al Raybould again, am I right?"

"Hear me out, okay?"

Howson checked his watch. "All right, but make it snappy. I've got a meeting."

Hicks got up and started pacing around the office. "Okay, on the surface it all looks neat and tidy. Fag junkie tries to roll a suit for dope money, but things don't go as planned. The suit resists and the queer goes ballistic. There's a struggle, and when the dust settles the suit looks like a dissected frog but still manages to pump three rounds into his killer. Okay, mystery number one: Where'd the gun come from? Thin air? Frankly, I don't see Flexner as the type to pack a weapon with the serial number filed off. And if it was the queer's gun, why'd he try to roll Flexner with a knife? Why not use the gun? And how'd Flexner end up with the damn thing? The queer's prints weren't even on it."

Howson stared at him noncommittally.

Hicks said, "See, Stan, I remember Swain from my tour in Morality. He's a pillow biter, pure and simple. No way he could rip a man open like that. He doesn't have the instinct or the brute strength."

Howson said, "Look, Rodney. I don't like to bring this up, but you've got some personal issues with Raybould—"

"And I'll be the first to admit it," Hicks said, "but this has got nothing to do with that." He leaned over the desk again, playing his trump card. "I saw the fucker get out of the widow's car last night, all right? Right here in the underground lot. What was that about?"

"Maybe he's a friend of the family. Maybe—"

But Hicks didn't want to hear it. "And what about the half-dozen other murders I've brought to your attention over the past four years? All prominent men on one or the other side of the law, all with people in their lives'd be happy to see them dead. Would *profit* from their deaths. And every one of them airtight. Almost artful, if you keep an open mind and honestly consider the possibility. Raybould always just…lurking on the sidelines. And what about the fucking chalet he's got in Switzerland?"

"The what?"

"You ought to see the place. He owns it, too, lock, stock and barrel."

"I've never heard him mention anything about that," Howson said, glancing at Mayer. "How would you know about it?"

Hicks' lips stretched into a guilty grin. "I followed him."

"Come again?"

"Last summer, when he went on holidays. Right after the key witness in the Corsino case turned up dead. I cashed in some bonds and followed him."

"To *Switzerland*? And you're trying to tell me this isn't personal?"

"Okay," Hicks said. "All right. Nobody'd be happier than me to see him go down. But I was his partner for three years, Stan. I *know* this guy. He's smart, cunning. Fucking ruthless. You know his methods. And he was always griping about the crooks getting rich while he had to live in a crummy third floor apartment and drive a Volkswagen. He said if he could play it both ways and get away with it, he would."

"He still lives in a third floor apartment, Rodney."

"I said he was smart." He sat in his chair, fixing Howson's gaze with absolute earnestness. He and Howson had been on the street together back in Division, Hicks the man's senior by a couple of years, training him. Stan turned out to be a fast-tracker, every move geared toward promotion, status; but underneath all that he was a good shit, and it was that part Hicks was appealing to now. He said, "Stan, we go back a ways, you and I. You know me. I'm a good detective. All I'm asking for is a couple weeks."

After a long silence Howson said to Mayer, "You with him on this?"

"Hell, yes."

Howson stood, checking his watch again, then looked firmly at Hicks. "One week, Rodney. Seven days to show me something concrete."

Hicks nodded. "Thanks, Stan. Thanks a lot."

"Don't get overheated. You're gonna carry your usual case load, both of you." Both men nodded. "It's not a holiday. Now get out of here. And Bryan, take that dog's breakfast with you."

Mayer folded his paper plate into a wet ball and followed Hicks out of the office.

Kate gasped when she saw her dad, mummified in surgical gauze, what little skin she could see already beginning to bruise. There were huge casts on his legs and what looked like a kid's erector set sprouting from his pelvis. Three of the fingers on his left hand had been splinted and a line of raw looking sutures peeked out from beneath the turban-like dressing on his head. IV tubing snaked out of both arms, the one on the left a deep maroon color from the blood they were running into him. The bank of monitors and equipment that surrounded him looked sufficient to service an entire ward.

But what shook Kate most was the sight of his face. It was utterly still. Were it not for the steady green blip on the heart monitor she would have thought him dead.

She hovered in the doorway, breathless, uncertain, fighting the urge to shout his name, run to his bedside and try to shake him awake...

Instead, she curled her hands into fists and breathed, the throb in her head taking on a new intensity. And when at last she spoke, though the words were tremulous and barely audible, she deliberately deepened her voice to a male timbre.

"I ask you to note that, uh, I did not call you callous-assed strumpets, or low-borne gutter sluts..."

Though Keith did not open his eyes, the ghost of a smile appeared on his lips. Kate smiled too, tears overspilling her eyelids. She approached the bed and continued.

"But I did call you whores, no escapin' that..."

"And for that slip of the tongue," Keith whispered hoarsely, "I apologize."

Kate touched his hand and Keith opened his eyes.

"Paul Newman," he said, and God love him he tried to invest his words with the same playful cockiness he always did when he was showing Kate who was boss. "*The Life And Times Of Judge Roy Bean*, nineteen-seventy-two. Piece of cake."

Kate bent over the bedrail and rested her head on his chest, relieved tears pouring from her eyes. Wincing a little with the motion, Keith brought his good hand up and patted her head. "It's okay, sweetie," he whispered. "Everything's gonna be okay."

Detective Raybould double-parked in front of a Queen Street cigar store and went inside for a deck of smokes. His beeper went off while he was paying the clerk, the display showing a familiar number, the sight of it inducing a vertical groove of concentration between his eyebrows. When he finished with the clerk he went outside to a phone booth at the end of the block and called the number on his beeper. While it rang he peeled the cellophane off the cigarette package and got himself a smoke. He set it between his teeth but didn't bother to light it.

One of Corsino's monkeys answered, an obnoxious little prick named Paulie. "Yeah, what."

Raybould said, "Paulie. You beeped."

"That was quick."

"That's why your boss pays me so well. What's on your mind?"

"A favor."

"That what we're calling it now?" Raybould chuckled. "Feast or famine, eh Paulie?" Nothing for six months, now two in the same week.

"The Vienna Café on Bloor, across from the—"

"I know it."

"Day after tomorrow, nine AM."

Raybould hung up and lit his smoke. Then he walked back to his car.

5

INVESTIGATIVE SERVICES OCCUPIED THE third floor of the Metro headquarters building on College Street, the different squads—Homicide, Holdup, Sexual Assault, Crime Stoppers—honeycombed around a central bank of elevators. Aretha, the receptionist in Sexual Assault, spotted Steve as he got off the elevator. She got up from her desk and met him at her office door.

"My eyes. Is that the young Constable Seger?"

"None other," Steve said, blushing as he always did when Aretha made a fuss. Aretha'd changed more of Steve's diapers than his mother had. She got right in there and gave him a hug. "How you doing, Reeth?" Steve said. It was what he'd called her when he was little, his first crack at her name, and it just sort of stuck. "Say, have you lost weight?"

Aretha gave him a swat. She'd weighed in at a solid two-eighty as long as Steve had known her, most of it in her can. "You really think so? I been eatin' those Slim-Fast dinners, bagels for lunch, cuttin' back on the greasy stuff."

"Well, keep it up, girl. You're a shadow of your former self."

Beaming, Aretha said, "Boy, you lie like a rug. Lookin' for your mom?"

"Yeah, you seen her?"

"She had a lecture with a bunch of rookies at nine." She glanced at her watch. "Should be through by now, though. I was you, I'd check the coffee room."

Steve said, "I'll give it a try," and started away. "Nice seeing you, Reeth."

Her big voice followed him into the corridor. "You too, baby. And hey, next time you come by, wear the uniform!"

Smiling, Steve headed for the coffee room.

His mother was there, running one of her scams on a pair of rookies. She saw him come in and winked, an impish glint in her eye that got him grinning right away. He joined a small group of detectives gathered by the coffee machine to watch her perform, all of them playing dumb, like straight men, knowing what was coming.

Whatever she'd told them so far, the rookies still looked skeptical.

"Whoa, Sergeant Seger," the taller one said. "Lemme get this straight. You're saying with one hour training and a maga*zine*, a woman about to be raped by two guys can inflict enough damage to just...walk away? She don't have a handgun or nothin'?"

Liz Seger said, "Okay, boys, first thing. Lecture's over, this is the coffee room. Call me Liz." She got a dig in next, razzing the bigger one in front of his buddy. "And no, she don't have a handgun or nothin'. They don't teach English at police college anymore? Now pay attention." She picked up a Newsweek off the counter, rolled it into the shape of a baton and stood between the two men, her back to the taller one. She said, "I'm four-eleven. How 'bout you, Stretch?"

"Six-five," the taller one said to her back.

"And your partner?"

The other rookie said, "Six-foot even, ma'am."

"Okay, I'm willing to bet—say, twenty bucks apiece?—you and Stretch here can't grab hold of me long enough to lift up my skirt."

"You're not wearing a skirt," Stretch said.

"If I were, then. Use your imagination. Get my belt off if you need a trophy. Care to give it a shot?"

75

Stretch looked over Liz's head at his partner. "You in?"

"I'm in."

They both looked down at Detective Elizabeth Seger, fifty-one, Coordinator of VI-CLAS, Violent Crime Linkage Analysis System. She stood at ease, the rolled-up magazine in her right hand, smirking at them.

"Whenever you're ready, boys."

"Go easy on her," one of the spectators said.

Then Stretch made his move, not mad but goaded, the way Liz wanted him. She let him put a choke hold on her while his partner reached for her belt. With a twitch of her hip she pushed the end of the magazine into the partner's gut, not as hard as she could but hard enough, and heard the wind go out of him, watching as he sank to one knee, at the same time reaching back and getting hold of Stretch's baby finger. She gave it a crank and felt the strength go out of him. The poor guy actually screamed.

Liz said, "You're mine now," turning to face him, positioning him between herself and his winded accessory. "Wherever I point your pinky—" she twisted it toward the windows "—that's where you go." The big guy lurched toward the windows. His partner was on his feet now, deciding if he was through yet. Liz said, "If your accomplice still feels frisky—" She torqued on the finger again and the rookies butted heads. "Believe me now?"

"Yes!"

"Give up?"

"YES!"

She let him go and stuck out her hand. "Okay, officers. Ante up."

Steve watched her take the money from the rumpled rookies and stuff it into her pocket, a street hustler with a detective's badge and a fifth-degree black belt in karate, the traditional discipline of *Go-ju Ryu*. Her obsessive love of the martial arts was the main reason Steve's father had thrown her out when Steve was eight. Every chance she got Liz was off to Okinawa to train, often for months at a time. Her father, also a martial artist, living in Memphis where Liz was born—you could still hear the trace of an accent when she got excited—got her started when she was only five. He'd spent his life teaching karate, and though he'd trained Liz himself, he'd always encouraged her to learn from the source. Her longest stint over there, which began when Steve was eleven, lasted two-and-a-half years, with brief trips home for birthdays and holidays. Following the divorce and his father's descent into alcoholism and depression, Steve had lived with his maternal grandmother, a wily old gal who at the time employed Aretha as a housekeeper. The job advancement had been Liz's doing, in appreciation of Aretha's help raising Steve. And though Steve had missed his mother mightily during her absences he'd never resented her for it, often in spite of his best efforts. Bottom line, she loved him and she always did her best. And she was just so damned much fun to be with, who could stay mad at her? He'd never tell anyone this, but his mother was his hero.

The show over, the other detectives went back to their coffees. Liz let the rookies down gently, telling them a bit about herself, then came over to join Steve. She smiled at him like a school girl, arms wide open for a hug.

"There's my big copper."

"Hi, Mom," Steve said, returning the hug briefly, then backing away. Why did the women in his life insist on embarrassing him? "People still fall for that routine?"

"All the time, sweetheart. You saw it yourself."

"What do you do with the money?"

"Cigarettes."

"I thought you quit."

"Yeah, but I got tired of it. So what's on your mind?"

"What do you mean?" Steve said, acting innocent. Christ, she knew him so well.

"I mean, that's about as much small talk as I've gotten out of you since you were nine. So what's on your mind?"

As Steve composed his opening line Liz asked him if he wanted a coffee and Steve said no. She suggested they talk in her office and Steve said okay. They were barely out the coffee room door when one of the detectives who'd been watching fell in beside them, matching their stride. He put his arm around Liz's shoulders and smiled. Steve could tell right away she didn't like it.

"Want me to show you how I'd get your skirt up?" the detective said.

Steve realized he was witnessing something he'd never seen before, his mother intimidated.

"No thanks, Al," Liz said. "You know all my tricks."

"Yes, I do." He took his arm away and looked at Steve. "This your boy?"

Liz made the introductions as they reached her office door. "Al Raybould," she said, avoiding his eyes, "this is my son, Steve. He's a constable with the O.P.P. now."

Steve accepted the man's handshake, surprised by his gentle, almost effeminate grip. "Pleased to meet you, sir," he said.

"You too, son. And call me Al." He cocked his head at Steve. "O.P.P., huh? Why not Metro like your mom?"

"Nicer cars."

Raybould laughed. "Nicer cars. I love it." He winked at Liz, saying, "If you change your mind, Liz..." and walked away.

Steve said, "Creepy guy."

"You have no idea," Liz said and left it at that.

Steve followed her into the office. Liz lit a smoke and Steve told his tale, doing his best to downplay his feelings for Kate, making it sound all business, one cop to another. When he was done, Liz said:

"And you believe this sad story?"

"Yes, I do."

Liz said, "Okay, let me put it this way," the Memphis accent coming through. "Are you thinking with your head right now or your johnson?"

Steve gave his neck a twist, like he was working a crick out of it, the way his old man used to show his irritation. "Okay, yes, I like her. But I believe her, too, and I'd like to help."

Liz squinted up at her son, a big strappy guy of six-foot-one, six-two in his Prospectors, towering over her. She planted her fists on her hips and inhaled, holding it in, the way a thousand pressing verdicts in Steve's life had been reached. He felt about ten years old.

"Come on," she said, finally exhaling. "We'll talk to Gord Brown over in Fraud. He's worked with the lottery people before." She led him out of the office, saying, "We'll have them detain who-

ever shows up with the ticket, assuming he hasn't already cashed it in." She grinned at him. "Then we'll have a talk with the creep.
"Now, tell me about this girl."

Kate's doctor discharged her from the hospital later that morning. He gave her a prescription for Tylenol 3, which she filled at the hospital pharmacy, and suggested she see him again if the headache persisted more than a couple of days. The pain in her arm was the worst—she sometimes got the feeling the broken ends of bone were grinding against each other in there, the sensation bringing beads of sweat to her face—but with a couple of the codeine-laced Tylenol on board it all backed off into a vague drone. Her only other complaint was a persistent itch under the cast, which she quickly learned to control with the small metal nail file she kept in her bag.

She returned to ICU just before noon and asked to speak with the doctor looking after her father. A nurse parked her in a small conference room near the unit and a few minutes later a red-headed woman in a white lab coat came in and introduced herself as Dr. Sutcliffe. She had an open, girlish face and wore a stethoscope around her neck like a jock's shower towel. Kate liked her right away.

"What can I do for you, Ms. Whipple?" the doctor said, her voice, like her gaze, steady and confident.

"Call me Kate."

The doctor smiled and Kate wondered how old she was.

"Okay, Kate."

"I was just wondering, you know, how he's doing. His injuries have been described to me, but I don't really know what to expect. Is he in a lot of pain? How long is he going to be..."

The doctor placed a warm hand on Kate's forearm. "He's not in any real pain, Kate, okay? That's number one. He's got what's known as an epidural catheter in his back. You may have heard of them in connection with obstetrics."

Kate nodded. A girl she worked with had given birth to twins recently and had told Kate the epidural was a life saver.

"Well," the doctor said, "since most of his serious injuries are below his waist, the epidural handles the pain beautifully. There's a continuous infusion of narcotic being pumped into him, so his discomfort should be minimal. Now, as far as how long it's going to take him to recover, he's got some nasty fractures and those take time to mend. Since his head, chest and abdomen are all fine, however, I'm expecting to move him into the Stepdown Unit by tomorrow, the following day at the latest."

"Stepdown?"

"It's a parallel unit we use, one stage before transfer to the ward. It's quieter in there and he'll rest better." She squeezed Kate's arm. "He's going to be fine, Kate. You were both very fortunate. He'll need a lot of physio and he'll probably have to walk with a cane the rest of his life, but barring anything unforeseen, he *is* going to walk out of here. I'm quite confident of that."

"Thanks," Kate said, water coming to her eyes. The doctor handed her a tissue. "How long will he be so dopey?"

"He'll sleep on and off for the next eighteen hours or so. He was ventilated overnight, just as a precaution, and we sedate our ventilators pretty heavily. He should be bright as ever by tomorrow, though."

"Can I go see him again?"

"Sure," Dr. Sutcliffe said, standing. "Come on. I'll take you to him."

Kate sat in a chair and watched him sleep, her oldest friend and companion. For the most part he seemed to be resting peacefully, but from time to time he moaned or twitched restlessly, as though he were dreaming and the dreams were unpleasant, even frightening. It upset Kate to see him this way. Outside of the usual run of winter colds and viral illnesses he'd never been sick a day in his life, and in a child's way Kate had come to think of him as invulnerable. Now he looked so beaten and frail. Diminished. It shook her all the way through, forcing her to envision a life without him in it. It made her reflect on her own life and the way she'd been living it. In hiding.

He awoke occasionally, groggy but full of questions: "Hi, kiddo. What happened?" She told him. "An accident? Really? Are you okay?" Yes, just a broken arm. "How about your car?" It wasn't my car. "Really? What happened?" And round and round, the same run of questions every time he opened his eyes. A nurse told Kate it was because of his concussion and the sedation, nothing to worry about, probably gone by tomorrow. He seemed to have forgotten about winning the lottery and for that at least Kate was grateful. She wasn't looking forward to breaking the news.

She took a break for lunch around two, grabbing a dry roast beef sandwich and a Swiss cream soda from the vending machines down the hall. While she nibbled she made a few phone calls, notifying relatives about the accident. Most of them wanted to come in right away, but Kate advised them to wait until tomorrow, repeating what Dr. Sutcliffe had told her about the sedation. The last call she made was to her boss. Former boss.

"Panther Courier," Morris said. "Mo Brooks speaking. How can I help you?"

Kate almost hung up. She didn't know how to play this, hadn't really thought it through. Morris was going to need some stroking, and Kate's tail didn't fit all that well between her legs.

"Panther Courier," Mo repeated, getting ready to hang up.

"Morris, it's Kate."

"Kate! Say, how you doing? You're the talk of this place, let me tell you. Like a movie star or something. Glad to see you haven't forgotten your friends."

Friends, right. "Do you really consider us friends, Mo?"

"Hell, yes. I mean, being the boss and all, it's up to me to maintain a certain distance, you understand. But yeah, I always considered you one of my favorites."

Lying little shit. "I'm glad to hear that, Mo, because...I need my job back."

Dead silence.

"Mo?"

"You're shitting me—right?"

"I've never been more serious."

"Okay, gimme a minute here, okay? You and your old man, you just won ten million big ones, tax free—and you want your eighteen-buck-an-hour *job* back?" He snorted. "You got a weird sense of humor, Kate, I'll give you that."

Kate took a deep breath and told him what happened, the whole story, hearing nothing from the other end of the line but silence; she could feel it around her neck like a yoke made of wet cement.

Finally, Mo said, "Oh, that's rich. Little miss millionbucks waltzes in here five minutes ahead of her shift on the busiest day of the week and announces she's quitting. So long, Morris, go screw yourself. But hey, now she's broke, just like the rest of us, and what—I'm supposed to feel sorry for her? Hand her job back on a silver platter and maybe kiss her ass while I'm at it?"

"Mo, I—"

"Listen, Kate, bottom line, I need people around here I can depend on. The job's been posted, you're welcome to reapply. When you get back from Disneyland drop in and fill out an application. In the meantime my pregnant wife is running your route."

He hung up.

Kate cradled the receiver and thought: Shit. Then she returned to her father's room.

What Steve wanted was to go back to the hospital. At least this time he had an excuse, news of his progress on the theft. His mother's friend Gord Brown in Fraud had set up a sting with the security people at the Lottery Corporation, fixing it so that nobody could cash in the ticket now without being detained, forcibly if necessary. He wanted to tell Kate about it and see her smile, feel her fingers warm on his arm as she thanked him.

Instead, he stopped off at the Queen Street Blockbuster and picked up a movie: James Cameron's *Titanic*. It was a long mother and he'd seen it twice already, but it would keep him occupied, maybe even help him sleep. Good excuse or not, he knew that showing up at the hospital again today would be pushing it. Kate would want to be with her father and his presence would only be an intrusion.

He'd drop by tomorrow. Early.

Steve rented a loft apartment on Pine Street in Toronto's east end, something he'd lucked into through one of the guys he met at police college. The guy's father owned the building and charged him a very reasonable rent, considering the size of the place and its location, so close to the downtown core. The catch was, starting in the fall he had to coach a junior A hockey team the father sponsored, something he enjoyed doing anyway. The place was huge and hard to heat, clunky old rads and a high ceiling crisscrossed with I-beams and air ducts, spider heaven up there. But the floors were hardwood, laid in by the previous tenants who'd used it as a dance studio, and the walls were sandblasted brick, nice and rustic. Steve loved the place. He had a small gym—free weights and a heavy bag—set up in a corner walled with mirrors, again compliments of the dancers, an oversized poster bed he picked up at a fire sale, a sturdy pine kitchen he put in himself, a huge bathroom with an antique clawfoot tub deep enough to snorkel in, and still enough space for a comfy living area and a regulation size pool table.

He came in late that afternoon with an armload of parcels and a few bags of groceries, enough to carry him through the holidays. Once he'd put everything away, he took a slow tour through the loft, at first to get reacquainted with the place, then picturing Kate in it... Tucked in beside him on the worn leather couch, watching movies together, trying to come up with quotes to stump her father. Standing next to him at the chopping block in the kitchen, watching him dice onions for a late-night omelet maybe, or pop corn in a pot with a tablespoon of oil, the way Aretha taught him. Kate leaning over the pool table in a pair of tight jeans, smiling at him over her shoulder before taking her shot, hustling him, beating the pants off him. Literally.

Stretched out next to him on his bed...

He got into his sweats and hit the weights, the exercise easing the pent-up tension. Afterward, he showered and cooked himself a meal, then popped the video into the VCR. He lay on the couch in the drafty lot, hands laced behind his head, watching the movie but not seeing it. He kept seeing Kate's face, replaying bits of the conversation they'd shared, wondering if when she said, "Will I see you again?" she meant in a professional sense—he was a cop, after all, and there was a fortune at stake—or more personally?

He hit the sack early, exhausted but unable to sleep. Something fundamental inside him had shifted, some basic navigational tool gone awry. The plan had been simple: no serious entanglements for twelve months. Date, sure, if the occasion arose, but beyond that, stow it until the end of his probationary year. How hard could that be?

But Kate had struck him like a meteor streaking out of that cold winter sky. He had no precedent for a situation this, nothing to measure it against. It all seemed so adolescent, stumbling around like a smitten teen. He'd had girlfriends before, plenty of them, even believed he was in love with one or two—but he'd always been able to call the shots. Turn it on or turn it off. What was it about her, anyway? She was attractive, sure. Those green eyes, like summer moss; nice facial features, a snug athletic body; that blond hair, the real thing. But he'd never gone for blonds, he'd always lusted after those smoky brunettes with the round figures. And shit, they'd barely exchanged a hundred words. If he thought about it hard enough he could probably jot them all down. He knew almost nothing about her, and could almost hear her telling him as much: "Steve, don't be silly, you don't even know me." But there was no escaping it. Whatever it was he'd already committed himself to seeing it through. He was involved now and that felt like the right way to be.

When he finally slept he dreamt of the boy in the Spiderman pjs, saw himself chewing the kid out for showing up at hockey practice in his pajamas.

IA Detectives Hicks and Mayer sat in darkness down the block from Raybould's brick-faced apartment building, Mayer at the wheel of his wife's gray Volvo with the engine running, Hicks hunched next to him, staring up at Raybould's third-story window through a pair of police-issue binoculars. The lights were on up there and from time to time Raybould's shadow could be seen passing the curtained window. Raybould's car was parked at the curb in front of the building, not going anywhere. According to the dash clock—fluorescent green digits with a colon that flashed off the seconds, driving Mayer crazy—it was twelve minutes past eleven in the PM. Mayer's ass was numb, he was hungry, tired and bored, and his wife, Donna, was going to murder him. He'd told her he'd be back two hours ago. It was time to pack it in.

He said, "Rodney, what say we call it a day? It's late and I gotta take a leak. Tomorrow's another day." Hicks lowered the field glasses but said nothing. He pressed his knuckles into his eyes, rubbing them. Mayer said, "I've got it all set up with Perry for the morning, bright and early. The least I can do is show up rested so I can pay attention." Perry Campbell had been Mayer's partner when he worked surveillance. After getting the go-ahead from Howson, Mayer had told Perry what they were into and Perry said he had just the thing, a state-of-the-art miniature transmitter with a five hundred yard range. He also said if they fucked it up he'd personally shoot them both. A good shit, Perry, but quirky. "Rodney?"

"Let's give it another few minutes. He might still go out. The guy never sleeps." He took a quick squint through the binoculars, the lights still on up there, then looked at Mayer. "Midnight, okay?"

"All right, midnight, but not a minute longer." He shifted in his seat, grimacing. "God damn, my ass is numb." He reached across Hicks' lap, opened the glove box and took out a bag of salted sunflower seeds, saying, "Ah, that's my girl." He held the bag out to Hicks, who shook his head. Mayer scooped out a handful for himself, dropped the bag into the V of his crotch and cracked the window an inch, popping a seed into his mouth and crunching it. "Donna, she's like a chipmunk, always munching on these things." He spit the shell into his fingers and flicked it out the window. "Tasty, but it'd take a year to make a meal out of 'em. I wish we'd picked up some sandwiches or something. You gonna be this much fun 'til midnight?"

Smiling a little, Hicks said, "Sorry, Bryan. It's just, sitting here, brings back a lot of bad memories."

Mayer said, "How long have we been friends? Close, I mean."

"I dunno. Four years and change?"

"Yeah. And in all that time we've never really talked about this. Why you got it in for this guy. What I know is what I've heard around the shop and I don't trust that kind of information. Never have. Now, this thing we're doing; you're my friend and I'm glad to help. But I gotta tell you, I'd feel a lot better about this hearing it from you. I mean, I know the guy. I see him around. I know SIU's on his ass right now over that crackhead he dropped a few months back and I also know he's squirmed out of that kind of situation before. He's a shooter and a smart one. Rumor has it they might bag him this time, but hey, they might not. I know he and your wife—"

"I trusted that fucker, Bryan. That's all you need to know. I trusted him."

Mayer crunched another seed, the silence in the car suddenly dense, seeming to thin the oxygen. He glanced at the clock, that flashing fucking colon—11:19—and jumped when Hicks said:

"Sally was addicted to cocaine. You probably heard that around the shop, too."

Mayer had, but he said nothing. He'd met Rodney's wife only two or three times before she split on him and Rodney came over to IA from Morality, where he'd been partnered with Raybould. Their association prior to that had been limited to bull sessions at Franklins', the police bar down the street from headquarters, and the occasional police function, Hicks always showing up alone. Hicks was a private person and Mayer respected that.

Hicks said, "When I found them I couldn't believe it. In our own fucking bed." Not looking at Mayer now, not looking at anything. "Even now, after all this time, I still can't believe it."

Mayer listened to Hicks tell it, watched him relive it...

Hicks blinked and saw his wife's naked back, the look she'd given him on that muggy August afternoon four years ago, languidly turning to see who it was. That stoned, amused grin. "Why don't you come ahead in, Rodney." Breathy, coked-out. "See how a real man does it."

He could see the mirror on the bedside table, the neat white lines that had nearly ruined their marriage a hundred times already, ranked in readiness across its surface.

It took Hicks a moment to credit what he was seeing—his wife in their bedroom in the middle of a Tuesday afternoon, naked and more stoned than he'd ever seen her, riding an enormous erection.

"Sally, what...?"

To this point he hadn't been able to see the face of the man she straddled. All he knew was the fucker was dead. Sally had been clean for sixteen months, a feat that had taken seven years and as many treatment centers to achieve, never mind the heartache. And whoever this dead man was, he'd gotten her started again. He'd gotten her stoned and then fucked her. And under the law according to Hicks, that was a capital offense.

He drew his sidearm and jacked a round into the chamber. That was when the man's head came up off the pillow. It was Raybould, his partner of three years. Smirking at him.

"Rodney. I thought you had a dentist appointment."

"Tomorrow," Hicks said, jamming the muzzle into Raybould's cheek. He shoved his wife off Raybould, whose erection was unflagging. "My appointment's tomorrow!"

Raybould raised his shoulders off the bed in an impish little shrug. Hicks could see the puckered scar on his chest where he'd taken a bullet. "Oops."

"I can't believe this," Hicks said, the tendons creaking in his trigger finger. He glanced at his wife, back on the bed now, stroking Raybould's erection. "Sally, stop—"

Then pain detonated in his wrist as Raybould seized it and twisted, the gun dropping to the floor like a hot coal. Raybould swung his legs off the bed, continuing the merciless pressure, forcing Hicks to his knees as Raybould rose to his feet.

"Never hesitate," he said, punctuating his words with agonizing pressure on Hicks' wrist. "You know that, Rodney. Three years with me, you haven't learned anything?" He kicked the gun under the bed. "Now normally, when someone points a gun at me, I kill him. But you and me, Rodney, we've got history. We've...bonded. And you're going to let a coke-head cunt fuck all that up?"

"How *dare* you!" Sally screamed. She launched herself across the bed at him and Raybould backhanded her hard. She landed on the floor on the opposite side of the bed and didn't get up.

Raybould said, "I did you a favor here, Rodney. I showed you what you've been decorating and calling a wife."

"How...long..." Hicks said, groaning against the pain in his wrist and in his heart. He'd genuinely believed he and Sally had turned a corner, that they'd grow old together, retire in Florida someday like his folks. What a chump.

"Couple months," Raybould said, "give or take. That's part of your problem. You don't pay attention."

Then Raybould's fist had come down and put his lights out. When he awoke Raybould and his wife were gone. He found a scrawled note on the kitchen table: *I love him, Rodney. Goodbye...*

Bryan could see the tears on his partner's face, shiny slashes of pain in the street light. He wanted to say something, touch him maybe, but he couldn't.

"I haven't seen or spoken to her since," Hicks said, facing him now, beyond shame or embarrassment. "Christ, Bryan, we've known each other since our teens. She didn't even drink back then." He shook his head. "I got her started on the coke. Took some off a snitch one time and decided, what the hell, give it a try, see what the attraction is. It didn't do shit for me, just froze up my face and made me more fucking hyper. But Sally, she couldn't get enough of it. And she was so much fun on the shit, I just kept...bringing it home. I didn't realize she had a problem 'til it was way past too late." Bryan had to look away, Hicks' features so distorted now he scarcely recognized the man. "I was her fucking pusher, Bryan. Her fucking pusher..."

Hicks leaned over his knees, sobbing, letting it come. Mayer reached out and held the back of his neck.

"Okay, partner," he said. "We'll stay as long as you want. And if this fucker's dirty, I'll help you nail him to the cross."

Cold fingers touched Kate's shoulder, snapping her awake, a voice behind her saying, "There's a family room, you know. With a bed and a TV and a fridge."

Kate squinted up at the nurse, disappointed the touch had not been Steve's. Her back was killing her. "What time is it?"

"Midnight," the nurse said, smiling in the low light. "We've been making bets, how long before you'd fall out of this chair."

Kate looked at her dad, still sleeping with the oxygen tubes in his nose.

"He's fine," the nurse said, "sleeping like a baby. Come on, I'll get you fixed up." Kate didn't move. "If anything changes or he wakes up and asks for you, we know where to find you."

"You'll come get me?"

"We'll come get you."

Kate rose stiffly from the chair, leaned over the bedrail and kissed her father on the forehead, his skin cool against her lips.

"Sleep well," she whispered, then followed the nurse out of the unit, down the hall to the family room.

It was small and chilly, the walls paper thin, but it had a bed and Kate found *Miracle On Thirty-Fourth Street*, the original, playing on the twenty-inch color TV with the plaque on top that said: Donated by the Ladies' Auxiliary. She watched until her eyes got heavy and she fell asleep that way, fully dressed under the thin blankets, images in blue light playing over her face.

6

MARTY SMALL CAME AWAKE all of a sudden, morning light piercing his eyes like heated needles. He had no idea where he was. Then he felt Earlene's warm ass spooned into the small of his back and he remembered. He should've been delighted, but his head hurt too much for anything else to really matter. He glanced at the bedside digital: 6:22 AM. Shit. He'd finally passed out around three, with a bellyful of pretzels and cheap wine; he could feel it sitting in there now like a sauna rock.

He sat up a little at a time, getting his feet to the carpeted floor. He gave it a moment, aware of a tense bladder now, then stood, his entire being suddenly seething with need. Standing, getting his head up in the air like that, seemed to bring the feeling on like a cold sweat. He *needed* something...

He shuffled into the living room and began sifting through the detritus of the night before. He found an open cigarette package and something inside him sighed, but the sucker was empty. He tossed it into a drift of shredded gift wrap and swirled a couple of the wine bottles that lay on the coffee table like slain soldiers, hoping for a little hair of the dog. No such luck. Even the coke was gone, the glass table top they'd cut it on bearing only the smeared sweeps of Earlene's spit-wet fingertips.

Marty dragged himself into the john, avoiding the mirror. He swayed in front of the bowl a minute, trying to get his plumbing started, then gave it up and sat on the seat. He propped his elbows on his knees, lowered his head into his hands and cursed his mother for bringing him into the world. God damn, what had he been thinking? He hadn't partied like this since his teens: thirty-six non-stop hours of booze, balling and drugs.

But Jesus, didn't they have fun? Staying stoned, Earlene up for anything. "It's your dime, sweetie, you call the shots." He'd kept her naked or nearly naked the whole time, not that it took much coaxing, and managed to convince himself that at least part of the proceedings were spontaneous, just a guy and his gal hangin' loose.

While he dribbled Marty replayed scenes in his head: Earlene standing in the bathroom doorway that first night, naked as a jaybird and giving him that smile, most of it just a working girl's pleasure at an easy score, but a hint of the woman underneath shining through. Using his first name like that, a part of her warming to the idea of playing house for a couple days, being fussed over and spoiled, Marty a willing spoiler. Late champagne breakfast in bed. An hour-long foot massage that seemed to please her more than the sex. Keeping the coke mirror stocked and her wine glass full. And at one point, while the sun was still high in the sky, doing a stand-up routine in his skivvies, getting her so giddy she almost wet the bed. "Marty, you make me laugh!"

Last night she'd heated up some leftover spaghetti, and while she was in the kitchen Marty snuck a peek in her closet. When he saw some of the outfits she had in there he hollered out to her from the bedroom. He couldn't help himself.

"Jesus, Earlene, lookit this shit. Where do you shop?"

Earlene hollered back, "See anything you like, try it on."

"Yeah, right."

He couldn't believe some of the get-ups she had. For the sick-fuck regulars, he supposed. He wondered how they'd feel dropping by with him sitting in the La-Z-Boy watching *All in the Family* reruns. The fuckers. He pulled out a leather and vinyl number, studded with what looked like tiny light bulbs or maybe LEDs. He found the battery pack on the belt and switched it on. Colored lights began to flash over the length of the outfit in random sequences. He held it up and shook his head. "Hey, Earlene, I wouldn't mind seeing you in this little number. Fuckin' Elvis meets Elvira."

Earlene stuck her head in to see what he was talking about. "I can do that. No water sports, though."

See? Making jokes. Warming up to him.

Marty said, "Got any inflatable dolls?"

"No, Marty. I work alone."

"I got a friend has an inflatable doll. Calls it Toni. Know what he does when it turns white?"

"I give up."

"He empties it," Marty said, and heard Earlene giggle in the kitchen.

"You are fucked up, Marty. Now come and eat..."

Now, with his head aching, Marty got off the john, not bothering to flush. He walked naked into the living room and raised the blinds, shading his eyes against the winter glare. An errant breeze swirled snow off the roof, the motion teetering something inside him, and for a long moment Marty was sure he was going to spew his guts into Earlene's Yucca plant.

He closed his eyes until the feeling passed, leaning on the sill. When he looked outside again he noticed a corner confectionery across the street. Yaghi's Market.

He shuddered and went to look for his clothes.

Kate opened her eyes to the shrill of an alarm followed by an atonal voice over the PA system: "Code Blue, ICU, Code Blue, ICU." Dad! she thought, panic slapping her wide awake. She whipped off the covers and burst out of the family room in her socks, startling an elderly volunteer by the elevators, skidded across the hall to the unit and plowed through the automatic doors, heading for her father's cubicle at a dead tear. "Ms. Whipple," a nurse said, Kate darting past her into the cubicle to find an empty bed. She turned and saw a guy pushing a defibrillator cart toward a cubicle on the other side of the unit.

The nurse who'd tried to intercept her came into the room. "Your father was transferred out this morning before change of shift," she said. "He's in the Stepdown Unit now, back through the main doors, down the hall to your right. Now I'm sorry, Ms. Whipple, but I'm going to have to ask you to leave."

A couple more staff members headed for the action across the unit.

"Of course," Kate said. "I'm sorry. I was asleep, I heard the alarm..."

"No problem," the nurse said, "I understand." She held her arm out, showing Kate the door. "Now please..."

"Of course. Excuse me."

Kate left in her sock feet, glancing into the cubicle over there, seeing a man's bare chest, barrel-shaped and hairy, and a set of black defibrillator paddles, somebody threading a tube down the man's throat. She looked away, thinking, Thank God, thank God...

She didn't breathe until she was out of the unit. Her headache was back with a vengeance. The elderly volunteer was still waiting by the elevators and Kate saw what she had in her hands: a gold chalice balanced on a red satin pillow. Kate turned toward Stepdown, then remembered her shoes and changed directions. As she passed the elevators the old woman in the yellow volunteer's jacket said, "Is everything all right?"

Hiding in her hair, Kate said, "Yes, thanks," and went back to the family room for her shoes. While she was there she washed her face and brushed her teeth with her finger, then sat on the john and peed. She got the Tylenol out of her bag and washed one down with some apple juice she found in the counter-top fridge. Then she went out to find her dad.

When the racket began at the front of the store Tarek Yaghi was hunched in the back of the display cooler, arranging bags of milk so that those closest to their expiry date were stacked at the front. He looked through the cooler's glass doors and saw some crazy guy standing out on the stoop, yanking on the door handle like he couldn't believe the place wasn't open yet. His boots were unlaced and his overcoat unbuttoned, clutched across his chest in one frost-reddened hand. His dark hair looked like rodents had nested in it.

Yaghi came out of the cooler shaking his head. He went to the door and pointed at his watch. "Not open yet," he said through the glass. "Fifteen minutes."

"Come on, man," the guy said, stamping his feet. "It's freezin' out here. A deck of smokes and I'm outa your hair."

He looked at Yaghi with such need, such desperation, Yaghi found himself unlocking the door. In spite of the expensive overcoat, the guy looked the way Yaghi felt these days—worn out, ready to say fuck it and walk—and the sight opened a vein of pity in him.

Marty hustled inside, trailing a wake of cold air. "Thanks a million," he said through chattering teeth. "You're a life saver."

Yaghi locked the door and scooted behind the counter, wishing now he'd made the guy wait. "You better not be a thief," he said with his thick, Middle-East accent. The guy had those quick, sneaky eyes, taking everything in. Like his wife. "Four times this year I got robbed. God damn cops, good for nothing."

"Hell, no," Marty said. "Just gimme a deck of Players mild." He took out Keith's still-fat wallet. "Wait. Make that a carton."

Yaghi put the merchandise on the counter and punched it in. Instead of paying, Marty wandered off down an aisle and came back with a bottle of extra strength aspirin. He bit off the childproof cap, shook a few tablets into his mouth and started chewing.

Yaghi punched in the aspirin. "That'll be..."

But Marty was gone again, this time to the candy rack. He returned with a couple of Turkish Delight chocolate bars, a package of Clorets chewing gum and a jumbo bag of ketchup-flavored potato chips.

Getting annoyed now, Yaghi said, "Will that be all?"

"That'll do her," Marty said. He fished a couple of twenties out of the wallet and slid them across the counter. He noticed the lottery ticket in there and slid it over, too. "Be a sport and check this puppy out for me while you're at it."

As Yaghi made change the guy wandered off again, this time to the drink cooler. He grinned as he brought a six-pack of Pepsi to the cash.

Yaghi punched it in, then counted out Marty's change.

Marty said, "You're Lebanese, right?"

Yaghi nodded, thinking, no, jackass, I'm Japanese.

"Know why they don't let Lebanese guys play hockey?"

Yaghi shook his head.

"'Cause every time one of 'em gets in a corner, he opens a fucking store!"

Marty brayed laughter. Bagging the purchases, Yaghi remained poker faced. He slid the bag across the counter.

"Anything else?"

Marty said, "Hey, man, nothing personal." He hefted the bag and started for the door. Yaghi got there ahead of him and unlocked it.

Marty said, "Thanks for letting me in," and stepped out into the cold. Yaghi shut the door behind him, gooseflesh rising on his arms. Before he had a chance to turn the key, Marty was pushing the door open again. "I almost forgot," he said. "You check that ticket for me?"

Yaghi muttered something unpleasant in his native tongue and stalked back to the cash. Marty returned to the counter and set the bag down. Yaghi fed the ticket into the machine, which immediately began to bleep and hoot like a pinball machine. Yaghi's face seemed to actually fall open.

"What?" Marty said. "I got a free ticket?"

"Holy-fuck-me-jesus!"

"What?"

Yaghi plucked the ticket from the machine, gaping at it with great excitement. "Ten million dollars! Ten *million* dollars!"

"Get the fuck outa here."

"I'm not lying!"

Marty put his hand out for the ticket. "Well hand it over, man! I gotta see this with my own eyes!"

Yaghi said, "I can't believe it. Eight years I got this machine, nobody win nothing." He leaned forward and actually kissed the machine. "Ten million dollars..."

Getting testy, Marty said, "Yeah, well, listen Sahib, it's *my* ten million dollars, so hand it over. You're bending the fuck out of it."

Yaghi started to do just that. The rules of fair play and propriety he'd learned since coming to this country demanded no less. But as he held out the ticket, something dawned inside him in a glorious sunburst, burning off a twelve-year fog. His was a proud people, a warring people, and in the many years he'd been isolated from their influence, chained to this counter under the watchful eye of his wife, he'd forgotten that part of his heritage, that part of himself. It came back to him now, though—oh, yeah—big, bright and unstoppable. In his mind's eye he saw the events of the next few seconds with total clarity.

He reached down and switched on the surveillance camera. Then he looked squarely at Marty. "The door's unlocked. Open it and get out. We're not open yet."

Marty said, "Hey!" sticking his hand out. "Are those ears painted on? Gimme the fuckin' ticket!"

Cool as hell, Yaghi said, "What ticket?" tucked it into his shirt pocket and folded his arms across his skinny chest. Case closed.

"You're cute," Marty said. "A fuckin' comedian. Now give it up before I get ugly."

Yaghi let his arms drift to his sides, like a gunslinger. "Get out or I call the cops."

"All right, greaser," Marty said, pulling the switchblade from his hip pocket. "Last chance." The blade whipped free, six inches of razor-sharp steel gleaming in the sunlight. "Hand that fucker over *now*, or I swear to God, I'll gut you like a trout."

"In my country we pick our toes with a toy like that," Yaghi said, bating him. "This is *your* last chance. Get out of my store or I throw you out."

"Okay, fuckface, we'll do it the hard way."

Marty launched himself at the counter and started scrambling over the top. In one smooth sweep, Yaghi drew a sawed-off shotgun from under the counter and shot him in the face. In the force of the blast Marty went airborne in a spectacular reversal of momentum, arcing out like a diver leaving a platform, but with none of the diver's grace. He was dead before he slammed into the candy rack. The bag containing his purchases flew off the counter with him, the six-pack exploding on the floor, Pepsi fizzing out to join a spreading puddle of Marty's blood.

Deafened by the report, Yaghi ran to the door and locked it, then sagged to the floor behind the counter. He laid the shotgun beside him and fished the ticket out of his pocket with trembling fingers, barely noticing the freckles of Marty's blood on his forearms. He could hardly breathe.

Ten million dollars, he kept thinking. Ten million dollars....

Kate couldn't believe it when she saw him, sitting up in bed in the Stepdown Unit, a nurse on either side of him and a grin on his face, sipping ice water through a straw with that turban on his head, a sultan flirting with the house girls.

One of the nurses saw her come in and said, "You must be Kate. Your dad's been telling us all about you. He says you're going to be a famous screenwriter someday." She smiled, having fun. "He's got us playing your movie trivia game. Isn't he a whip?"

Kate said, "Be careful what you bet him." And to her father, "Dad, you behave."

"Ladies," Keith said, his voice still hoarse, "excuse me, if you will. The princess beckons."

The second nurse, olive-skinned and petite, said, "Okay, Keith, just one more. Get this one and I'll rub your feet." She scrunched her green eyes to slits, looked flatly into the distance and said, "'We're all gonna die.'"

Keith chuckled. "Fetch the Baby Oil, Rose. *Predator*, nineteen eighty-eight. What Billy, the big Indian says. Best line in the movie."

"'I ain't got time to bleed,' is my favorite," Kate said, capturing her father's full attention. The nurses took it as their cue to leave. Kate pulled up a chair and took his hand. "So how you doin', *Keith*? You old smoothie."

He grinned at the gentle rib. "Not bad, you know, considering the mileage. This epidural's a wonder. And they gave me a shot this morning for my fingers. They throb some." He noticed her cast for the first time. "What about you? You broke your arm?"

Kate rapped her knuckles against the cast. "Yeah. Aches a little. Itchy. No biggy." It amazed her how bright he was this morning. "How much do you remember?"

"I remember the accident. And that big bugger in the orange jumpsuit trying to stick something down my throat. After that, not much 'til this morning. What about what's-his-name—Bernie—the limo guy?"

"He didn't make it."

Keith looked at his broken legs, considering this news. He said, "Then we were lucky, you and I."

"Yes, we were."

He gave her a wan smile. "Some millionaires, huh?"

Here it was, then. She squeezed his hand and said, "Dad, we're not millionaires anymore."

"What do you mean?"

"We were robbed. On the highway, after the accident. Some guy, he stopped and took everything, including your wallet. I didn't want to tell you right away, but…"

Keith's faced tightened, a blankness coming into his eyes. He said, "No, Katie, I'm glad you did." He sighed and Kate thought she'd never heard a more defeated sound. It broke her heart. "Got everything, huh?"

"Pretty much."

"Even Janey's Big Bird?"

Kate blew air through her nose, as close to a laugh as she could muster. Even in the face of such abysmal news her father was trying to make light of it. "No, he didn't get Big Bird. But I got blood all over it."

Keith shook his head. "You know, honey, it almost seems just. I got greedy. And afraid. All that money, I just couldn't wait to get my mitts on it. I should've waited. We could've driven down later, once the weather cleared. I'm sorry. I got your hopes up for nothing. I even jeopardized your life."

"Dad, please. I was just as excited as you."

That terrible sigh again. "Did you report the theft?"

"Not—"

"Yes, Mister Whipple." Kate turned to see Steve standing in the doorway, jacket slung over one shoulder. He came in and stood at the foot of the bed. "To me."

"Oh, Dad," Kate said, flushing a little. God, she couldn't take her eyes off this guy. "This is Constable Steve Seger. He was at the accident."

"Pleased to make your acquaintance," Keith said.

"Same here, sir."

"So tell me, Constable, are we out of luck here?"

"Maybe not," Steve said. "I put out an unofficial report on the computer with a list of stolen items. You had some expensive merchandise there, sir, but it's not much good to a thief unless he can fence it. It's a long shot, but it might turn something up. You should file an official report, though, as soon as you can. We also put a call in to the Lottery Corporation. They said you can file an appeal for payment without the actual ticket, but it's complicated. The good news is, they agreed that if our boy shows up trying to cash it, they'll detain him and notify us. That's how I think we're going to catch him."

Keith said, "Wouldn't it be his word against ours?"

"If it comes down to that, Mister Whipple, you let us worry about it." He pulled on his jacket. "Anyway, I just wanted to pass that along. I'm going to go now, let you two visit. Nice meeting you, sir."

"Likewise," Keith said. "And thanks for your help."

"Glad to do it," Steve said. He turned to Kate. "Uh, if your dad's okay, it probably makes sense to file that ticket claim as soon as possible. I was thinking, if you'd like, I could drive you there later this morning."

Caught off guard, Kate said, "That'd be great," feeling her face turn three shades of scarlet. Her father always said she got that from her mom. She glanced at Keith, who nodded, a sparkle in his eyes she couldn't help notice. "Sounds like a good idea," he said.

"Okay," Steve said, a little red-faced himself. "They open at nine. What say I meet you back here at quarter to?"

"Sounds like a plan."

He gave her a cheerful smile and left. Keith caught Kate's wistful gaze as she watched him go.

"Finally," he said, grinning. "Grandchildren."

"Dad!"

FINDERS KEEPERS

Tarek Yaghi got to his feet. He'd been slumped behind the counter since the shooting, twenty minutes, maybe more, his mind going a mile a minute: rehearsing what he'd tell the police, deciding on the best way to deal with his wife, picturing what it was going to be like to be handed a check for ten million dollars. He hadn't felt this alive since his teens, running wild in the streets of Beirut, living by his wits in those days, stealing food from vendors' stalls, finding shelter where he could. And later, after fleeing Lebanon for the Greek islands at the age of fifteen, trading sex for money in the tourist hotels. Soft American women with a taste for brown boys. He had a purpose back then, a mission: to find his fortune and return to Beirut, to his parents and three baby sisters, to liberate them from the squalor of the slums. And no matter how far fate had taken him from his homeland, no matter how many empty years had gone by since those heady days, that dream had never left him. He'd prayed and he'd believed. And at last, Allah had answered.

Yaghi gazed at the ticket with bitter-sweet tears in his eyes, thinking, Twelve years. Twelve years since he first set foot in this godless store, an illegal immigrant of twenty-six, one short step ahead of the law. Claudette sitting at the till on that rainy September afternoon—a fine big woman in those days, before she blew herself up to three hundred pounds in front of the TV—looking up from one of her romance novels as he entered, lizard eyes eating him whole even then; Yaghi asking in his broken English about the HELP WANTED sign in the window. Claudette hired him on the spot, treating him with affection and respect in those first sweet months. So sly, drawing him slowly, almost willingly into a life of slavery. Within a year, luring him first with rich food and wine, then with the most exciting sex he'd ever had, she found her hook, offering citizenship and security in exchange for a contract of marriage. "Marry me, Tarek, and I'll look after you. And someday soon, your family, too." Signing documents in front of her lawyer—partnership papers, she told him—changing the name of the store to Yaghi's Market, filling him with pride; Yaghi finding out only years later, after threatening to leave her for lying about his family, that what he'd signed was a prenuptial agreement. "You go out that door, Yaghi, you go with the clothes on your back." Penniless if he left her, nothing to show for his years of servitude. So he stayed, biding his time, skimming what he could to send to his family, still living in the same rat-infested tenement in Beirut.

He said it out loud, "Twelve years," letting it build. Twelve years working six-thirty to eleven, seven days a week, Claudette coming up with new and thinner excuses each day for not pulling her weight. "My arthritis is bad today, Tarek, I don't think I can make it in." "Mother's heart is acting up again, she needs me close." "Michael Douglas is gonna be on Oprah this afternoon and you know how I just love Michael..." And on and on, until she just stopped bothering. The only time she did come in anymore was to run one of her surprise inspections on him, like he was an employee instead of her husband.

He couldn't wait to get even. And it was going to be so easy. Just show her the ticket and walk.

He looked over at Marty and felt his gorge rise. The guy's face was...gone. Luckily no customers had come to the door. He only wanted to have to explain this once.

He tucked the ticket into his shirt pocket and got moving, dragging a dusty tarp out of the back and throwing it over the corpse, then going to the phone and dialing a number from memory.

"Come on," he said as it rang. "Be home...be home..."

It was picked up on the eighth ring, the breathless, sing-song voice warming his heart: "Hello?"

"Marilyn, it's me."

"Tar! Oh, it's so *nice* to hear from you! I was just in the shower." She pitched her voice low and sexy. "I was thinking of you."

Yaghi squirmed, turned on in spite of the circumstances. Maybe because of them. He said, "Listen, I need you tonight."

"But honey, what about your wife?"

"Everything's changed. Will you be there?"

"Of course I will."

"Okay, good. See you later." He cut the connection and dialed 911.

Lee Merrick, the eldest of Keith's three siblings, showed up at eight-thirty that morning with a black duffel bag and a large Tim Horton's coffee. She plunked the bag on the bedside table, then the coffee, then bent to give Keith a noisy kiss on the mouth. She turned and gave Kate one, too. She said, "Have you ever tried to find a parking spot at this place?" looked at Keith's legs and started to bawl.

"Hey, come on," Keith said. "It's not that bad. Really, we're fine."

"I know, I know," Lee said, accepting Kate's hug. "It's just such a shock." She sniffed—a small, angular woman of sixty-four with deep-set eyes the color of worn denim—said, "Okay, enough of that," unzipped the duffel bag and started unloading. "We got a deck of cards for Crazy Eights. The bible according to Leonard Maltin." She slapped the fat movie guide on the table next to the cards. "If I can't stump you with this thing, I give up. We got a jumbo bag of Werther's Originals, your favorite. A stack of movie magazines—sorry, little brother, no skin books in your condition." She winked at Kate. "Some home-made butter tarts for when you're eating again. Lose the Tupperware and I'll kill ya. Warm socks— they're Dale's, but don't worry I soaked 'em in Javex overnight— and a couple of Stephen King paperbacks." She said to Kate, "I've been trying to get him to read King's novels since the seventies. See if he can squirm out of it now."

Finished with the bag, Lee sat in a chair next to Kate. "So tell me," she said, "what's it like to be filthy rich?"

In a somber voice Keith told her what happened, Kate filling in the details that were sketchy for him. Lee listened, white as a ghost.

When he was done Kate said into the silence, "I'm going to try calling my boss again." She'd told Keith earlier about her chat with Morris. "Before Steve gets here."

Keith said, "Do you think it'd help to talk to him in person?"

"Yeah, maybe, but..."

Lee looked back and forth between them, puzzled.

Keith said, "So why don't you take a run home. I'm in good hands here. If you think it'll help you get your job back, you should go."

Lee said, "I'm lost. Who's Steve? And honey, you got fired?"

Keith said, "Lee, I'll explain it all later." And to Kate, "Have you got enough money for bus fare?"

Lee said, "To Sudbury? On the bus? Forget it, honey, if you're going you can take my car. And don't worry about your dad. I'm staying right here. I can nap in the family room, I already checked. When Dale gets hungry enough, he'll eat. I'm more worried about the dogs."

Kate said, "Then maybe I will," thinking how good her father was at reading her. "Morris is an ass, but I need the job. And I can get us some clean clothes and stuff while I'm there."

Keith said, "Yeah, bring my shaving gear. And my trades, I need my magazines."

"All right," Kate said. "Thanks, Aunt Lee. If I can set something up with Mo for tonight I'll leave right after I file the claim."

Lee said, "Now who's—" just as Steve walked in.

"I'm a little early," he said, his eyes on Kate. He'd been wandering around the lobby drinking coffee, watching the clock, thinking how slowly time passed when you wanted it to.

Standing, Kate said, "Aunt Lee, this is Steve Seger. He's with the O.P.P."

Lee stuck her hand out and smiled, her curiosity stretched to the limit now. "Oh. Hello, Steve."

Steve shook her hand and said hello.

"Okay," Kate said. "You two have a nice visit. I'll be back in an hour or so for the car." She looked at Steve and smiled. "Shall we?"

When they were gone, Lee said, "Oh, my. Sparks flying there."

In the hospital lobby Kate said, "Would you mind if I made a quick call?" and Steve said, "Of course not. I'll bring the truck around and meet you out front. It's a green Cherokee, lots of rust."

She went to a bank of public phones near the tuck shop and used her calling card, dialing Mo's office number from memory. His wife Roxanne picked up.

"Panther Courier, Roxanne speaking, how can I help you?"

"Rox, it's Kate."

"Kate, hi! Please tell me you're coming back to work."

"That's why I'm calling. I already talked to Mo and—"

"I know, believe me, I heard about it. I love the man, Kate, but he's full of shit. You know that."

"I was thinking about driving home today, maybe meet with him?"

"That'd be the way to do it."

"You think he'll see me?"

"I'll make him. Seven months pregnant he's got me driving a goddam truck. What time suits you?"

"I was thinking six-thirty, seven o'clock."

"Meet him at Eddie's at seven. Buy him a beer, nod your head and I'll do the rest."

"Thanks, Rox."

"Don't thank me, thank you. How's you dad?"

"Pretty wracked up right now, but they tell me he's going to be fine."

"Glad to hear it, Kate. Gotta go."

Kate hung up and walked outside, her arm starting to ache inside the cast. Steve was waiting for her at the bottom of the steps, opening the passenger door.

By nine o'clock that morning Yaghi's Market had become an official crime scene, the entire block barricaded off, a half-dozen cop cars angle-parked in front of the store. A forensics team was busy doing its thing, shooting pictures of the body, dusting for prints, whatever else those guys did. Yaghi watched them with patient disinterest. He stood in his usual spot, thinking he'd never have to work the till again or freeze his ass off in that cooler, never have to watch some old granny count through her pennies or chase dogs out of the garbage out back. The thought filled him with the sweetest serenity.

Hunkered down at his side, viewing the video footage of his encounter with Marty Small, was a beefy homicide detective by the name of Jack Cullen. Yaghi had liked the man right away. Huge guy, towering over Yaghi's slight frame, but not the least bit intimidating. His hand shake had been friendly and warm and, considering his size, surprisingly gentle. Unlike most of the cops Yaghi had come in contact with since coming to this country, all swagger and attitude, this guy didn't make him feel like a criminal.

"Jesus," Cullen said now, watching as a grainy, black-and-white Marty Small did a half gainer into the candy rack. "You sure tagged his ass." He stood, his knees popping like firecrackers.

Yaghi said, "I got any trouble for this, officer?"

Cullen smiled. "I wouldn't lose too much sleep over it, Mister Yaghi. Heck, if I get my way they'll pin a medal on you. You'll have to come down to headquarters, of course, make a statement, but with this video we should be able to get you back on the street in a matter of hours."

Yaghi nodded gratefully, his hand going to his shirt pocket of its own accord, touching the bounty inside. At Cullen's request he retrieved the video cassette and handed it over into evidence. Then Cullen told him to get his coat. It was time to go downtown.

7

THE LOTTERY CORPORATION WAS located on Bloor Street, ground floor of the Xerox building. Kate was surprised at how unspectacular the place was. A cramped waiting area with a row of chairs against one wall, the word WINNERS suspended above them in foot-high silver characters. A pair of red-velvet ropes slung through brass posts forming a cordon for customers to file their way up to the semicircular cashiers' counter. And as a nod to the season, an artificial tree and some cheesy looking Santa faces strung across the low ceiling. Kate didn't know what she'd expected, but this sure wasn't it.

At the moment there was only one cashier on duty, a rail-thin brunette in her twenties, and they had to wait behind an old guy with a stack of winning tickets, one of which was hefty enough to warrant a check. During the five or so minutes it took to cut the check the old guy told the cashier about his dead wife, his condo in Palm Beach and how lonely it got down there sometimes, all that hot sand and sunshine and no one to share it with. While they waited Kate and Steve made whispered bets, how long it would take the old boy to invite the girl down to Florida. Disappointing them both, a balding guy with a Zorro mustache brought out the check and interrupted the proceedings. The old man took his winnings and left.

Steve said, "Too bad. I think she was ready."

Kate said, "Please. You're making my skin crawl."

"Can you picture it? The two of them cuddling on the beach in the moonlight—"

The cashier said, "Can I help you?"

Kate stepped up to the counter, trying to erase an image of that bandy-legged old dude and this young, gum-chewing clerk naked together on a Daffy Duck beach towel. She shook her head and bit back a grin. For the first few seconds she couldn't look the girl in the eye.

She said, "Yes, I was wondering what the procedure is for claiming on a lost winning ticket. Stolen actually." The cashier seemed uninterested until Kate said, "It was the Saturday draw."

"Hold on," the cashier said, serious now, "I'll have to get my supervisor." She got out of her chair. "Can I have your names, please?"

"I'm Kate Whipple and this is Steve Seger."

The girl nodded, eyes raised for a beat as she logged the names into memory. Then she hurried off into a back hall lined with offices, leaving them alone at the counter listening to synthesized Christmas music. She reappeared a minute later, said, "Come this way," and lifted a hinged section of the counter.

Steve said, "You want me to wait out here or…?"

"Would you mind coming in with me?" Kate said.

Steve said of course not and followed her through the gap in the counter.

The girl led them to a cramped back office and got them seated in front of a metal desk. "Mr. Tasker will be right with you," she said and made a quick exit, pulling the door shut behind her. The air in here was stuffy, stale cigarette smoke and cologne. There was a framed photo on the desk of three bland, unsmiling children, a phone and not much else.

Kate whispered, "I feel like I'm in the principal's office."

"Nervous?" Steve said.

"Mm-hm."

"Makes sense, there's a lot at stake. But remember, you're in the right here. You and your father won that money fair and square and you were robbed. You're only claiming what's rightfully yours."

Kate gave him a grateful smile, realizing only then that she had been feeling oddly ashamed about being here. Like she was begging or about to plead some hopelessly pathetic case.

Tasker came in then, a big ex-linebacker type with a flashy PR smile and a firm handshake, which he promptly bestowed on each of them, leaning over Kate to do Steve first. He addressed them by their first names, like they were old pals, introduced himself as Jim Tasker, "Call me Jim", and Kate thought, Oh boy, I can see how this is going to go.

He sat behind his desk, glanced at the photo of the kids with a look Kate couldn't quite read, then folded his hands on the desk in front of him. Kate noticed the clunky team ring on his finger. Jock, all right.

Tasker said, "Sandy tells my you folks are here to file a claim on a missing ticket?"

Steve flashed his badge. "That's correct, Mister Tasker. I'm Constable Seger. An associate of mine, Detective Sergeant Brown, spoke with a Ms. Harris yesterday morning regarding—"

"Yes, of course," Tasker said. "I was off yesterday. Mary-Lou—Ms. Harris—told me about it this morning. We've agreed to detain whoever shows up with the ticket." He pulled an official looking document out of a drawer and set it on the desk, squaring it with those big hands. "I've got the declaration form right here. I should ask you though, is the ticket in question yours?" Speaking to Kate now.

"Well, officially it's my father's, but—"

"See, there's our first problem. To start a case, to actually initiate a claim, we need to deal directly with the ticket owner. If not, we're into power of attorney, privacy restrictions, that sort of thing."

"My father's in the hospital right now, Mr. Tasker. We were involved in a serious traffic accident." She showed him her cast. "He won't be available to come in here probably for weeks, so he's asked me to act on his behalf."

Tasker said, "I understand, Kate, and I'm not saying we can't discuss the specifics, you know, familiarize you with the procedures involved. But to actually get the ball rolling—there's a whole investigation that needs to be done, a number of official bodies that have to consider your claim based on specific points of evidence—for that we need the ticket owner, in this case your father, or legal proof that you are empowered to act on his behalf." All of this in his annoyingly cheerful sports announcer's voice.

Kate said, "That shouldn't be a problem. Though it does seem an unnecessary delay. It would be nice to...get the ball rolling before too much time has gone by."

"Frankly, Kate," Tasker said, "even if this whole thing pans out in your favor, the Corporation won't pay out on this claim for a full year from the date of ticket purchase. Unless, of course, the ticket turns up."

"Okay, let me put it this way," Kate said. "Say I come back here in an hour with power of attorney. What happens then?"

"You'll fill out and sign the proper forms, then we'll ask you to provide us with all the information you have about the ticket. Stated bluntly, Kate, to convince us the ticket is yours. By the way, did your father sign the back of the ticket and make a photocopy? The instructions are clearly stated on the back of all our ticket stock. And the retailer's machine should have issued a claim form when the ticket came up a winner."

Kate could feel herself blushing. "My father's paranoid about those machines. He doesn't trust them. He always checks his tickets by hand, from the store display or the newspaper." And she was willing to bet he'd never read the back of a ticket in all the years he'd been playing the lotteries. She never had. Those tiny red letters, almost illegible. He probably had no idea he was supposed to sign the damned thing. Everyone played, but who ever really expected to win? And even if he did know, in all the excitement he'd probably just forgotten. "But he plays the same numbers all the time," Kate said. "Some are family birth dates, others correspond to other important dates in his life. And he always buys them at the same store, unless we're out of town for some reason. The guy who runs the place is a friend of his, he could tell you." She shook her head. She was spinning her wheels here. She glanced at Steve, but his eyes were fixed on Tasker.

Tasker said, "All right. Here's the situation from our end. As you know, we're talking serious money here. To protect ourselves we have to rule out the possibility of a fraudulent claim. It only makes sense."

"Are you calling me a liar, Mr. Tasker?"

"No, Kate, of course not. All I'm saying is, it happens. Everything's been tried, from the sublime to the ridiculous, believe me, but because our security measures are so strict the Corporation hasn't yet lost a dime to fraud. If what you're telling me is true, it's understandable that you're upset—"

Kate said, "I'm not upset, Mr. Tasker, but if you suggest one more time that I'm a liar, I will be."

Tasker began to fidget. "Okay, Kate, let me start over. Look, here's what I suggest. Arrange for power of attorney, as we've already discussed. Then come back, we'll complete the necessary paperwork and you'll be allowed to build your case. If we feel there's validity to your claim, it will be passed on to a group of senior people in the Corporation who form a claim review committee. They will then decide whether or not the claim should be paid. How does that sound?"

Steve said, "Why the one year wait?"

"Because we still have to allow that someone else might come forward with a legitimate claim to the ticket." He shrugged and smiled, his hands tied.

"All right, Mr. Tasker," Kate said, standing. "I apologize if I was short with you. It's been a trying couple of days."

"No problem, Kate," Tasker said. "I hope everything works out for you." He stood. "Come on, I'll show you out."

Kate said, "That could have gone better."

The whole scene with Tasker had got her head aching again. On the way out of the Xerox Building she'd dry-swallowed one of the Tylenol 3s, but it wasn't helping. Her head felt like something was trying to punch its way out from the inside. They were in Steve's Cherokee now, heading back to the hospital.

Steve said, "That's the trouble with PR men. It's like talking to the wall. Run a background check on a guy like that, dimes to donuts he comes up an ex-realtor or a used car salesman." He gave her a chin-up smile. "But hey, it could still work out in your favor. From what you've told me, your father should be able to prove the ticket's his, no problem. The lottery people know which machine it was issued on, no way the creep who robbed you's going to know that. The only down side is you'll have to wait a year to collect."

Steve's right hand rested on the gear shift and Kate touched it, meaning only to thank him for his help. The touch must have startled him because he flinched slightly and Kate heard a breath dart into him and stop. She opened her mouth to say the words and watched her fingertip trace the veins on the back of his hand, feeling the thrill of it in places that had been asleep too long. There was an unexpected intensity to the sensation she hadn't experienced since her first trembling breaths of sexuality as a girl of eleven or twelve, playing spin the bottle or holding hands on the porch-swing while the adults played euchre in the kitchen. It lasted only a moment, as far as she could tell, before she changed it to the grateful pat she'd intended and took her hand away.

"I'd like to thank you for all your help," she said, her voice breaking, betraying her.

"It's really no trouble," Steve said, glancing at her as he swung right onto the Gardner Expressway on-ramp. "I'm glad to help."

There was a charged silence then, almost anticipatory, Steve driving, Kate tapping her toes to the tune on the radio, Johnny Lang's, "Lie To Me." As they merged into traffic she looked out her side-window at the gray shaft of the CN Tower, not really seeing it, hiding her face in the delicious fear that Steve could read her thoughts.

"You like the blues?" he said, forcing her to look at him.

"Sure."

"Yeah, me too. Did I tell you my mother's from Memphis? Home of the blues?"

"Really? Have you ever been there?"

"Lots of times. We were there just last summer. My grandfather's a big karate guy, has a dojo down there about five minutes' walk from Graceland."

Kate said, "Get outa town! I *love* Elvis."

"I met him."

"You're lying."

"God's truth. I was five, maybe six, and he was already all bloated up and everything. My grandfather used to teach him sometimes. Elvis was a karate nut and my grandfather's pretty well known in that circle. Elvis came into the dojo one afternoon while I was there, watching my mother and grandfather train."

"Oh, my God! Did you get his autograph or anything?"

"I was five. I didn't know Elvis from Castro. All I remember is he had beautiful eyes. He gave me a Cadillac, though."

Kate said, "Now I know you're lying," wanting to touch him again, feeling like it was permitted, like she'd been doing it forever and had for some reason simply forgotten.

"Okay, there's no Cadillac, but I did meet him. I'd swear to it on a stack of bibles. My grandfather's got an autographed picture of the two of them in their gis right there on the dojo wall. Elvis with those big old sideburns. My grandfather's a musician too, plays a mean blues harp. I spent most of my summers with him in Memphis when I was a kid. He'd drive us over the border into Mississippi sometimes to a place called Junior Kimbrough's—an actual juke joint, it's still there—no sign on the place, just a shack on the side of a dirt road. My grandfather'd get up sometimes and jam, keep me up half the night. My mother still doesn't know about those trips. B.B. King's got a night club right there on Beale Street. I saw Jerry Lee Lewis there last summer, the guy set the piano on fire with a can of lighter fluid." Steve looked at her and smiled, raising his eyebrows. "And if you're into voodoo, you've got Schwab's Dry Goods right down the street. Eye of newt. Bubble, bubble, toil and trouble."

Kate thought, Wow. The codeine must be kicking in. She giggled.

Steve said, "You know, Kate, there's a great blues club near my place. The Blue Room. I go there all the time. I was thinking, you know, if you're going to be around a while anyways, maybe we could..."

Kate touched his hand again, to hell with it, giving him a coy smile. She said, "Constable Seger, are you putting the moves on me?"

"Why, yes, Miss Whipple, I believe I am."

"Well," Kate said, excited by her boldness, "you have the court's permission to proceed."

"So..." he said, waiting. "Would you? Like to?"

"I would. But it can't be tonight."

"Of course not," Steve said, like the thought had never occurred to him. "Some other night. Once the dust settles. What are your plans, anyway? You have a job to get back to?"

"As a matter of fact, I'm planning to drive home later today to see if I can get my job *back*. When Dad won the lottery, I quit. Stupid move."

"How are you getting home?"

"My aunt's car."

"You know what? I could drive you. I'm on holidays anyways, nothing else planned."

"A police escort?" Kate said, smiling. The poor guy was blushing. "That'd be great."

"Then it's settled."

Kate left Steve in the truck while she ran into the hospital to let her dad know about the change in plans. He and Aunt Lee were playing cards, Lee winning as usual, Keith looking tired but comfortable, propped up in bed against a mound of pillows. Kate told them what Tasker had said about power of attorney and Lee jumped right in.

"Kate, your uncle Fred—Dale's brother—remember him?"

Kate said she did. She hadn't seen him in years but she remembered him, his cold hand sliding too low on her back when he hugged her at a family reunion, hard liquor on his breath. She couldn't've been more than twelve. The guy was a pig.

"Well, Fred's a lawyer," Lee said. "Not a very good one, but he could do this for you. I'll make him. I'll set it up for tomorrow. And if he asks for money, you tell him to take it up with me."

"Okay," Kate said. "Thanks, Aunt Lee." What the hell, she'd keep her distance.

She told them next about Steve's offer to drive her home and Keith said fine, I'm sure he's a good driver, call when you get in. Kate promised she would, said she expected to be back late tonight, then kissed them both goodbye.

She stopped off in the tuck shop on the way out and picked up some snacks—chips and Cheezies, bottled juice and chewing gum—then joined Steve in the truck.

"All set?" he said.

"Ten-four," Kate said. And they were off.

The roads out of the city were wet but bare, the only evidence of Sunday night's blizzard the huge snow banks that lined the shoulders and a procession of road signs shrouded in ice. The day was sunny and mild and the two-day forecast for the Toronto area promised more of the same.

By the time they reached Barrie, Steve had already told Kate about his mom, his stint at police college and some of the mischief he'd gotten into down there.

"So why the police force?" Kate said. "Because of your mom?"

Steve shook his head. "The real reason?"

"Are there any others?"

"Okay, but if you laugh, it's a long cold walk to Sudbury. Dirty Harry."

"You're a cop because of Dirty Harry?"

"Yeah! Man, when I was a kid I must've watched that movie a hundred times. The others, too, but the first one was the best."

"Agreed."

"And the kicker? The movie was released on the day I was born. Like Karma or something. Not only that, my folks were *at* the movie when my mom went into labor."

Kate turned her face away, hiding a grin.

"Clint," Steve said. "The dude is so cool. Even now. This is dumb, huh? But damn, I'd watch Dirty Harry and I'd wanna be him so bad. I used to practice that look, that squinty thing he does? I'd practice it in front of the mirror, use it on the hard cases at school."

"Did it work?"

"Froze 'em dead in their tracks."

"And now?"

Steve's smile faded. In his mind's eye flare-light played over the dead boy's face, making the Spiderman figures on his pajamas seem to caper.

"Now...well, it's different when the carnage is real." After a brief silence he said, "So what about you? You like your job?"

"I like it well enough. I enjoy scooting around in the van, the people I work with. And I meet lots of interesting folks on deliveries. My real ambition, though, is to write for the silver screen. You know, 'Screenplay by Kate Whipple'."

Steve looked at her and smiled, impressed. "Really? You're a writer?"

"Well, not officially. I haven't sold anything yet. But I intend to."

"That's so cool. I can barely write a grocery list." He looked back at the road. "Screenplays, huh? Did you take a course or something?"

"Just a summer thing, locally, with a traveling film institute. But I'm sure I've seen more movies than any six normal people, and I've downloaded dozens of scripts off the internet. I read them the way other people read novels. They're fun, and not all that hard to put together once you get the hang of it. And I've read a bunch of how-to books."

"Any nibbles?"

"I did a girl-buddy thing around the time *Thelma and Louise* came out that got some attention from a small indie company."

"That's fantastic."

"Yeah, I thought so, too. But the company went bust and the film never got made."

"That's bad luck. But it's only a setback, right? I mean, they wanted to make the film. And—" Steve was startled into silence by the sudden change in Kate's expression.

"Look," she said, pointing through the windscreen. "Over there."

They were coming up on the spot where the limo plowed into the rock cut. The snow down there was all churned up, bits of gift wrap snagged in the branches of a broken sapling, a jagged scar of white paint on the ancient granite. A few hundred yards farther along, on the opposite side of the road, the snow was melted in a huge crater shape, the exposed ground charred black from the flaming tanker.

Steve switched the radio off, its tinny cheerfulness suddenly an intrusion. He accelerated discretely, Kate turning for a last look as the scene dwindled behind them.

They were quiet for a time, then Kate said, "I was convinced I was going to die out here. I kept fading in and out, and I'd see my father lying out there in the cold, not moving, the snow covering his face..."

"It must have been terrible," Steve said, touching her hand, ice cold under his fingertips.

"I kept wishing I'd made more of my days, you know? I've been on cruise for so long now, just...marking time. Emotionally." She faced Steve, wanting to get this said. "I'm not all that religious, I admit that. But I prayed to God for another chance. I asked Him to spare me and my dad." She took his hand, squeezing it. "And he sent you."

"Funny," Steve said. "I've been thinking it was the other way around."

Kate gave him a half smile, wanting to savor the tenderness of this moment but feeling she had to go on. "Have you ever read the story 'The Monkey's Paw'?"

"The one about wishing for money and getting it the hard way?"

"Yeah," Kate said, her face reddening. "I used to do that a lot."

"Who hasn't?"

"But I mean a lot. Like it was some kind of answer. I'd think, if only I had money, all my problems would be solved."

Facing her, Steve said, "That's not really anything to be ashamed of though, is it, Kate? The way our society's set up, money *does* solve a lot of problems. It's a nice thing to have. I can flip through a *People* magazine and get jealous as hell, seeing the way some folks get to live."

Kate said, "But what I'm getting at, I didn't really have any problems before that ticket came along. I had a job, a future planned, a father with two strong legs. Now..." She paused, thinking for the second time since meeting him, Why am I telling him all this? "The excitement of it, Steve, winning...it was incredible. Your entire life changing in an instant, everything you ever dreamed of suddenly right there, within your reach. It was like a drug." She looked at their linked hands, then into his eyes. "But it changed more than just my life. It changed me. In ways I'm not very proud of."

"How do you mean?"

Kate averted her eyes. "When we were driving down in the limo the driver asked my father what he was going to do with all that money. Dad started talking about buying a condo for his mom, giving big chunks to the rest of our family, dozens of them, and I'm thinking, Shit, Dad, slow down. What about me? Don't give it all away. Like a greedy kid. And then such a sick feeling after realizing we'd lost it, like my life was over—and we'd never even seen a dime of it. This huge emotional stir over a piece of paper, something that never even materialized."

Steve looked at her and smiled, a gentle, empathic smile. "Aren't you being a bit hard on yourself, Kate? I mean, these are pretty much normal feelings we're talking about here. I'm sure I'd've felt the same way. Truthfully? I've had feelings at different times in my life I wouldn't tell a priest. The point is, having these feelings and not liking them, isn't that how we grow?"

Kate had to smile. "How'd you get so smart?"

Steve said, "I'm quoting my mother," and laughed.

They chatted comfortably after that, filling the time with facts and feelings, offering snapshots of separate lives now intersecting. Their hands remained linked until they reached the outskirts of Sudbury, the sun just beginning to sink in a riot of furnace red.

Tarek Yaghi sat on the flower-print couch in the living room of his mistress' apartment and stared at the winning ticket. Marilyn was in the kitchen, busting ice cubes out of metal trays. She was making one hell of a racket out there, chattering away, but Yaghi tuned her out. All he could think of was waving this ticket in his wife's face. With any luck the shock would kill her.

He glanced at his watch: 4:46 PM. She must have heard about the shooting by now, it was all over the news. Some of the local stations were even dubbing him a hero, 'a welcome vigilante in a neighborhood rife with violent crime'. He liked the sound of that.

Getting out of the police station had taken longer than Detective Cullen predicted, though true to his word the man had done everything in his power to speed up the process. Some bullshit about the legality of using a sawed-off shotgun for personal protection. Cullen had told him there would be an investigation, possibly even some minor charges down the road, but Yaghi could care less. By this time tomorrow he and his sugar plum would be high over the Pacific Ocean in the first class section of a 747, sipping liqueurs and feeling each other up. Bound for Australia. He'd wanted to go there ever since he saw the movie *Crocodile Dundee*. He loved Mick's accent—and that jacket. He'd have to get himself a jacket like that, with boots to match. They would have been in the air tonight, but by the time he'd finished with Cullen, the detective dropping him back at the store, the lottery office had been closed.

He'd show Claudette the ticket tonight. Or even better, wait until *after* he cashed in the ticket, show the bitch the check instead, drawn in his name, with all those lovely zeros. That'd do her in for sure—

Marilyn banged through the saloon doors from the kitchen, an aluminum ice bucket in the crook of her arm, an open bottle of champagne leaning inside.

"Just think of it," she was saying, Yaghi tuning her in now. "No more sneaking around. You don't need her anymore, Tar. You don't need her store, you don't need her apartment, and you sure don't need her penny-pinching bullshit. You're free!"

"That's right, my sweet."

Yaghi soaked her in with his eyes, a bleach-blond, buxom girl of twenty-three, heavily made-up and chubby, the way he liked his women. A strong whiff of perfume preceded her into the room. The sight of her filled his heart. She'd been a regular at the store almost a year before coming right out and asking him if he was married, that sweet face turning such a deep shade of crimson Yaghi had thought she might faint. He'd been admiring her since the first time she came in, but could never muster the courage to make the first move. He sometimes wondered if Claudette had forked out for the expensive surveillance equipment just so she could keep an eye on him. She had a way of inducing that kind of paranoia.

Marilyn minced over to the antique Welsh dresser and got out a pair of her finest crystal goblets. She set them on the coffee table beside the ice bucket, sat next to Yaghi on the couch and clutched his arm while he poured. She started chattering again, dreaming out loud, saying what they'd do when they got to Australia, see a Koala bear maybe or go snorkeling on the Great Barrier Reef. But Yaghi was someplace else.

"I can't wait to put this in her face," he said, gazing at the ticket again.

"Why bother, baby? Just disappear."

"No. I want to see the look in her eyes. So bad I can taste it. Then it's over." He looked at Marilyn, touched her round face. "Sugar Plum, when I'm free of her, I want us to be together."

Marilyn smiled. "Tar, are you proposing to me?"

"Yes," Yaghi said, taking her hand, "I am."

Marilyn bounced in her seat, giving him a big wet smack on the lips. "Oh, Tar, this is so exciting! You can file for divorce as soon as we get back."

"That's what I wanted to talk to you about," Yaghi said. He gulped down his champagne, watching as Marilyn refilled his glass, then topped up her own. "If you accept my proposal we won't be coming back."

This seemed to please her. "You mean we'll be staying in Australia?"

"No," Yaghi said. He opened his wallet and took out a dog-eared photograph, the image faded with years and repeated handling. "My family," he said, showing it to Marilyn. She leaned in close, pointing a delicate finger at the boy posed there with his parents and three baby sisters: a slim, shirtless lad with jet black hair and a dazzling smile, dark eyes full of mischief. "You," she said and Yaghi nodded. "Your mother's beautiful." She touched the face of the plump, stern looking woman in the photograph.

"I haven't told you about my past," Yaghi said, "because I try not to think about these things. But now, with this ticket…" He looked into her bright eyes that always seemed a bit startled. "We'll leave for Australia tomorrow, stay as long as you want. Then we go to Beirut, to my family. We buy a big house there and live like royalty, with you as my wife." He kissed her softly, whispering, "How does that sound?"

"Like a dream," Marilyn said, breathing the words into his mouth. "Of course I'll marry you, Tarek. You know I will. And I can't wait to meet your family."

"Good. Good…"

Leaning into him, Marilyn said, "Let's make love," her knowing fingers slipping under his shirt. "Right here, right now…"

"No," Yaghi said, pulling gently away from her. "I want to be free of her first." He drained his champagne glass and stood, the decision made. "Keep the rest on ice for me. I'll be back in an hour."

Though unhappy about it, Marilyn let him go. When he got like this, an idea in his head, there was no point standing in his way. She busied herself after he left, corking the champagne and putting it back in the fridge, fixing her face, watching TV; but she couldn't shake the dreadful feeling that had come over her as she locked the door behind her sweet Tarek.

She'd seen his wife, and she was afraid he would be no match for her.

Kate and Steve pulled up in front of the Whipple residence at a quarter to five that afternoon. During the final leg of the trip a low cloud cover crept in and now a light snow was falling, downy flakes drifting to earth on the still air. Steve followed Kate up the snow-choked path to the front door, admiring the snug fit of her jeans as she climbed the steps. After a brief struggle with the lock—that bulky cast on her arm was going to take some getting used to—she pushed her way into the foyer the two levels shared and kicked off her boots. Steve closed the door and slipped past her, their hips brushing. He sat on the steps to the upper level and unlaced his boots while Kate unlocked the door to her father's place.

"I'm just gonna get some things for my dad," she said. "He's a bear about staying clean shaven. And he'll go crazy without something to read."

Steve placed his boots side by side on the slush mat and stood.

"Come in," Kate said, opening the door. "Have a look around."

Steve followed her in, watching as she tossed her coat over the arm of a chair, took off through an archway and disappeared. Leaving his own coat on he strolled into the room, admiring the impressive home entertainment center, the comfy looking furniture and the framed movie posters on the walls: *Psycho*, *Attack of the Fifty Foot Woman*, *The Pink Panther*, *The Body Snatchers*, five or six others.

Loud enough to be heard, he said, "Is this stuff stolen?" referring to the stack of stereo components and the huge video library alphabetically arranged along a series of recessed shelves.

"That *stuff*," Kate said, "represents years of scrimping and pooled resources—and it's still not paid for. It's the eighth wonder of the world. My dad's in front of it nearly all the time." She chuckled. "I'm almost as bad."

Steve ranged further into the room, peeking through an archway into the kitchen and the bedrooms beyond. He could hear Kate rummaging around back there somewhere. He poked his head into a room off the living area that was obviously Keith's study, a small office set up in there with a Dell computer, an old dot matrix printer and a vast photo gallery covering nearly every inch of wall space.

He took a few steps into the room, examining the photographs, many of which were black and white. He found one of Kate as a baby of perhaps eleven months, cradled in the arms of a woman who was obviously her mother. Steve saw right away where Kate had gotten her smile and that forthright gaze. She'd been a chubby baby and, as he saw in an adjacent picture, a scrawny, tomboyish girl. The photo showed a kid of about nine in a *Yankees* jersey two sizes too big for her, drilling a baseball at someone off-camera. From the mischief in the child's eyes Steve was pretty sure the unseen target was her dad.

He'd just found a color shot of Kate and her senior prom date when Kate slipped up beside him, a small leather suitcase in her good hand.

"Found the rogues' gallery, huh."

"These are great," Steve said, looking now at a shot of Kate at about three, pedaling a tricycle, smiling over her shoulder at the camera. "Who's the cameraman?"

"The early ones my mom did. She was a professional photographer. Had a shop downtown for years. Family portraits mostly, but she did work for the mines, shooting underground, and some catalogue work for the old Beamish stores. She did forensic stuff too for a couple years. Murder scenes, accidents, grisly stuff like that. The rest were taken either by my father or my aunt Lee."

"Who's this guy?" Steve said, tapping the prom scene with a fingernail.

"Tucker Ward. Jock douche bag, to quote my father. He was right, too. Son of a bitch tried to feel me up before we even got to the dance."

"What'd you do?"

Kate showed him her right hand, fingers curled into a fist around the molded end of the cast. "Socked him in the jaw and went to the dance with one of my girlfriends." She tapped him on the chin with the fist. "So be advised."

"Duly noted."

"Come on," Kate said, smiling. "Let's go upstairs."

Yaghi's wife, Claudette, was on him as soon as he came in through the apartment door. "Where the hell were *you* all day?" Thudding toward him down the hallway in her white cotton nightgown, big as a parachute. "I must've phoned the store nineteen times."

Yaghi unzipped his coat, savoring the moment. "You didn't hear?"

"Hear what." Not a question, an order. But it stopped her.

"You didn't have the TV on? The radio?"

"I was on my back with a migraine all day." She squinted at him, suspicious. "What didn't I hear?"

"We had another robbery—"

"Those *mother*-fuckers!" Flapping those big arms now, fanning b.o. at him. Oh, this was rich. "Did you have the camera on? Did you call the cops? How much did they get?"

"There was only one guy," Yaghi said, still standing by the door. "He pulled a knife on me so I shot him."

"You shot him? You mean...?"

"He's dead. You didn't lose a penny. I spent all day at the police station."

Claudette clutched his arm, massive breasts shifting under the thin fabric of her nightgown, broad face brightening as the news sunk in.

"Tarek, this is fantastic! My God, why didn't you call me?" She gave him that look, narrow-eyed and sort of pouty, the one she put on when she wanted sex. Well, he was going to fuck her, all right. She said, "You know, honey, what you did, it's going to be so good for the store. Once word gets around, those hoods'll think twice before—"

"Store, store, store!" Yaghi said. He jerked his arm away from her, fed up. "That's all you ever talk about. Twelve years I got to listen to you go on about that store." Shouting at her now, letting it come. "You want to know some things about your store? There's rats in the basement, big bastards like beavers, and that sink in the back? I piss in it. Kids shoplift? I don't give a shit, let them. You don't want to do your share, that's how it is. I let my friends play poker in the store room. And once a week on Wednesdays Pedro from the laundry brings a whore in there for a piece of tail. How do you like these apples?" Claudette's eyebrows went up, but she said nothing. "You want to know what I *think* about your store? *Piss* on your store—" He pulled the ticket out of his shirt pocket and finally, gloriously, wagged it in her face "—and piss on you, too."

"What's that."

"A ticket," Yaghi said, triumphant. "To freedom."

Claudette cocked her head, squinting at him with one eye, a sniper sighting down a rifle barrel. "We won the lottery?"

"Not we," Yaghi said, the whole scene playing out exactly as he imagined it in the car, that piece-of-shit Vega she made him drive. "Me. *I* won the lottery. So you can stuff your *store* up your shit locker, because I am gone."

He slipped the ticket back into his shirt pocket and turned to leave. As he reached for the doorknob Claudette's hand closed around his wrist like a manacle. With surprising dexterity she plucked the ticket out of his pocket and held it over her head, out of Yaghi's reach.

"Nope. Uh-uh."

Yaghi made a grab for it, bouncing off her prodigious flank. "Give that back!"

"Forget about it, Yaghi. You think I don't know about your little love nest? Your scrawny *girl*friend? You asshole." She snapped the ticket between her fingers like castanets. "If you're a millionaire, then I'm a millionaire."

Real low, Yaghi said, "Okay. You want to play rough? I've been waiting a long time to do this." Then he punched his wife with everything he had, the blow coming all the way up from his balls. Claudette barely flinched. Frustrated, Yaghi hit her again, a straight-ahead pile driver this time, shredding his knuckles on her teeth. He saw blood spurt from her bottom lip and began to pinwheel his arms in a frenzied attack, slamming his fists into her moon face in vicious salvos, Claudette making only the most halfhearted attempts to avoid the blows, something in her eyes almost inviting it.

He stopped when his hands hurt too much to continue. He looked and saw Claudette smiling at him through the blood.

"You through?" she said, cuffing gore off her chin. "Because if you are, I gotta tell you—you just hit the wrong lady."

Claudette let fly with a hummer of a roundhouse. Yaghi ducked and Claudette's fist slammed through the drywall. She made a grab for him and he squirmed past her down the hall, outgunned, looking for a weapon.

"You're gonna give me that ticket," he said, his breath coming in thin gasps. "If I have to get another gun and shoot you, too, you're going to give me that ticket."

Still standing by the door Claudette stooped at the waist, grabbed the edges of the hall runner and yanked with all of her considerable might. Tacks flew, the runner came up like a curling wave and Yaghi's feet whipped out from under him. He did a midair flip with a half twist, landing on his back facing his wife, the wind knocked out of him.

Claudette put her head down and charged, her rolling shoulders barely fitting in the narrow corridor. Five feet before she reached him Claudette went airborne, landing nimbly astride him on all fours, her broad face a hovering planetoid above his, framed in stringy black hair. Her breath reeked of barbecue chips and cheap wine.

"You have no idea who you're fucking with," she said. "Do you. You never really did."

Claudette straightened at the waist, letting her knees take her weight. In mock seduction, she raised the nightgown off her belly and lowered her rump onto Yaghi's chest, leaning forward as she did so that Yaghi's nose and gasping fish-mouth were engulfed in the apron of flesh that was her abdomen.

Yaghi grunted and kicked for a while, thinking oddly of Crocodile Dundee and that snappy lizard-skin jacket. It never occurred to him that Claudette had no intention of relenting until an intense white light burst nova-like inside his head and abruptly faded to black. Then he lay still.

8

KATE'S PLACE WASN'T MESSY exactly, Steve thought; it was more a kind of casual disorder. Things on the floor that didn't belong there, the chairs at the glass and brass table left this way and that, a pair of gym socks balled up on the mantle. He peeked into the kitchen and amended that assessment: Maybe a little messy. But there were lots of healthy plants, a picture window overlooking the lake and a fresh selection of movie posters: *Predator*, *Alien*, *Terminator 2*, *The Replacement Killers*. Not the sort of favorites he would have expected for a woman, but that was part of what made Kate so interesting to him. She wasn't like any of the women he was used to. Not even close. She had a kind of youthful exuberance, tempered by a relaxed self-possession that held up even under the recent pounding she'd suffered. The accident, losing all that money, Christ, he'd've been a basket case if the same thing happened to him. But Kate was taking it all in stride, putting the pieces of her life back together, and he admired her for that.

He continued exploring. There was a fish tank full of mutant goldfish in the living room; some exercise equipment in a side room that also served as her office, a computer in there and a rank of tightly stocked book shelves; a spacious kitchen with a big cooking island, brass pots on hooks hanging from the overhead vent canopy. It was a comfortable place, Steve decided, airy and bright with its pastel walls and polished oak floors, and he half-wished they could stay.

He took a closer look at the fish, eight or ten of those bloated, genetically engineered cartoons. Raising his voice he said, "Where'd you get these fish—Chernobyl?"

Kate's voice came out of the back, "You're a riot, Alice," followed by a flat thunk and a stifled curse. "Shit. Steve? Could you give me a hand in here, please?"

Steve started down the hall toward the room at the far end. He could hear her struggling with something back there. He passed a bathroom with a see-through shower curtain and felt his imagination surge ahead into an intimacy that didn't exist between them, yet seemed so inevitable. He could almost taste the sweetness of her lips, parting as they pressed against his...

He gave his head a shake and went into the bedroom.

Nice big comfy-looking queen size in here...

Jesus, Seger, keep it in your pants.

Kate was kneeling on the floor at the foot of the unmade bed, trying to drag a fat blue Samsonite suitcase out from underneath. Steve said, "Hold on," and lifted a corner of the bed, the suitcase sliding free. He took it from her and hefted it onto the bed.

"Thanks," Kate said. "I don't know how I got that thing under there." She turned the clock radio on, tuned to a local FM station, opened a bureau drawer and got busy stocking the suitcase with clothes. Doing a neat job of it, too.

Good, Steve thought. Staying awhile.

He stuck his hands into his pockets and looked around the room. The same cheerful disorder. Lots of framed photographs, like in her father's study. Clothes everywhere. A bunch of athletic trophies arranged on a glass shelf.

Kate noticed him checking out the trophies. "So I was a tomboy," she said. "Wanna make something of it?"

"Hey, no," Steve said, "this is great." He broke into a respectable Inspector Clouseau. "I'm something of an ath-u-lete myself, you know."

Kate laughed. "Say, that's pretty good."

Steve moved to a shot of a teenage Kate in track gear, throwing a discus, the image caught as she released the heavy projectile, at the end of that powerful, spinning wind-up.

"Discus?" Steve said.

"Yeah, discus!" Kate said, strutting over to him, flexing a biceps. "Provincial champ three years running. They were afraid to let me throw against the boys."

"You would've, too, wouldn't you."

Kate gave him a playful shove. "Why not?"

Steve stumbled over something on the floor. It was one of those stupid, inelegant things that sometimes happened. Kate put her good hand out to catch him and lurched into him instead, her added weight bearing them both to the floor. Kate landed on top of him, her cast bopping him on the forehead.

"Ow!" Steve said, laughing. "That thing's hard as a rock!"

They lay there a moment, giggling, Steve spitting Kate's hair from his mouth and rubbing his forehead, Kate rubbing it too, laughing even harder. Then she flipped her hair aside and looked into his eyes. They both stopped laughing.

Kate kissed him lightly on the mouth, tasting him, as Steve had imagined tasting her. He raised his head for another and Kate obliged, the embrace heating up—

Until Kate started giggling, her mouth still pressed against his. She turned her face away and buried it in his shoulder, giggling helplessly.

More than a little hurt, Steve said, "Geez, talk about your great rape deterrent."

Kate reached up and increased the volume on the clock radio. "The song," she said. "Listen to the lyrics…"

The song was "Mouth" by Merrill Bainbridge. Steve tuned into the lyrics that had shattered his crystal moment:

'When I kiss your mouth, I wanna taste it. Turn you upside down, don't wanna waste it…'

Steve laughed in spite of himself. "You wanna turn me upside down?"

Kate kissed him on the chin, whispering, "Maybe when I know you better," playful, and Steve put his hand on the back of her neck, feeling her warmth.

It could've happened then, easily, each of them on the verge...but the embrace cooled off, Kate drawing away, Steve letting his head sink back to the rug. He looked into Kate's eyes and saw her desire shaded by doubt, maybe even fear. He wanted her—at this moment more than anything—but not this way. If it was going to happen, it had to feel right for both of them.

Smiling, he said, "Wow."

"Yeah," Kate said. She rolled off him, rising to her haunches beside him.

Steve pushed up on one elbow to face her. "That was..."

"Close." She leaned over and pecked him on the cheek. "And nice."

"At the very least."

Reddening, Kate said, "I'm sorry, Steve. I've rushed into things before—"

Steve put a finger to her lips. "Me, too. Let's just get you packed."

Kate nodded and got to her feet. Steve got up, too. There was another clumsy moment, Steve feeling like he should get out of her bedroom but not wanting to just walk away and appear sulky, when a weather warning came on the radio. Kate listened to it with unveiled alarm. In tandem, they looked out the bedroom window and saw that the light snow had turned to sleet.

"Shit," Kate said. "Shit, shit, shit."

Claudette sat at the kitchen table, weeping miserably, hunched shoulders quivering with shock. Putting on a show for the coppers. She'd always believed she could do a better job than those willowy fakes on daytime TV and here was her chance to prove it. She was still wearing her nightgown, nicely bloodstained from her scrap with Yaghi, but for discreteness sake she'd pulled a housecoat on overtop, belted loosely around her waist. The knot of Kleenex in her fist was soaked with tears and blood.

There was a team of them out in the hall, fussing around Yaghi's body, a couple of guys in blue jumpsuits from the Coroner's office waiting by the front door with a zippered bag and a stretcher. They'd left a lady cop in the kitchen with her, a hard-looking broad with her tits strapped in tight under the dark blue uniform. All that shit hanging off her belt, standing there by the fridge with her hands behind her back. A comforting presence.

Before dialing 911 Claudette had called the lottery hotline to make sure Yaghi hadn't been shitting her—she wouldn't put it past the little prick—carefully writing down each number with a pencil as the computerized voice rhymed it off. She compared them to the numbers on the ticket maybe ten times before letting out a yelp and dancing around the kitchen table, tracking her own blood all over the tiles with her bare feet.

Unbelievable.

She got the tears flowing again, heavy footsteps coming up behind her now. She couldn't wait to get this over with.

Detective Jack Cullen came into the kitchen and sat across from the dead guy's wife, Claudette. He glanced at her as he flipped open his notepad, thinking he'd never seen a more pitiful sight. The dame's bottom lip was split, the raw, fleshy sight of it making his skin crawl. Blood had crusted over her nostrils, one of which had to be packed with gauze by the paramedics to stem the bleeding, and her eyes were already starting to blacken. It was hard to believe the little guy in the hall had managed to wail on her so hard—and freaky beyond belief the same son of a bitch had blown away a bandit on Cullen's day shift. When he took the call tonight and recognized that name, *Yaghi*, he'd thought, no way, couldn't be the same guy. But there he was, laid out in the hall like a strip of bacon.

"Okay, Mrs. Yaghi," Cullen said, "why don't you tell me what happened here tonight. Take all the time you need."

Sniffling, Claudette raised her head to look at him through red eyes swollen to slits. "He came home smelling of booze," she said, snatching another tissue from the dispenser on her lap. "Furious over something...the shooting at the store, I guess. I told him how worried I'd been—he didn't even call—and..." She dissolved into tears for a few seconds; then, in a baby-girl voice, "...he hit me. It wasn't the first time, but I never told anyone. He threatened to kill me if I did."

"He's beaten you before?"

Claudette nodded. "Just never this hard." She fixed him then with an expression of such bewildered helplessness Cullen had to look away. "He knocked me out, detective, and I...fell on him. When I came to, he was..." But she couldn't go on.

"I understand, Mrs. Yaghi," Cullen said, thinking, Yeah, that'd do it, all right. He closed his notepad. "Don't worry, okay? We'll get everything looked after. Take a few minutes here to collect yourself then we'll drive down to headquarters. I'll take your statement and it's over."

Claudette covered her eyes and sobbed. Cullen got up and moved away from the table, waving the female officer over, nodding discretely at Claudette. "Sit with her a minute," he told her, "then help her get dressed. Drive her downtown, I'll meet you there in an hour."

Cullen rejoined the investigative team and told them to wrap it up. In his view the creep's death had been accidental, and from the look of things, well deserved. What he wanted now was to bail out of this stuffy apartment and go get some drive-through. Working doubles like this always got him craving junk food, and at the moment a big sloppy Wendy's burger seemed about right. With onion rings, fries and a jumbo Coke.

The Coroner's crew bagged Tarek Yaghi and carted him away. Cullen followed them down the steep staircase, his belly grumbling for grease.

Three hours and forty minutes later Claudette sat next to Detective Cullen in the front seat of his eight-year-old Buick, a maroon Le Sabre that smelled of cigars, telling him where to go when he lost his bearings in the maze of dead ends and one-way streets that was her neighborhood. She'd turned on the waterworks a couple more times during her statement—conducted in a cramped, soundproof room with pink walls and metal chairs made for midgets—and had believed Detective Cullen afterward when he told her she'd done very well. It pleased her that he'd volunteered to drive her home.

"Here we are," Cullen said, gliding to a stop in front of her apartment block, a five-story brownstone with a ratty spruce tree on the lawn, trimmed with Christmas lights. "I used to live near here when I was a kid. You think I'd know my way around."

"It's tricky," Claudette said, giving him a restrained smile. Mustn't forget she was in mourning. "Thanks for the lift, Detective," she said, shifting to face him. "You've been a saint through all of this."

Cullen smiled, his deeply-lined face tinted orange in the street light. "All in a day's work, Mrs. Yaghi."

Claudette touched his arm. "After all we've been through this evening, Detective, I think you can call me by my Christian name."

"Claudette, then."

"Do you mind me asking your name?"

"Not at all. It's Jack."

"Jack," Claudette said, as if tasting the word. "I've always liked that name." She smiled at him, letting it fade as she looked up at the drab apartment block, the number 516 in peeling gold foil centered on the steel and glass door. "Well, I guess I should be going in."

"You sure you want to spend the night here? After what happened, I mean."

"What did you have in mind?"

"What I meant, you have a friend or something you want to spend a few days with? Or I could drop you at a hotel."

She gave him a sigh, deep and long-suffering. "No, I'm better off in my own bed, I think, Jack. Thank you, though. Would you mind seeing me to the door?"

"'Course not," Cullen said.

Claudette watched him get out and hustle around the hood to open her door. He offered his hand and Claudette told him thanks, she could manage, grabbed the edge of the door frame and pulled herself out. Cullen closed the door and took her arm, falling in behind her when they reached the shoveled walk, not enough room for the two of them between the tidy banks of snow. At the entrance Claudette turned to face him.

"Thanks again, Jack. I hope I haven't put you out."

"Glad to do it," Cullen said, handing her something. His card. "Call me if I can be of any further assistance." He pointed at the card. "My home number's on the back."

"I will," Claudette said, opening the door. "'Night, Jack."

"'Night, Mrs. Yaghi."

"Claudette."

"Yeah," Cullen said, smiling. He started away. "Claudette."

She watched him walk back to his car, a solid, droop-shouldered man in his forties with a good belly on him and no rings on his fingers. He gave her a wave as he opened his door, wiggling blocky fingers, then he was gone, the faded maroon car rolling down the street, turning left on Craig and out of sight.

Claudette pushed her way inside, filling the stairwell as she clomped up the wooden risers, out of breath by the time she reached her second floor apartment. She kicked off her boots and hung her coat on the hook, almost tripping on the uprooted runner as she made her way to the fridge, the ticket waiting for her there under a magnet in the shape of a pear. She plucked it free and kissed it, then looked around for a pen to sign the back with. She found one by the phone, bent over the counter to sign the thing and thought, No, do it tomorrow at the lottery office; it'll make a great publicity shot. She tucked the ticket folded into the fleshy chasm between her breasts and tossed the pen on the table.

She got a king can of beer out of the fridge, lit a Cigarillo and drew herself a hot bath. While the water ran she opened the medicine cabinet door, angling it so the mirrored surface faced the tub, and tucked the ticket into its beveled edge. The final touch before she stripped and lowered herself into the steamy bath was her boombox radio, which she rested on the toilet seat and tuned to her favorite top forty station. The song that came on as she cracked the oversized beer can and took a cool swallow couldn't have been closer to perfect had she called the request line and asked for it herself: "If I Had A Million Dollars" by the Bare Naked Ladies.

Admiring her fortune—wrinkled now, looking somewhat the worse for wear—tucked into the edge of the mirror, Claudette sang along in a soaring voice:

"If I had ten million dollars..."

Her imagination roamed a glamorous spectrum as she lay there smoking, drinking and singing, and before she got out of the tub she decided that when the Hollywood moguls came sniffing around after the movie rights to her story, she'd insist on playing herself. After all, who else could fill the role?

The thought made her laugh out loud.

9

RAYBOULD WORKED THE HEAVY bag, the sound of his barefisted blows resounding through the headquarters gym. He liked it down here this time of night, eleven-thirty, twelve o'clock, the gym always abandoned. His workouts were intense and he preferred to do them without people gawking. For variety he threw in the occasional savage kick—front, spinning back, roundhouse—tricks he'd picked up from an upper echelon martial artist he sometimes trained with. Twice his weight, the bag jiggled and jived on its chain.

Sharpening his focus, Raybould pictured the prosecuting attorney, those superior eyes staring bullets at him across the safety of the courtroom. He imagined the man's soft body, stripped of its thousand dollar suits, and drove his fist into the bag, instead of the flat impact of knuckles on canvas feeling the satisfying give of human tissue, the snap of bone under vicious assault. He didn't like the way the man made him feel, a sensation so alien to him he had difficulty giving it a name. It wasn't fear; that was something he understood, a precise weapon in the right hands. It wasn't even helplessness. It was more a kind of uncertainty, a distressing confusion as to how to proceed. It made him feel cornered, persecuted, angry. He wanted to lash out against a situation that demanded restraint, make personal issues that were coldly impersonal. Even if he did go after the prosecutor—kill him, scare him off, whatever—they'd just send in another.

He shifted focus, not liking where his mind was going, thinking now of Corsino, wondering what new breed of asshole the old man was sending him. The little games they played, first trying to justify, then sanitize the act of murder by contract. Well, Raybould had his own little games—as the widow Flexner so recently discovered—with his own set of rules. And once a person played, he owned them forever. He concentrated on that. Thinking about it quelled that free-floating anger. He tried never to act in anger because when he got angry he stopped thinking. And when he stopped thinking he made mistakes.

He threw combinations into the bag, one-two, one-two, his wiry hundred-and-eighty pound frame dripping sweat. When the feeling began to leave his fingers he headed for the locker room for his weight lifting gear.

Hicks stood outside the door to the headquarters locker room and gym. He could hear Raybould in there, pounding the heavy bag. Probably pretending it was the head of some doper or pimp. Sounded like he was pelting it with a Louisville Slugger.

He checked his equipment again: a small flathead screwdriver and the tiny remote transmitter Mayer had given him, microscopic circuits imbedded in plastic, the whole thing smaller than a dime. He'd practiced planting it a dozen times with Mayer before coming down here, using a Glock .45 identical to Raybould's, with the heavy rubberized grips Raybould preferred. Mayer had checked the log for Raybould's locker number: 203. Everything was set. It was a simple matter now of going in there and getting it done. As long as he could hear Raybould working the bag he'd be okay.

He pushed the door open and paused, listening into a sudden silence. Then Raybould was slamming the bag again.

Hicks took a deep breath, already tacky with sweat. Alone here in the face of what he intended to do, he was forced to confront his fear. He could think of no one he was more afraid of—and no one he despised with a deeper passion.

He went inside and started looking for Raybould's locker, the wrist Raybould had injured throbbing with the beat of his heart. He scanned past the 100's into the 200's, rounded a corner and there it was, locker 203. Unlocked, as Hicks had known it would be. Hicks had asked him about that once, why he never locked up his stuff. He recalled Raybould's cocky remark: "Who do you know fool enough to touch anything of mine?"

He listened for the bag and didn't hear it.

"Rodney, I never took you for the fitness-conscious type."

Hicks spun and there was Raybould, shirtless, gleaming with sweat, the engorged veins in his arms standing out with brute vitality.

"Jesus," Hick said, "you shouldn't sneak up on a person like that."

Raybould smiled. "I came in here like a bull in a china shop." Getting into Hicks' space now, backing him up. "Not paying attention again, Rodney."

Hicks' hands curled into fists. This was the first time he'd spoken to the man since that day in his bedroom. Now, it was like it happened only yesterday. Hicks wanted to drop him where he stood.

He said, "Preoccupied, I guess," flashing on an excuse. He backed up another half step, Raybould's good-buddy proximity raising his hackles. "I grabbed a shower down here last night and forgot my watch in one of the lockers." He'd left it on the back of the toilet at home this morning.

"Which one?"

Hicks turned to the rank of lockers opposite Raybould's, stepped over the bench separating the rows and opened the first unclaimed locker he saw. "This one right here."

Raybould stepped over the bench with him, peering inside. "Hmm. No watch."

"Stolen, I guess."

"In a cop shop," Raybould said with an ironic chuckle. "Is nothing sacred?"

"Just a twenty-dollar Timex," Hicks said. He wanted out. "No harm, no foul."

"You sure this is the locker?" He opened a couple of others, checking inside.

"That's the one, all right."

"Oh, well."

"Yeah, well, listen Al, I gotta be going."

"Okay," Raybould said. He was in Hicks' space again, showing that warm smile. "But before you go..." The smile was replaced with an expression of contrition, convincing as hell. "I never got a chance to apologize. You know, for what happened." Hicks clenched his teeth so hard they hurt. "Things got out of hand there for a while. Way out of hand." He put his hand on Hicks' shoulder; Hick's could feel its heat through his shirt, its coiled power. "I just wanted to say, I'm glad you could be a man about it."

"Water under the bridge."

The hand came away. Hicks breathed.

"How is Sal?"

"We split up," Hicks said. "Last I heard she moved to Toledo to live with her mother."

"Sorry to hear that. I hope it wasn't because of..."

"It was because of a lot of things."

"Yeah, well." Raybould's expression changed again, a light coming into his eyes. "Say, you want to spar?" He smacked a fist into his palm.

"No thanks." Hicks said. He stepped over the bench and started away. "I've got a bum wrist."

"Nice talking to you again, Rodney," was the last thing he heard.

It had been three hours since the nurse gave Keith an injection for the pain in his fingers. They were killing him now, really throbbing. He could barely concentrate on what his sister was telling him. Some new antic of his brother's.

"He invited them in for lunch—"

"Who?"

"These three Jehovah's Witnesses. Dragged them right into the kitchen for soup and crackers and ended up selling *them* about a hundred dollars' worth of Amway."

Unable to endure the pain any longer, Keith interrupted Lee's story and got her to go fetch a nurse. When the nurse came in he asked her if there was any way they could move his injection up a bit; it wasn't due for another hour. The nurse went out to ask Dr. Sutcliffe, returning a few minutes later with a computerized med-pump mounted on an IV pole.

"It's a PCA pump," she told him, setting it up. "Patient controlled analgesia. A morphine infusion you control yourself."

Lee watched the nurse load the pump with a fluid-filled syringe fixed to a length of slender tubing that ended in a fine needle, which she deftly inserted into the skin of Keith's chest. Keith let out a squawk when the needle broke the skin and Lee said, "Big baby," watching as the nurse taped it into place.

"Okay," the nurse said, handing him what looked like a call button attached by a length of gray wire to the pump. "No more needles. When it hurts, just press the button."

"I can't overdose myself?"

"Nope." She patted the fancy pump. "We limit how much you can give yourself; a small amount every fifteen minutes. There's a loading dose going in right now, so you should start to feel better very soon."

Even as she said it Keith thought the throb in his fingers had backed off a little. He put on a pained grin for his sister. "Ain't technology grand?"

Lee returned his grin, watching the nurse leave the room. "So before you're too high on drugs," she said, "tell me more about this young policeman."

"Not much to tell," Keith said. "I only met him today. He seems nice enough, though. Katie took a shine to him right away."

"Well, I can't say too much."

"Considering you married one."

"And I'd do it again in a minute."

"How is Dale?"

"Bored since he retired. He's gone back to the accordion."

"Now I know why you're here."

They shared a private laugh, Keith wincing, splinting his ribs with his hand.

The phone on the bedside table rang, startling them both. Lee picked up the handset and said hello, then handed it to Keith. "It's Kate."

Keith said, "Katie, are you all right?"

"Yeah, Dad, I'm fine. We're still at the house. There's another storm up here and—"

"Well, you just stay right there, then. Lee's here and I'm fine. They've got me hardwired to a case of scotch and I'm getting drunk as a lord."

"What are you talking about?"

"I'm pulling your leg. Don't worry about me. Stay there 'til the weather clears. Your friend can sleep in my place."

"I thought I'd put him on the couch upstairs."

"I'm sorry, sweetie. I didn't mean..."

"I know, Dad."

"You're a grown woman." He cleared his throat. "Did you see your boss yet?"

"I'm meeting him at Eddie's in twenty minutes."

"Got your lips puckered?"

"Like a rosebud."

"Taking Steve along? Police presence?"

"No, I've got him reading my screenplay. Besides, Mo likes to be the biggest cheese on the platter."

"He'll take you back."

"I hope so, Dad. Sleep well. I'll call you in the morning."

"Okay, kid."

"'Bye," Kate said. "Say 'bye to Aunt Lee for me."

"I will, hon. 'Bye for now."

Lee took the handset and replaced it in its cradle. Keith looked at her and chuckled.

"Look at you," she said with a wry smile. "You *are* drunk." She patted his hand. "How's the pain?"

"Backing off some, I guess." He sighed, shaking his bandaged head, the drug shifting his mood. "You know, Sis', I feel so bad for Katie. She was so delighted about the money."

"Don't be silly. She was a happy young lady before you became Donald Trump, she'll be a happy young lady again. When you think about it, except for the accident, nothing's really changed."

"I changed. I went crazy. I feel like this is all my fault. Why couldn't I've just waited?"

Lee said, "That's not important now. What is important is that you and Katie are alive. Money's just money. Remember what Mom used to say? The root of all evil?"

"It's just... I've always wanted to be able to give her so much more, you know? Since her mother died, there's been such a hole. For both of us. And I think she's tried to fill part of that for me."

"As you've done for her."

"That's different. I'm her father. She's a great companion, but she's given up so much to be with me. I've always urged her to get out, meet new people. That's why I gave her the place upstairs when she turned eighteen, so she could have her privacy. But she's such a dreamer, always with her head in a book or tapping away at that computer." He smiled in spite of his distress. "Or watching movies with her old man. She used to call them flick-tunes when she was a kid. 'Hey, Dad. Wanna catch a flick-tune?' I have no idea where she picked that up... And with all that money, I thought... I could stop worrying about her. She's a bright girl, Lee, she doesn't belong driving around in a truck. The money would've..."

"You're right, little brother," Lee said, stroking his brow. "She *is* a dreamer. That's her nature and no one can change that. But she's a talented dreamer. And a determined one. She's young yet and she knows exactly what she wants from life. She got those things from you. A hundred million dollars couldn't buy that for her. She's going to be fine."

"I hope you're right..." He was beginning to nod off.

"Of course I am." She bent and kissed him on the forehead. "You rest now. I'll be here when you wake up."

But Keith was already fast asleep.

Hicks waited outside the locker room door until he heard the bright hiss of the shower, then he crept back inside. He had a bad moment when a radio came on in there, blasting out "Gimme Some Lovin'" by the Spencer Davis Group, Raybould's big voice singing along, amplified by the cavernous shower room. Cursing to himself, Hicks waited until he heard the splash of water off Raybould's body, then he returned to locker 203.

He opened the door and slipped Raybould's service pistol out of its holster. He pulled back fractionally on the slide, unsurprised to find a round already chambered. Working quickly, he unscrewed one side of the rubberized Pachmyer grip and inserted the remote transmitter, wedging it into the lower corner of the metal frame, the way Mayer had shown him. Then he replaced the grip, being careful not to score the black-painted screws, and returned the gun to its holster, the whole operation taking less than a minute. He left the steamy room in a hurry, the welcome coolness of the hallway air flooding his lungs.

Mayer was where Hicks had left him, one floor up in Internal Affairs, hunched over the surveillance receiver—a compact portable unit built into a stainless steel case the size of a carry-on bag—fiddling with dials and guzzling coffee.

Hicks said, "It's done."

"Excellent," Mayer said. "Took you long enough. Any trouble?"

Hicks shook his head. "What's the range on this baby again?"

"Five hundred yards, give or take."

"See if you can pick him up."

Mayer made a few adjustments, fine-tuned—and got Raybould's voice, singing along to the radio in the shower.

The detectives traded smiles.

Steve looked up from Kate's screenplay to watch her come in. She had on a red wool toque, snow crusted into the weave, and a couple of plastic grocery bags in her good hand. Her cheeks were rosy from the cold. He'd finished reading the script only minutes ago, rooted to the couch the whole time Kate was gone, flipping the pages as fast as he could read them. He couldn't wait to talk to her about it.

Kate tossed her jacket onto a chair, getting snow all over everything, then walked over to stand in front of him, the grocery bags still in her hand, waiting.

"So?"

"Kate, this is fantastic. I'd go see this movie in a minute. I feel like I just did."

"Really?" She set the grocery bags on the floor and took off her hat, getting a strand of hair out of her face with a toss of her head. "It wasn't too far fetched?"

"Not at all. I've always said there's not enough good science-fiction out there. And your lead characters, the way you bring them together, I loved it. I had no idea they were going to be abducted by aliens." He handed it to her. "It blew me away. So descriptive, and the dialogue's really snappy."

Kate gave him a smile. "How would you like to represent me?"

"I'll pitch it to Spielberg in the morning."

She put the screenplay on the coffee table and plopped down beside him on the couch.

Steve said, "So how'd it go?"

"Well, I got my job back. Without belting him. Bugger didn't even blink when I picked up the check." She scratched absently at the snow frozen to her hat. "It's really coming down out there."

Steve nodded, hoping they'd be snowed in for a week. "Want to order out for pizza or something?" He'd lost track of the time reading and now he was starved. Eight-thirty already. Normally by this time he'd be scrounging around for an after dinner snack.

Kate pointed at the grocery bags. "I thought I'd cook."

"Even better," Steve said, veiling a sudden apprehension. He was strictly a meat and potatoes man and dinner invitations always made him nervous. A Bahamian girl he'd dated briefly had cooked for him once, their second date, plunked a boiled kidney down in the middle of this big wooden plate. No vegetables, no starch, just this big wet kidney the color of a bruise. He'd poked at it a bit, then faked an attack of appendicitis and got the hell out of there. "What's on the menu?"

"I make a mean spaghetti sauce."

Steve smiled. "Sounds great."

He got right in there and helped, chopping vegetables, showing off some of the knife handling skills he'd picked up in his teens working summers as a salad chef at a sidewalk café. Kate prepared the meat on the gas range behind him, Steve sneaking peeks at her backside in those snug jeans, the little gyrations it made as she stirred the hamburger in the frying pan. He couldn't keep his eyes off her, couldn't stay focused, his mind leaping forward into the evening ahead, playing out different scenarios, all of them in direct contrast to the awkward agreement they'd made earlier in Kate's bedroom. His inattention ended in a cut finger, Steve letting out a surprised yelp when the stainless steel Henckels blade drew blood, startling amounts of it. Kate dressed the wound with a butterfly bandage, told him he was gonna live then kissed the tip of his finger.

They dined by candlelight, Eric Clapton providing the music, the "Unplugged" album, Steve toasting the cook with white wine decanted into stem glasses. The sauce was fantastic, the conversation relaxed, each of them offering anecdotes and opinions, testing their fit. Inevitably the subject of future plans came up and Steve went first, letting her know as subtly as he could that after his probationary year he could pretty much apply for assignment anywhere in the province.

That was when Kate dropped the bomb.

"If everything works out I'll be moving to California in the fall. I've been accepted into the film school at UCLA."

Goddam. Bullet through the heart.

Steve said, "Really?" trying to give it some zest. "That's great." The promising part, Kate seemed bummed about it too, the implications dawning on her as she said the words. "Maybe you could come visit," she said and Steve said sure, he'd love to. They let it go at that, the whole thing too far in the future to dwell on right now. After a third glass of wine and a second helping of pasta, Steve had pretty much put it out of his mind. They were here now, together, and that was just fine.

When they were done—hot apple pie and ice cream for desert, followed by coffee—Steve insisted Kate relax while he cleaned up, clearing the table, stacking the dishes in the dishwasher, scouring the big sauce pot and frying pan by hand. By ten o'clock they were downstairs in Keith's living room, flipping through the video library.

Kate said, "How 'bout this?" holding up *Dirty Harry*, and Steve had to grin. They nestled together on the couch to watch it, Steve giving a running commentary, pulling Clint faces and putting Kate into stitches. When the movie was over, almost midnight before Harry capped the psycho with his magnum, Steve started thinking again about the sleeping arrangements.

Yawning, Kate said, "The couch upstairs all right for you? It's a fold-out."

Steve said, "Perfect."

"My father said you could have his bed—"

"Couch's good."

"Then maybe we should turn in. I'm bushed and weather permitting, I'd like to get back on the road first thing."

"Yeah, I'm pretty bagged myself," Steve said. He manufactured a yawn that fell a bit shy of convincing. He'd've been just as happy to sit up with her all night, watching movies and talking. Sleep was the farthest thing from his mind.

Kate shut off the TV and led the way upstairs. Steve helped her make up his bed, then sat around in his jeans and undershirt waiting for his turn in the john. Kate came out after a quick shower in a silk brocade night dress the light shone through, handed him a bath towel and a new toothbrush, still in its package, and told him he could grab a shower if he wanted. He took the fastest shower of his life, toweled off, brushed his teeth and got back into his undershirt and jeans. He found Kate seated in front of her computer in the dark, pecking away at the keys.

"I had an idea for a story," she said, looking up at him, the pale blue light from the monitor casting her in soft shadow.

"What's it about?" Steve said, towering next to her in his sleeveless CK undershirt, the warmth of the shower still on him, rekindling his mild high from the wine.

She smiled. "It's about a girl who can't control herself."

She turned off the computer and stood, Steve stepping back to give her room. Leading him into the living room now, to the fold-out bed, a subtle scent to her, clean and floral. Turning to face him in the low light, twisting a strand of hair around her baby finger, spun gold in the lamp light. Waiting.

Come on, dummy. But he couldn't move.

"Goodnight, Steve," Kate said, rising on tiptoes to kiss him on the chin. "Thanks for a fun evening."

"'Night," Steve said.

She tilted her head, playing with her hair again, a sparkle in those green eyes.

"See you in the morning," she said and walked away, lingering in the archway a moment before disappearing, one hand sliding down the molding, a slow caress and then gone.

"See you in the morning."

He was a long time falling asleep.

Kate lay in the middle of her bed with her arms around a pillow thinking: I'm a slut. Had she really struck that cheap Marilyn Monroe pose in the archway just now? On *purpose*? Then hovered there out of sight for like what, five minutes? Listening to see if he'd taken the bait? Oh, God, then it *had* been on purpose. And that toothbrush, brand new in its package like she kept a dozen at the ready, you never knew who might spend the night. She wanted to go out there right now and explain—one of her friends was a dental hygienist, always bringing her stuff like that, toothpaste and floss, brushes and whiteners, samples the salespeople left. He was probably lying there thinking she had a selection of condoms waiting somewhere, too, all colors and sizes.

God, she was so clumsy at this stuff. Why did it have to be so hard?

But it was fun, too. The buildup. The anticipation. She'd caught him checking her fanny in the kitchen and put a little more shimmy on it for him, liking the attention. She wanted him to notice her. Everything felt so right with him, it seemed almost ridiculous to be sleeping apart. Yet she'd barely known him forty-eight hours, the only thing preventing her from traipsing out there right now and snuggling in next to him.

She heard the creak of footfalls in the hall and held her breath...but they stopped at the bathroom door, the light going on out there. A few minutes later the light went out and she heard him again, padding back to the living room. Shit.

Kate turned on her side and hugged her pillow, her restless gaze touching every now and again on the luminous digits on the clock, chronicling the night's slow passage.

She finally drifted off around three, waking abruptly two-and-a-half hours later, stiff but surprisingly rested. The first thing she did was look out the window. Not bad. Dense clouds, but no snow falling now; not much accumulation, the streets already plowed. The worst of the storm must have given them a pass.

Anxious to get under way she opened the linen closet in the hall, a narrow thing with a balky bi-fold door, hoping the noise would waken Steve. She dug out a fresh towel and went into the bathroom, slipped out of her night dress and yelped when a knock came at the door. She heard Steve chuckle in the hall.

"I didn't mean to startle you," he said. "I was just wondering, bacon and eggs okay for you? I noticed last night you've got some in the fridge."

Standing there naked Kate said, "Sounds great. How long have you been up?"

"Half hour. I was trying out your stepper. You really work it at that kind of tension?"

Kate smiled, wondering what he'd do if she opened the door. "Buns of steel, baby."

"Impressive," Steve said, doing a really bad Arnold. "Go ahead and finish, then we'll eat. That way we can be on the road by six-thirty or so, back at the hospital by eleven at the latest. How do you like your eggs?"

"Over hard and ugly."

"I thought I was the only one."

He served her in the kitchen by the corner windows, at an antique oval table that had belonged to her mother and Kate now used for a big hibiscus that flourished there in the sun. They sat in folding deck chairs Steve found on the landing to the back stairs, sipping pulpy orange juice and nibbling toast, each claiming to have slept like a baby. Kate said to leave the dirty dishes in the sink, but Steve rinsed them off and stacked them in the dishwasher, which he'd already cleared of last night's dishes. They left the apartment in silence, sharing a kind of quiet melancholy, clumping down the stairs to the exit with the suitcases Kate had packed. Steve helped her clear the snow off her car—a '96 Corolla she'd bought used from a girl at work, dark gray, still in nice shape—and followed her out of town in the Cherokee. Kate drove slowly, checking her rearview at every stoplight to make sure she hadn't lost him.

They stopped in Parry Sound for gas and were back on the highway by eight-fifteen. The low cloud cover had finally dissipated, the sun beating down full force now, warming Kate's face through the windshield.

Her mind wandered as she drove, focusing on the day ahead for a while, then drifting again. She'd have to get busy on that power of attorney thing as soon as she got back, find out if Aunt Lee managed to set something up with Uncle Fred the lawyer. She hoped Steve would go back to the Lottery Corporation with her, help her with that guy Tasker. She hated jocks. She imagined her first date with Steve, hoping it'd be soon. The blues club he'd mentioned maybe, then back to his place.

Kate shook her head, laughing at her own lack of resolve. The frightened part of her, the hurt part that had slammed on the brakes yesterday in her bedroom when they were so close, that part was quickly losing its voice. Something in her experience in the wreckage had freed her from that fear, helped her see how baseless and self-defeating it was. And now, some other part wanted out. It was a new feeling, scary in its own right, almost wild.

"Jesus," Kate said out loud, laughing. "Get a grip."

She turned on the radio. Elvis again, doing "Blue Christmas". Her eyes started to mist with tears. She turned it up and sang along, looking at the back of Steve's head in the Cherokee, ahead of her now, wondering if he was tuned to the same station.

10

CLAUDETTE AWOKE A HALF hour ahead of the alarm. She'd slept with the ticket under her pillow, rousing periodically from a restless sleep to assure herself it was still there. Following her usual pancake and syrup breakfast, she dressed in her best print shift, accented with a matching silk scarf knotted loosely around her neck. A bit springy, perhaps, but that was how she felt on this bright December morning. Plus, if they wanted photographs, for publicity or whatever, she always looked slimmer in colors. She carefully applied make-up, doing her best to hide the scrapes and bruises, then doused herself with perfume. The finished effect, she decided, appraising herself in a full-length mirror, was perfect. She looked...pampered, a woman accustomed to the privileges of wealth.

Ten million dollars. The mere thought of it made her heart flutter. The only thing she had to worry about now was what to buy first.

She tucked the ticket into a zippered pocket in her purse, stepped into her Kodiaks and pulled on her winter coat, an ankle length wool job she'd had for years. As she left the apartment she realized there'd be no one to open the store this morning and she said out loud, "Who cares?" drawing a look from the landlady, Mrs. McEwen, busy swamping out the main foyer with a mop. Claudette bugged her eyes at the woman and laughed.

The day was sunny and cold, the sidewalks scabbed with ice, and Claudette picked her way cautiously to the bus stop a half-block away. She moved with that rocking, side-to-side gait characteristic of the extremely obese, her sheer girth taking up the entire sidewalk. She'd stopped buttoning her coat years ago, partly because of the near impossibility of the task, but also because the cold didn't faze her anymore. As she lumbered along, she drew stares from those forced to shrink against walls or scale snow drifts to let her by. Claudette could care less.

She decided her first extravagance would be one of those extended European tours, hopping from country to country in the first-class section of a private jet, hitting the big cities first, taking in the shows and hot spots; then on to the countryside, sipping vintage wines from goblets on the turrets of ancient castles, cruising the cobbled streets of quaint historic villages in horse-drawn carriages. Perhaps she'd meet a gentleman whose tastes ran to the more generously proportioned and she would initiate him in the raptures of excess.

The bus pulled up to the curb and with difficulty Claudette climbed aboard. She'd never understood why they made these doorways so damn narrow you had to be a super model to squirm through. She flashed her bus pass at the driver with a surly scowl. This would be the last bus ride she ever took.

Puffing, she said to the driver, "How close do you go to the lottery office?"

"Right across the street," the driver said.

Without thanking the woman Claudette labored to the back of the bus, eyeing the other passengers as she passed, purse clamped to her breast in a greedy bear hug.

Two more fares hopped aboard as the driver shut the doors, a pair of hard looking punks, real rough trade. The first one's head was shaved bald save a thin, beet-red strip that ran along the midline of his skull like a vivid scar. He wore baggy army pants and, in defiance of the sub-zero temperatures, an unbuttoned jean jacket hacked off at the shoulders, scrawny arms sheathed in a pair of fishnet stockings with finger holes cut in the ends. His face looked like an open tackle box, pierced in so many places he jingled. His companion was closer to human, a full head of spiky, lemon-yellow hair and a single gold hoop in each ear. He at least had been sensible enough to wear a coat, a raggedy old cast-off Claudette was betting he'd shoplifted from the Sally Ann.

They flopped into the center-facing seat across from hers, Fishnet's narrow eyes finding her right away.

"Hey, Tommy," he said to his pal, jerking his chin at Claudette. "Eighteen wheeler."

Tommy gave her a look, foggy eyes widening. "Whoa. More chins than a Chinese phone book."

"Give it a slap and ride the wave in."

Great, Claudette thought. The comedy team of Martin and Lewis.

Tommy said, "Would ya?"

"If I was fucked up enough?" Fishnet said, considering. "Not even with your dick."

The punks cracked each other up, but quickly lost interest when they failed to get a rise out of Claudette. Tommy returned to his original haze, working a zit on his cheek with a black-painted fingernail.

But Fishnet, easily the more predatory of the two, couldn't help noticing how jealously the fat bitch was guarding that purse.

He leaned over and whispered something in Tommy's ear.

Hicks and Mayer sat in an unmarked surveillance van on the north side of Bloor Street, waiting for something to happen. Raybould had been sitting in the window of the café across the street for over an hour now, sipping coffee and smoking. He was reading a paperback, but even with a pair of high-powered binoculars Hicks couldn't make out the title. That irritated him. Much as he hated the man, Raybould intrigued him in some morbid way and that part of him wanted to know what kind of book a man like Raybould would read. He sat facing the street and Hicks could see his face clearly enough, but he couldn't quite get that title...

He angled the Zeiss-Icon lenses up to Raybould's face: a picture of self-possession. Hunched over his book like some erstwhile coffee shop scholar, flirting with the waitress when she came by to freshen his beverage. Hicks decided then, looking into that placid, unaffected face, that when the shit went down and if the chance presented itself, he'd shoot the fucker dead.

Mayer said, "Heads up."

Hicks lowered the binoculars and saw a silver BMW glide to a stop in front of the café. A Hispanic male, early thirties, wearing a gray cape over a sea-blue leisure suit, got out of the back seat and strode inside. The Beemer nosed ahead a few feet to idle at the curb, the driver invisible behind tinted glass.

Hicks said, "That's gotta be a contact."

"Definitely," Mayer said. He took a sip of his coffee then focused on his equipment, saying, "Can you close your window? I'm freezing my nuts off over here."

"In a minute," Hicks said. He watched the Hispanic through the binoculars, swaggering up to Raybould's table in his reflectorized shades, swishing that god awful cape off his shoulders, easing into the chair across from Raybould and fucking up Hicks' view.

Hicks shook his head. "Greaser asshole. Look at him."

Mayer looked up from his equipment. "Say what?"

"Nothing. You picking them up?"

"Loud and clear."

Mayer flipped the headphones down around his neck and switched to speaker. The first voice they heard belonged to the Hispanic. Addressing the waitress.

"Coffee, black. Toast, white bread. None of that grainy health-food shit."

"Would you like jam with that, sir?"

"Did I ask for jam?"

Mayer switched the tape recorder on. "Sweet guy."

A city bus chuffed to a stop behind the BMW, obscuring their view, temporarily squelching-out the reception. Mayer cursed and bent over his dials. A few passengers debarked and the bus pulled away. Then Raybould's voice came in clearly.

"Hold on, lemme make sure I got this straight. You want me to wax your priest?"

Mayer said, "Now it's getting juicy."

Hicks watched through the glasses, a grim smile on his lips.

Raybould had to chuckle. Where did Corsino find these guys? The spic'd been here less than a minute and already he was almost pissing himself with rage.

"That cocksucker's no priest, man. He *fucked* my wife. Fucked her right in her *ass*! The bitch loved it, too. I can't believe it. I want some of that I gotta go down to the strip and pay for it."

He dug some glossies out of his coat and handed them to Raybould, who slid them out of their envelope, fanning them out on the table between them.

The spic said, "Lookit that *puta*. For a dime I'd put her name on the contract too."

"Jesus, amigo, you're right," Raybould said, rubbing a little salt into the wound. "Lookit the equipment on that boy."

"Yeah, whatever. I want the *cono* buried."

Raybould sleeved the photographs and handed them back. "The man told you what I get for this kind of work?"

"Yeah."

"This'll cost you double."

"Double! Why double?"

"I'm a Catholic."

Hicks and Mayer exchanged grins, Hicks saying, "You get all that on tape?"

"Every sweet syllable."

Hicks returned his attention to the binoculars. "All right. Let's see if we can pick up the details."

There was a prolonged silence, sounds of cutlery and background chatter, the Hispanic munching his toast. Then the Hispanic's voice: "I gotta take a piss."

Hicks watched him strut to the bathroom, that swaggering, body-proud walk those guys had, giving Hicks an unobstructed view of Raybould again. Christ, look at him. Cool as a summer breeze. He'd just agreed to kill a man—a priest—and Hicks could read no more tension in his face than if he'd agreed to sell his car. The thought of this animal in bed with his wife made his skin crawl.

Another bus pulled up, blocking his view. He lowered the binoculars and rubbed his eyes.

Claudette was out of her seat before the bus came to a full stop and she stumbled slightly, swaying toward the two punks seated across from her. The one with the stockings on his arms flailed back in an exaggerated pantomime of alarm.

Claudette thought, Have your fun you little dinks, I'll buy the roach ranches your mothers call home and burn them to the ground. She pivoted on a chrome post, heading for the rear exit.

Behind her Fishnet sprang up from his seat and bulled past her into the stairwell, out onto the sidewalk and out of sight along the flank of the bus. Tight on his heels, Tommy did the same.

"Rude shitbugs," Claudette said. She slung her purse over one arm and lowered herself onto the first step, using the handrails to pull herself through. When her foot came to rest on the bottom step she grabbed the vertical safety bars for a final emancipating thrust. Suspended from her arm, the purse swung out into space—and Fishnet's spidery hands came up and seized it. The little prick had bad teeth and they flashed yellow at her before he turned to bolt. In her surprise Claudette let go of the safety bars and the purse-strap skidded down her arm to her wrist, nanoseconds now from whipping free. With a ferocious grunt she twisted her hand palm up and the leather strap snagged in her fingers. Her fist closed around it like a claw.

"No you don't!"

Fishnet made it to the elastic limit of the strap before his feet left the ground and his shoulder almost popped out of its socket. He looked up at Claudette and saw a snarling dragon, eyes shot red, blunt teeth bared in fury. She was reeling him in like a ten-pound pickerel.

Red-faced, Fishnet said, "Fat bitch, give it up!" wrapped his arm once around the strap and threw every ounce of his weight back, not caring now that if she let go his skull would probably crack like an egg on the icy sidewalk. "Give-it-*up*!"

Claudette heaved, setting the hook—and the strap broke. It snaked through her fingers, rope-burning her skin, but then she had it again. She braced herself for one last pull and Tommy appeared, something flashing in his hand in the hard winter sunlight as his arm slashed down between Claudette and his confederate.

Then there was only strap in her hand and Claudette toppled backward into the stairwell, wedging there in a heap, the spectacle of the two punks fleeing with her purse reaching her eyes through prisms of raging tears.

"*You little fuckers!*"

Like a beetle on its back Claudette flapped and twisted until she managed to roll onto her side. She reached up with her right hand, the leather strap still laced through her fingers, and got hold of one of the rails. A burly guy in a navy toque tried to give her a hand, but his efforts served only to bounce her out of the bus into a puddle of slush.

The doors flapped shut behind her and the bus pulled away.

Claudette was on her feet in a flash, slush dripping from her backside, big voice raised in fury: "Somebody help me!" She pointed after the fleeing purse snatchers with a flapping hand. "They got my ticket! *They got my ten million dollars*!!"

Waiting for his asshole client to return from the can, Raybould watched with amusement as the felony unfolded outside the café window. Like an episode of *Keystone Cops* or something. Despite his status as a police officer, he was not in the least inclined to intervene. The only thing he hated worse than doper punks was fat people. Not just fat, but the monsters like this one. How the fuck could a person do that to themselves? It wasn't just the why of it that baffled him, it was the how, the physical improbability of it. How could a person who had started out small enough to come into the world in the usual fashion bloat up into something so grotesque? How many tons of sugar and grease did it take, how many sedentary hours forking it in? It was a sick mystery to him and he felt content to just sit and watch. For a few seconds there, until Fishnet's accomplice waded in with the switchblade, it looked as if Tubby might win the tug of war. But the punks were away now, the beast up and rampant—

Claudette's voice, muffled by the café window, reached Raybould's ears, galvanizing him.

"They got my ticket! *They got my ten million dollars*!!"

Raybould put it together in an instant. The Lottery Corporation was right across the street. She'd won the lottery and the ticket was in her purse.

In a heartbeat he was out of his chair, heading for the exit at a run.

From the surveillance van Hicks had been blind to the entire fiasco. He first laid eyes on Claudette when the bus merged into traffic, a very large woman hoisting herself out of the slush, sheets of it dripping from her ass, the woman screaming blue murder. What was she raving about?

He gave Mayer a poke. "Hey, Bry, listen to this broad. Ten million dollars?"

Mayer leaned across him to have a peek. In the same instant Raybould burst out of the café and flashed the woman his badge.

"What the...?"

Mayer cranked up the volume on the receiver. "Goddam, get a load of this."

Raybould's voice: "Ma'am, I'm a police officer." His gold shield sending off sun flares over there. "Can I be of any assistance?"

Hicks watched Claudette check Raybould's I.D., then seize his wrist and point down the street. The punks had made it to the end of the block, about to dart around the corner now.

Claudette's voice: "Officer Raybould, thank God. Those two little bastards—they got my purse! There's a ten million dollar lottery ticket in that purse, officer. Get it back for me and I'll give you a million. *Two* million! Now go!"

Raybould gave chase.

Hicks said, "Shit!" dropped the binoculars and slammed the van into gear. He started to pull out, intending to cut across traffic in pursuit, but the light at the next intersection turned red and a graffiti-scrawled garbage truck locked him in. He jammed on the brakes and Mayer, who'd been holding his coffee, let out a shriek, the still-steaming liquid slopping into his crotch.

"HOT!"

Hicks shoved his door open to go after Raybould on foot, but a pizza delivery guy in a rusted Pinto decided there was enough room between the van and the garbage truck to slip through at thirty miles an hour. His front bumper creased the opening van door, slamming it shut and almost taking Hicks' head off.

Losing time, both men bailed out on Mayer's side and took off after Raybould on foot.

Raybould rounded the corner at the end of the block and saw them right away, a hundred yards ahead now, moving at a fast walk. Fishnet was already digging around in the purse.

Raybould crossed the street, pulling on a pair of leather gloves, continuing his loping run. Fishnet made him before he hit the sidewalk. He slapped his partner on the back, his words reaching Raybould's ears on the still winter air.

"Split up. Meet me at the arcade."

The partner broke into the street, veering left across the intersection, weaving through traffic in an attempt to lure him away from the prize. But Raybould stuck with the money.

The kid was fast, built like a long distance runner, and he led Raybould a merry chase, plowing through anything that stood in his way. A woman laden with parcels stepped out of a department store into his path and the kid knocked her sprawling, almost losing his balance in the treadless cowboy boots he was wearing. The edge of the open door saved him and he took the chase inside, bounding along the first aisle he came to, screaming like a banshee to clear a path, shoppers shrinking back from him. Hot on his heels, Raybould ran him into the exit on the opposite side of the store. He almost had him in the revolving doors. He caught one of the wings and jammed it with his toe, but the slippery bastard managed to squirm out through a space Raybould couldn't have squeezed his leg through. Then they were back in the street.

Raybould paced himself now, waiting for the kid to do something stupid. Fear always made people stupid, a fact he'd counted on more than once.

Sure enough, tiring, the kid ducked into an alley. Bad move. Raybould knew the alley; it dog-legged into a dead end.

He got out a cigarette and set it between his teeth, pausing at the mouth of the alley to glance up and down the street, alert for any attention their foot race might have drawn. But everything was business as usual. That was a beautiful thing about a city like Toronto: nobody ever saw anything.

He entered the alley, an icy, rutted corridor between a Thai restaurant and an abandoned warehouse. Sure enough there was the kid, leaning against a dumpster, looking every bit like he was ready to puke. No sign of the stolen purse.

Grinning, Raybould said, "You coke-smokers are out of shape. I've gotta be twice your age, I haven't even broken a sweat yet." He lit the cigarette, taking his time. "I could run your skinny ass all day. But since we're here, why don't you be an agreeable little reprobate and hand over the lady's purse."

"What purse?" the kid said. "Why are you on my ass anyways, man?"

Raybould took a step toward him. "I'm sorry, I must've given you the wrong impression. You think I'm in a playful mood? Fish the handbag out of the dumpster and hand it the fuck over. You reading me now?"

He took another step toward the kid, spitting distance now, and the kid pulled a knife. A switchblade, like his buddy's. Raybould smiled.

"The shape you're in, you're gonna fuck with me?"

"Back off, dickhead." Waving the blade. "I'll stick this in your heart."

Raybould flicked his cigarette into a mound of dirty snow. "Okay, kid."

Still smiling, Raybould dropped into a fighter's stance. Startled, the kid took a wild slash at him and Raybould's right hand came down like a broad-sword on his wrist, the knife twirling to the snow-crusted pavement. The kid huddled over his arm, breathing hard, wide eyes unable to comprehend the unnatural angle at which his wrist now jutted. Raybould picked up the knife and handed it back to him.

"Here," he said. "Take it." Fishnet accepted it with his uninjured hand. "Take another shot. Come on. Make me proud."

The kid hunched there a few seconds longer, clutching the knife, making up his mind. Then, cat-quick, he lunged at Raybould, trying to bury the blade in his throat. An instant before the steel found its target Raybould snatched the kid's wrist and twisted, spinning him around on his own arm. Then Raybould was behind him, one arm around his chest, the other holding the switchblade to his throat.

"Nice try, but nasty. Here's how it feels."

He plunged the blade into Fishnet's neck, driving it through the larynx deep into the cervical spine. The stab was precise and nearly bloodless, designed to suffocate rather than exsanguinate. Raybould relaxed his grip and the kid staggered away, clasping the knife with both hands, trying to yank it free. But it was in there for keeps.

The flat part of the blade stoppered his windpipe and after a few seconds of mute struggle the kid sagged to his knees. Ignoring him, Raybould propped open the dumpster and found the purse. He turned in time to see the kid go over like a felled tree, landing squarely on the butt of the knife, driving it deeper into his neck. The kid rolled onto his back, raising his arms to the white sky, a strange clicking sound coming from his throat.

Raybould opened the purse to a waft of stale perfume, rummaged through candy wrappers, loose change and the stale crumbs of a hundred squirreled snacks, and found the ticket in its zippered pocket. He folded it carefully into his wallet, then bent over a nearby manhole cover and lifted it free. He leaned the heavy disc against the dumpster. Then he stood over the dying kid, shaking his head. The kid's eyes could no longer hold their focus. Raybould grabbed him by the ankles and dragged him to the open manhole.

"In you go."

He folded the kid in ass first. There was a thudding splash but no other sound. After a brief look around he tossed the purse in after the punk, replaced the manhole cover and walked away.

Hicks was convinced they'd lost him. Trailing the pursuit by at least a minute, they rounded the first corner and saw no sign of Raybould or the punks he'd been chasing. Then Mayer spotted the woman Fishnet had bowled over, gathering up the last of her muddied parcels. They jogged up to her and identified themselves as police officers. Without further prompting the woman pointed into the department store.

Splitting up, the detectives fast-walked through the crowded store, scanning the aisles as they went. At the rear exit Hicks noticed a couple of teenagers standing outside the revolving doors, craning their necks and pointing down the street. He signaled Mayer and they ran out onto the sidewalk together, Hicks showing the teenagers his badge. "You see a couple of guys run through here?" he said and one of the teenagers said, "Yeah, man, they went thata way." Pointing south toward the Asian district. "What'd the dude do, kill somebody?"

Mayer said, "I see him."

A long block away on the other side of the street, looking this way briefly before strolling into an alley or a side street, hard to tell from this distance.

Hicks said, "Yeah, that's him," and sprinted off down the street. Mayer fell in behind him, breathing hard.

There was a liquor store across from the alley and the detectives went inside, Hicks loitering by the glass door while Mayer hunched by a cognac display, trying to catch his breath.

Several minutes later Raybould reappeared at the mouth of the alley. He paused to scan his surroundings, and for the space of an eyeblink his gaze fell on Hicks. Hicks lowered his head—a quick, startled gesture—hiding his face with his hand. When he looked up again Raybould had already started back toward the Lottery Corporation, lighting a fresh cigarette.

When Raybould was out of sight Hicks and Mayer headed for the alley. It dead-ended in a wide alcove bordered by two L-shaped buildings with a space between them Hicks couldn't fit his arm into. Set into one wall was a steel door with no handle. Mayer tried to jimmy it with his fingers but it was sealed tight from the inside. No fire escapes, no pipes or ladders to scale. The place was a bolt hole, nowhere to run.

After a few minutes scouting around they stood together by the dumpster.

"I don't get it," Mayer said.

"Yeah," Hicks said, "if the kid ran in here Raybould had him cold." He opened the dumpster, started poking around inside.

Still winded, Mayer bent forward at the waist, hands on his knees, letting gravity take the weight of his gut. He took a deep, wheezing breath and spotted something by the manhole cover. He limped over on an ankle that suddenly felt lame.

"Rodney. Take a gander at this."

Hicks walked over for a look. Smiling, he said, "Nice going, Hawkeye."

They bent over a single drop of fresh blood.

Hicks said, "Let's get this sucker open."

It took some doing, the damn thing heavy as hell, but they got the lid off and rolled it aside. Mayer brought out a penlight and aimed it down the shaft. Fishnet stared up at him with glazed eyes, the switchblade jutting from his throat. The fat woman's purse lay open on his chest, its contents strewn around him. His splayed legs, wedged across the frosted concrete shaft, framed his face in a khaki V.

Mayer sank to a squat, shifting the flashbeam to the open purse. He said, "The son of a bitch got the ticket."

"And I'd bet dimes to donuts he's back there right now explaining to the fat lady how this poor mutt outran him."

"Moot point," Mayer said, grinning at Hicks. "If we didn't have the man before, we got him now."

Hicks said, "That's a given." He squatted down to his partner's level. "But think about this a minute. He *got* the ticket. You said so yourself."

"Yeah? And? We got *him* for murder-one, right here, you're worried about theft?"

"You think he's back there handing that broad her ticket?"

Mayer glanced down at the dead kid. "That's a dumb question, Rodney. No, I'm fucking sure he's not back there handing the broad her ticket. But is that relevant? Am I missing something here?"

Hicks rose to his full height. "Ten million dollars, Bryan, that's what you're missing. Ten million dollars."

Mayer stood, saying, "All right, slow down a minute, tell me if I'm reading you right. Ten million dollars—split three ways, we all makes out like bandits and nobody's any the wiser? Is that what you're getting at?"

Hicks' eyes were rock hard. "Sweeter split two-ways," he said, facing Mayer dead on. "The rules of the game've just changed, Bryan. Do we agree on that?"

Mayer cast his eyes down, unnerved by what he saw in his partner's unblinking gaze. He'd been a police officer sixteen years, and apart from a solid bunch of friends on the force and two strong sons he doted over, he had little to show for it. He'd been an honest cop, mostly, holding as firmly as he could to standards that had been almost naively ideal when he took the oath. When he'd mentioned a three-way split just now he'd assumed Hicks was bullshitting, or maybe just dreaming out loud. But it was clear the man was not screwing around.

Mayer took a deep breath. He was being asked to cross the line here, all the way over, and it was his wife's voice, heard as clearly in his mind as if she were standing right next to him, that warned him off. He opened his mouth to say no, the only acceptable response he could make...but in that moment, like a man stepping up to the rim of the Grand Canyon for the first time, he got a clear vision of what was in it for him should he choose to go along. *Five million dollars...* The sheer enormity of it and all it could bring weakened his knees.

Agreed," he said, still not looking at Hicks. "Agreed."

Claudette's theatrics attracted a crowd that included a pair of uniformed officers, one of whom was attempting to glean a statement from her.

"Ma'am, can you describe the men who took your purse?"

Claudette looked at the cop as if he were from another solar system. "What's *wrong* with you people? Why are you writing? Will you for God's-sake go *after* them?"

Raybould shouldered his way through the rubbernecks, noticing his client's Beemer was gone. Not that it mattered anymore. He showed the cops his shield, but before he could speak Claudette had him by the arm.

"There you are. Did you get my purse?"

"I'm sorry, ma'am," Raybould said, oozing sympathy, "but they were just too fleet-footed."

"No!" Claudette said, tears squeezing from her blackened eyes. "You don't understand. You've *got* to find them. You've got too!"

The officers pried her off Raybould and led her to a waiting squad car, Claudette wailing all the way. Once they got her settled Raybould gave them a run-down of what had happened, describing how he'd witnessed only the last few seconds of the theft over his morning coffee, then engaged the perps in a foot race, which, unfortunately, he'd lost.

"Too much starch," he said, pouching out his plank-hard abdomen, patting it for effect. He took a drag off his cigarette. "And too many coffin nails." He finished his informal statement with a dead-on description of both punks. "That's from behind, you understand, at a full run."

He spent the next few minutes entertaining the boys with one of his standard Holdup Squad war stories and a couple more patiently answering the questions of the more junior of the two, who had aspirations of becoming a detective. He commended the fellows on their thoroughness and competent handling of a hysterical victim. Then, with a jaunty salute, he excused himself.

He walked a block or two in the hard winter sunshine, reviewing his actions. More spontaneous than he liked and definitely more public, but the situation had demanded it—the whole thing, SIU hunting him, his association with Corsino falling apart, only a matter of time before the old guinea decided to shut him down—and suddenly, like a lightning bolt, a solution appears. No time to do anything but react. Sure it could've been neater, given more time, but he was reasonably certain no one had seen him go into the alley. And the dead kid's friend would likely stay out of it, at least for the time being, that street rat mentality. And who else was going to miss the little fucker? If the ticket was legit—and God help that fat sow if it wasn't—he'd only need a day or two. Then he was gone.

He doubled back to his car, stopping on the way at a variety store for a deck of Lucky Strikes. There was a lottery display by the door and Raybould casually removed the ticket from his wallet and unfolded it. As he compared the numbers to the posted winners, his hand crushed the pack of smokes.

"Mother of God…"

On his way out he tossed the ruined smokes into a garbage can.

11

KATE AND STEVE PULLED into the hospital parking lot at ten forty-five that morning. They parked in adjacent spots and got Kate's gear unloaded, Steve hefting the bulk of it. As they made their way inside Steve said, "Something occurred to me on the drive back. What if this guy doesn't realize he's got your ticket? What if he never realizes it?"

Kate said, "I hadn't thought of that."

"Maybe we need to nudge him a bit," Steve said. "What's your schedule for the rest of today?"

"I thought I'd get that power of attorney thing straightened away. Go back to the Lottery Corporation and fill out those forms. Then, just hang with my dad I guess."

In the lobby Steve handed her the suitcases. "Can you get upstairs okay with these?"

"Sure. What have you got in mind?"

He started for the exit, walking backwards, giving her a cagey smile. "Baby, I'm gonna make you a star. See you this afternoon. Be ready. And wear something nice."

Intrigued, Kate watched him go, then lugged the suitcases into the elevator.

Lee was still with Keith, the two of them sharing a laugh over something on the TV Keith had rented from the hospital. Kate kissed her dad then gave Lee a hug. Keith looked great, his color coming back, and they'd taken that god awful turban off his head. He was all smiles.

"Hi, sweetie," he said. "How was your trip?"

"Fine. The roads were bare this morning, we made great time."

Smirking, Lee said, "I bet you did."

"That's not what I meant," Kate said, giving her aunt a poke.

Keith said, "Did you get your job back?"

"Yes, but only barely. And when he finally said yes he wanted me to start right away. Then we got into it again. Truth is the creep needs me. I called Trudy last night before I met Mo, she told me his wife screwed up the route so bad at least twenty customers called in to complain, asking where the usual girl was. I start January second. I took a shot at a raise but Morris almost had a coronary."

Keith said, "Good for you."

"I got you an appointment with that dope, Fred," Lee said. She looked at her watch. "He should be here any minute. I told him eleven o'clock."

Kate asked her father about his pain and Lee said he was on a permanent high, hitting the button on the pain pump every fifteen minutes on the dot, he didn't even have to look at the clock anymore. She said Kate better find a reliable heroin pusher up there in Sudbury because her old man was gonna need one.

They chatted about nothing in particular until Fred came in at 11:30, grinning from ear to ear. He shook Keith's hand—saying they should talk about the accident, too, sue the limo company into bankruptcy—nodded at Lee from a safe distance, then turned to Kate with open arms, showing nicotine-stained teeth. He pulled her into a bear hug saying, "Kate, my God, look how big you've gotten," his hand gliding down her back to the swell of her hip. Kate stifled the urge to knee him in the balls.

She said, "Hi, Uncle Fred, long time no see," and backed away. "So tell me, what's involved here?"

Fred glanced at Lee, staring bullets at him. "Piece of cake," he said, opening his briefcase. "I've got everything we need right here."

Hicks had to admire the man's cool. If the ticket had fallen into his hands he'd've gone straight to the Lottery Corporation to pick up his check, caution be damned. But Raybould spent the rest of the day performing his appointed rounds. Business as usual. Probably analyzing every angle in that iron trap mind of his, the way he'd done when Hicks was partnered with him. His deliberate approach to even the simplest thing used to drive Hicks crazy, though he had to admit, more than once that same methodical nature had saved their skins. "You don't go kicking the door down, Rodney, until you're damn sure what's on the other side."

They'd tailed him all day, Hicks growing increasingly agitated, Mayer unusually quiet. Now, at change of shift, they sat in the van in front of headquarters, Mayer working on a meatball hoagie, Hicks staring at the silent audio receiver. Raybould had entered the building ten minutes ago, but so far no conversation.

"So when do we move on him?" Mayer said around a mouthful of food.

"Tonight," Hicks said, "when he's all nice and cozy at home."

"What's our line gonna be?"

Hicks tapped the tape recorder with a finger. "We start by quoting from his conversation with the spic. If that doesn't shake his tree, we remind him about the garbage he dropped down the sewer."

"Think that'll do it? I heard he doesn't scare easy. Heard it from you."

"It's not about being scared, Bryan, it's about being cornered."

Mayer put his sandwich down on the consul, unfinished. "Know what a weasel does when you corner it?"

"What's he gonna do? Shoot us?"

"Maybe."

Hicks looked at the half-eaten sandwich. In all the time he'd known Bryan he'd never seen him leave food uneaten. "You gonna finish that?"

"Uh-unh." He made a sour face, burping softly.

"Okay, Bryan, what's up? Talk to me, man. Look, if you want out, now's the time to say it. I'll take the fucker alone and no hard feelings. I mean it. Shit, you can sit at home and I'll still cut you in."

Bryan sighed, the sound heavy and asthmatic. "No way. No charity. If I'm in then I'm in."

"So take your time," Hicks said. "Be sure. Then tell me: are you in?"

Bryan looked him in the eye. "Know what, Rodney? Ten years ago? Or if it was just me and Donna, I'd tell you 'Sorry, pal, you're on your own, I don't need the aggravation'. But my boys...Mick's gonna be ready for university in a couple years, Jerry's only eleven months behind him, and I don't think I'm gonna be able to afford the tuition. You know how that feels? Shitty's how it feels. I want the world for those boys, Rodney. Always have. And this is my chance to give it to 'em. So yeah, I'm in. Count on it."

Bryan was saying the right words, but Hicks still didn't like his tone. He said, "Bryan, we got him. He's fucked, and when I explain that to him he'll see that I'm right. You know what? You don't even need to come in. That's how sure I am. You can wait out in the hall, back me up if you hear any commotion."

"Stuff that bullshit, Rodney. We go in together or we don't go in at all."

Hicks smiled, the old Bryan talking now.

There was a pause before Bryan said, "If we pull this off, what're you gonna do with your share?"

"Quit this fucking job and get my wife back," Hicks said without hesitation. "If she'll have me. Then? I don't know. Travel. Stop worrying." He grinned. "Whatever the hell I want."

Bryan returned the grin, relaxing a little. "We tell everybody we've been going halves on tickets and we finally lucked out. Simple as that."

"Simple as that."

After another pause Bryan said, "Don't you think...?" and trailed off, looking unhappy again.

"What?"

"Don't you think it'd be smarter to cut him in? Ten million three ways, what's the difference? We do it that way, we're all sitting pretty, and we don't need to be looking over our shoulders the rest of our lives. I don't know about you, but a son of a bitch takes a fortune off me, I'm gonna be pissed. Forever. I don't know what I'm gonna do to him, but I know he's not gonna like it. I can see myself dedicating my life to that fucker's misery."

"I hear you," Hicks said, pretending to consider it. "Maybe you're right. Tell you what, we'll play it by ear, okay? See how he reacts."

Bryan laughed, no humor in it. "You're full of shit, Rodney. You're planning to kill the man, aren't you. You're fucking him out of a king's ransom here and it's still not enough for you." Hicks said nothing. "Well, here's the news. If that's the case, I don't want any part of it. Forget it. You give me your word, right now, we offer him a three way split and keep our cocks in our pants. Do it smart. He balks, we walk away and bust him for the dink in the sewer. The money goes to charity or down the toilet, I don't give a fuck. My kids get jobs and put themselves through school. That's the deal, take it or leave it."

Hicks said, "Okay, all right, we'll do it your way," surprised and a little touched by Bryan's ability to read him. "We'll cut the fucker in and I'll use part of the money on a stack of self-help books. Anger Management, Forgiveness Is Bliss, shit like that. Read 'em on the beach." He smiled. "Now will you relax?"

Bryan eyeballed him a moment longer, then picked up his hoagie and took a bite.

"That's better," Hicks said, shivering a little in the ensuing silence. He turned the heater up a notch, warming his hands in front of the dash vents. "Fucking winter," he said.

"I like winter," Mayer said, chewing noisily. "Suits my metabolism better."

"What's your metabolism got to do with it?"

"I sweat. Like a pig. You know that. I'm sweating right now, fuck sake. Summer in the city, pure hell. Allergies, can't breathe worth a shit in that heat. Grass to cut. And that cottage Donna's dad gave her? Fuckin' work camp. I can't get a minute's peace up there. Fix this, fix that. Busted pumps, rotten porch boards, mice in the goddam walls. And bugs? Black flies, mosquitoes, spiders everywhere. Moths. I've never seen anything like it. If you'd come up like I invite you every year you'd see what I mean."

"Your wife doesn't like me."

"What's that got to do with anything? *I* don't like you."

"Fuck you."

"And the horse you rode in on," Mayer said. He took another bite of his sandwich, a big one. "Fucking moths. Squadrons of the dizzy bastards, all shapes and sizes, bopping against the porch light like retards. Drive up there at night, the fuckin' car's coated in 'em. Jesus, that is one stunned creation. What're they good for? They like light so much, why don't they come out in the daytime?"

Hicks laughed. "You're a doorknob, Bryan, there's no escaping it. How'd you get out of grade school?"

A voice came out of the receiver, laced with static. Both men recognized it immediately.

"Hey, Al," Jack Cullen said. "Pull up a chair. You're gonna love..."

Then it was gone, swallowed in white noise.

"Shit," Mayer said, adjusting dials, frowning. "He's out of range." He looked at Hicks. "Wanna take it inside? See if we can pick him up from the office?"

"Naw. Let's just sit tight. How much trouble can he get into in a police station?"

After checking his messages Raybould cut through Homicide on his way to the gym. One last workout, a good night's sleep for a change, then the Lottery Commission first thing in the morning. After that, first class to Grand Cayman for a few days R and R, then the Concord to Europe and fuck all the rest.

It was five o'clock and a change-of-shift bull session was in progress around Jack Cullen's desk, five or six detectives forming a loose circle around Cullen himself. A small TV and a VCR sat on the desk amid a litter of Pepsi cans and Styrofoam coffee cups. Cullen had everyone's attention. Raybould couldn't stand the guy, just another bullshitter cop who'd never pulled his piece, except maybe in front of his bedroom mirror. His cronies in Homicide called him The Exorcist, saying he looked like that dark-haired priest from the movie, but Raybould couldn't see the resemblance. Dummy looked more like Linda Blair.

"Hey, Al," Cullen said, waving him over. "Pull up a chair. You're gonna love this."

Raybould grabbed a chair and sat down. What the hell. One of the men handed him a can of pop, which he tabbed but didn't drink.

Cullen got right back into it.

"So yesterday morning early I get this call. Lebanese guy shotguns an armed scumbag tryna empty his till. Straight-forward, right? The Leb even got it on tape. Then that slacker Fitzpatrick calls in sick, I gotta pull a double. I get this domestic call—it's the same Lebanese guy, comes home drunk and starts bashing on his wife. And, oh my, you gotta see this broad. Three hundred pounds if she's an ounce, this guy goes maybe one-forty soaking wet. Anyway, he starts wailing on the blimp and *pow!*, lucky shot, knocks her out cold. Now get this—she fucking *falls* on him! Can you picture it? By the time she comes to, this guy's clock has been punched. He's fuckin' dead!"

The men roared with laughter.

"But the plot thickens," Cullen said, looking at Raybould now. "This is the part you're gonna get off on, Al. The fat lady turns up at headquarters this morning with a couple uniforms claiming her purse got snatched, flapping about a stolen lottery ticket—ten million bucks worth of lottery ticket. Ringin' any bells, Al?"

Raybould said, "I made the lady's acquaintance."

"Well, here's the capper."

Cullen turned on the TV and slid a tape into the VCR, the men huddling around the screen. Cullen started the tape and a grainy Tarek Yaghi appeared, lips moving soundlessly in the moments before he turned the shotgun on Marty Small.

"See that?" Cullen said, using the stir stick from his coffee as a pointer. He indicated Yaghi's hand as it pocketed the ticket. "At first I thought nothing of it."

On the screen Yaghi shot Marty in the face.

"God damn Terminator," one of the men said.

"Then I get a call from Smitty over in Robbery," Cullen said. "Turns out the stiff at the store rolled some accident victims on his way home from a break-and-enter spree up north the other night.

Lifted their wallets and Christmas gifts right out of the wreckage and left them for dead. We turned up half the stuff in the guy's van and the other half in the apartment of this little sperm-guzzler he picked up at a strip joint—Jesus, the mouth on that one. The lottery ticket was in one of the wallets he lifted. Jagoff didn't even know what he had 'til the Leb blew his face off. Now I ask you, is that a daisy chain or what?"

"That's a hell of a tale, Jack," Raybould said, standing. "I was you, I'd send it in to *America's Funniest Home Videos*."

"I pity the purse snatcher when he shows up trying to cash in that ticket," Cullen said. "He is gonna get STUNG!"

Raybould left on the men's laughter.

Kate said, "You've got to be kidding," looking down the hospital steps at the camera crew standing by their red and white van, a reporter she recognized from the evening news having his bald head powdered by make-up. A few plump flakes were falling, landing on that shiny pate, vexing the make-up guy.

Steve took Kate's arm. "Don't worry, it'll be a snap. The cameraman over there, the guy with the bandage on his nose? That's Willy, hockey buddy of mine. He's a lousy hockey player, but a great guy. He set this up for us." He waved to Willy and Willy waved back, balancing the big Sony camcorder on his shoulder. Steve kept talking, coaxing Kate down the steps. "The whole thing's been scripted for you. All you've gotta do is read your lines. The idea's to let the guy know he's got your ticket, assuming he doesn't already know, then lure him in."

Kate said, "I hate having a camera pointed at me."

Steve laughed. "What'll you do when it comes time to accept your Academy Award? Think of it as practice."

"You come on with me then, tough guy."

"Oh, no. You're the star of this show. Tell you what, though, I'll stand right behind Willy so you can see me. Make some faces."

Kate wanted to say something more, but the crew was moving in on her now, the reporter shaking her hand—"Hi, Kate, I'm Leo Lang"—and she was stuck.

Leo Lang said, "There's nothing to this, Kate. Sandy over there'll be holding up some prompt cards for you. Just read them off. Act natural. It's a human interest story, it'll sell itself."

Kate said, "Okay, Leo, look. I'll do this, but I won't read any lines. I've got my own feelings about this. You ask your questions and I'll answer them. All right?"

Leo said, "Fair enough," and signaled the crew to begin. He stuck the mike under his chin and smiled for the camera.

Raybould said, "Fuck," and slammed the heavy bag with his fist, driving a kick into it, a quick combination, the bag jouncing on its chain. "Fuck!"

Exchanging a look, two young constables working the weights picked up their gear and headed for the showers, leaving Raybould alone in the small gym.

Oblivious, Raybould punished the bag, dumping his fury into it, clearing his mind. He needed options. Identify his options and go from there. This was just another problem. A giant motherfucking pain-in-the-ass problem, but still just a problem. And every problem had a solution. Most had several. All he had to do was identify them and then pick one. But fuck, it was maddening.

Better than federal prison, though, when you thought about it. The temptation to run straight across Bloor Street and cash that big honey in had been great. But some instinct had twitched, a warning whispered in a small voice he'd faithfully heeded all his life. Wisely. Waltzing in there with the ticket in his hand would've been the most spectacular blunder of his life.

He worked the bag, reaching for clarity, bathing his system with calming endorphins. Okay, cashing in the ticket was no longer an option, so stroke that. What else? Who *could* cash it? The original owner, but he had no idea who that was. He could find out, would find out one way or another, but that approach could get messy. What else?

It came to him then, a plan of such sweet simplicity he had to smile. It'd cost him, but when you were talking these kinds of numbers, what were a couple million here or there?

He eased up on the bag, satisfied, shaking the numbness from his hands. Dripping sweat, he went into the locker room and showered, standing for a long time in the splash and echo of the tiled shower stall, singing softly to himself.

"Gimme some lovin', gimme gimme some lovin'..."

Hicks said, "There he is."

Raybould came out of headquarters onto College Street, moving fast. He stepped onto the street, dodging traffic, and angled straight for the van. Hicks twisted his body away from the window saying, "Shit, he made us," and Mayer leaned over his gear, turning his face to the passenger door.

But Raybould cut behind the van onto the sidewalk. Mayer picked him up in his sideview mirror. "The fuck's he up to now?" he said, watching him go into a Burger King outlet.

Hicks opened his door, ready to tail him on foot, but Mayer said, "Wait a sec," and boosted the volume on the receiver. "Listen..."

The jingle of a coin dropping into a payphone.

"There's a payphone in the entrance," Mayer said.

"If anybody'd know that, it'd be you."

"What's that supposed to be, a joke? Some kind of slur on my eating habits?"

Hicks said, "Quiet."

Raybould's voice: "Paulie, it's me. Yeah, I need a meeting. Tonight." Pause. "Don't give me any shit, Paulie. Tell Mister Corsino it's worth two million, simple exchange." Pause. "Okay, put him on."

Mayer said, "God damn, looks like you were right about this guy."

"You had any doubts?"

Raybould's voice: "Yeah, Mister Corsino, it's a lottery ticket. Ten million." Pause. "Can't do it. Too much heat." Pause. "What...? No, I had to drop a guy to get it. All very public. The ticket's clean, but I can't show my face." Pause. "Paulie can do it, get his picture in the paper."

Mayer said, "This guy's got a death wish."

Raybould's voice: "A million cash, the other seven wired." Pause. "What's to convince? Can you think of a neater way to launder ten million dollars? And *make* two million while you're at it?

Think about it. I'm doing you a favor here. It's easy and it's legitimate." Pause. "Half! Are you fucking shitting me? You...no, Mister Corsino, don't hang up. I apologize. Jesus... Okay, five it is. But I still need the million cash." Pause. "Ten o'clock, I'm there."

Hicks grinned at Mayer. "The kitty just got a million bucks sweeter."

"Shit, Rodney, I don't know. This is getting dicey. I've got a family to think about, I can't afford to walk into the middle of a shit storm here."

"Bryan, if we're cool about this we'll be fine. Are we cool?"

Hesitating, Mayer said, "Yeah, we're cool."

The sound of another coin dropping into the payphone, then Raybould saying, "I need a flight to the Caymans, tomorrow afternoon."

"Prick's not wasting any time," Hicks said. He looked at Mayer. "Hey, Bry, when this is over I'll flip you for the plane ticket."

"Shit, Rodney, I don't know."

Kate said to Steve, "You don't see the double standard there?" looking him straight in the eye. They were alone in the elevator, heading back to Stepdown. The interview had gone better than either had expected, Kate a natural in front of the camera. And with the exposure the reporter promised, in a matter of days everyone in the country would know her story. It was the surest way Steve could think of to draw the thief out. "Take *Striptease* for example," Kate was saying. "Cinematic dreck, granted, but you guys get full rear *and* frontal views of all Demi's new software, the rest of us get what, two or three seconds of Mel's backside in *Lethal Weapon* and that's supposed to be fair?"

They'd been discussing nudity in film, using it as a kind of unconscious foreplay, when Steve made the mistake of calling male nudity gross, something he'd rather not see outside the precinct shower room. Even there if he could help it. Now instead of arguing, he was watching Kate's face, enjoying the way her nostrils flared when she got excited, the red spots that came up on her cheeks like a rash, the flash and sparkle of her eyes. She really cared about this stuff.

She said, "That's the part I don't understand. Why is it—" The elevator doors opened and they got off, turning right to Stepdown and in through the automatic doors. "Why is it considered such a big deal when a man takes his clothes off and—"

A gruff male voice boomed out of Keith's cubicle into the main hall: "Gabe, keep them *god*dam boots off the furniture."

Kate froze in her tracks. "Oh, shit, it's my uncle Garnet." She looked at Steve, biting her bottom lip. "I should warn you about him. He's my dad's older brother and he...stayed on the farm. He's a bit crusty."

The same voice said, "You gonna eat this shit or not?"

One of the nurses frowned at Kate.

Smiling, Steve said, "I like him already."

Kate said, "Okay, but don't say I didn't warn you."

They went into Keith's cubicle.

Garnet Whipple, a gaunt man of sixty-three with a scruffy white beard and eyebrows to match, stood next to Keith's bed in his bib overalls, eating a chicken leg off Keith's dinner tray. His wife, Myrtle, narrow peasant's face set in stone, sat in a chair at the foot of the bed with a glossy white purse in her lap, unshaven legs showing under a wash-faded cotton skirt. Gabe, their forty-year-old mentally challenged son, sat hunched on a stool next to his mother, biting a ratty finger nail. There was no sign of Lee. She'd either gone home or made herself scarce. She hadn't spoken to Garnet in almost fifty years, not since he pulled a ladder out from under her in the barn and broke both her ankles.

Kate rolled her eyes at her father, who gave a little shrug, then made the introductions. "Everyone, I'd like you to meet my friend, Steve Seger. He's a constable with the O.P.P."

Gabe grinned and scratched his eye. Myrtle said, "Hey, Steve," without looking up. Garnet, using his sleeve to wipe chicken grease off his chin, said, "Hey, officer. You didn't ticket my old deuce coupe out there, didya?"

"No, sir," Steve said, smiling. "I'm off duty."

Kate touched his arm. "Steve, this is my uncle Garnet and my aunt Myrtle. And this—"

"That's Gabe," Garnet said. "Not enough oxygen to the brainpan at birth. Told the wife we shoulda hit him in the back of the head years ago 'n' raised a pig. Least that way we'da had pork." He winked a merry eye at Steve, letting him know he was only kidding. Still, Steve had to wonder. "Ain't but one thing he's good for," Garnet said. "Gabe, sing for the constable."

Grimacing horribly, his few remaining teeth pearl-white in his ruddy face, Gabe raised his chin and broke into song, Roy Orbison's "Pretty Woman", his voice an almost flawless reproduction of Orbison's.

Steve said, "That's incredible."

Garnet said, "Ain't it?" spooning up Keith's ice cream now. "Like puttin' a nickel in a jukebox."

Myrtle said, "Garnet, leave the boy alone," and Gabe went back to chewing his nails.

After a brief silence Keith said to Kate, "So how'd the interview go?"

"Pretty good, I think," Kate said, looking at Steve.

"She was amazing," Steve said.

"The reporter said they'd start running the spot tonight on the six o'clock news," Kate said, "so hopefully the guy'll see it."

"Worth a shot," Garnet said. Keith had explained to him earlier what Kate was doing. "Goddam, for that kind of coin, I'd take a bare-ass swan dive off the CN tower into a tub of wet cow shit if I thought it'd do any good."

Kate whispered to Steve, "Now that you've sampled the Whipple gene pool, can't you just hardly wait 'til we have kids of our own?"

Steve stifled a laugh.

Finished with Keith's tray, Garnet removed his upper denture—casually, as if the entire civilized world did the same—and started sucking the stuck bits of chicken from between the teeth.

Keith said, "Garnet, for Christ's sake, that's disgusting."

"What."

Gabe broke wind, a damp gunshot pinging off the metal stool, then started singing again, this time in a child's voice, "Beans, beans the musical fruit…"

Steve lost it completely. Despite themselves, Keith and Kate did too.

Garnet seemed content to hang around forever, but Myrtle was beginning to fuss. "Garnet, it's time. We don't wanna be out on that highway after dark." Kate was glad when they finally got up to leave and could see her father was, too. Two and a half hours with Garnet and his clan had worn him out.

Garnet was pulling on his duffel coat, saying, "You get all that green money back, Keithy-boy, don't forget who pulled your skinny ass outa the silo that time. You'da been rat bait, sure as hell. I want *out* of the cattle business. Maybe get into poultry. The Kentucky Fried kind. Be a millionaire myself in half a year."

Myrtle said, "He ain't gonna forget his loved ones, Garnet. Now let's go."

Keith said, "'Bye, folks. Thanks for dropping in. I'll give you a buzz when I'm mobile."

Kate offered to walk them down to the lobby and Gabe took her arm, lumbering along beside her down the hall, all smiles.

When they were out of earshot Keith said, "God help me for saying this, Steve, but sometimes I can hardly believe I'm related to that man."

He's...colorful," Steve said. He picked up the chair Myrtle had been sitting in, walked it closer to the bed and sat facing Keith with his elbows on his knees.

"You're very generous," Keith said, chuckling. "Garnet's all right. He's just been out of touch for too long. When we were kids there was this crazy old coot named Misner used to live in a hovel across the field from us. Garnet thought the sun rose and set on that guy. Spent all his time over there. He wanted to be just like the man and now he is. All that to say, he's the way he is more through conscious effort than genetics. Sounds like I'm apologizing and I guess I am."

"No, Mister Whipple," Steve said. "I thought he was great. All of them. I haven't laughed like that in a long time."

"Let me put it this way, then. Can you imagine taking him to church? Or out to a nice restaurant? Sure, he's a giggle, but...it's a dose-related thing."

"Small doses only."

"Exactly."

Keith tried to change position in bed and couldn't manage. Steve got up and gave him a hand, hoisting him up by the armpits and adjusting his pillows. Keith thanked him, then pushed the button on the pain pump.

"I've been trying to cut down on this thing," he said, "but these damned fingers, they really throb."

Steve only nodded.

After a brief silence, both men watching for Kate to return, Keith said, "I wanted to thank you for driving Katie home yesterday, Steve. I was worried about her going all that way alone, so soon after the accident."

"I was glad to do it, sir," Steve said, afraid suddenly and for no rational reason that Keith could read his mind. He'd been thinking about that kiss in Kate's bedroom, running with it.

"So...you saw her place?"

Steve said, "Yeah," not sure where this was going.

"You didn't find it a bit...?"

"Disorganized?" Steve said, catching on.

Keith chuckled. "You really are generous. She gets it from her mom. God, that woman used to drive me crazy. And to look at her you'd've never guessed. Well dressed, always neat as a pin, hair just so. And she was a marvel in the kitchen, half an hour in there banging about and you sat down to a fabulous meal. You know the kind I mean, you want to put your feet up after and snooze?" Steve said he did. "But go out there behind her, it looks the place's been nuked. Cupboards hanging open, plates and utensils everywhere, puddles of sauce on the counter, the cooking island drifted with trash and that big black garbage bin right there beside it, closer to her hand than the island. God help me, she was messy. So unlike me. Left to my own devices...well, you saw my place."

"I did, sir," Steve said. "In that regard we're a lot alike."

"But you know what? I loved that woman from the first moment I saw her. Long as I live, I'll never forget it. It was a church social and she came at me out of the sun, lit up like an angel, and that smile. Green eyes aimed straight at me..." Keith stopped a moment, rubbing the corner of one eye. "But I never tried to change her, no matter how tempted I got to take a crack at it. She was perfect for me just the way she was. You know what I'm talking about, don't you, son."

Caught off guard, Steve said, "Yes, sir, I believe I do."

Keith smiled and gave him a nod.

"What're you boys talking about in here. Should my ears be burning?"

It was Kate. Steve stood up as she came in.

"Smart, too," Keith said, winking at Steve. "And call me Keith. I feel old enough without you young bucks calling me 'sir'."

Smiling at Kate, Steve said, "Excuse me a minute, folks," and left the room.

Kate sat in Steve's chair, feeling his warmth against the backs of her thighs. She looked at her father and said, "Steve asked me to go out with him tonight to a blues club. Would you mind?" Then cast her eyes down, feeling like a teenager again.

"Of course not, sweetie. Lee's coming in later to play cards anyways, so I won't be alone. You two go ahead, have a nice time."

"Thanks. I might even end up staying, you know, at his place."

"That's fine, Katie."

Kate reached into her handbag, taking out a small pad of paper. She tore off the top sheet, folded it in half and placed it on the bedside table. "I wrote down his phone number and address. His apartment's just a few blocks from here. His beeper number's on there too, just in case. If you need me...what?"

Keith was grinning, shaking his head. "You're just like your mother. You're your mother through and through. Stop being such a worry wart. I'm in the hospital, I've got my dope, I'm fine. Now go have some fun."

Kate stood up and gave him a kiss. "Thanks, Dad. Call me if—"

"Will you get out of here?" Keith said, laughing.

"Okay. I'm gone."

12

HICKS SAID, "OKAY, SLOW down, he's turning."

Mayer checked his rearview and decelerated, guiding the van onto the plowed shoulder. The transport that had been trailing them roared by on the rural highway, rocking the van. A half-mile ahead Raybould's sedan turned into Rideau Downs, the harness racetrack, closed now for the season.

"Why here?" Mayer said.

"Who knows," Hicks said. "Corsino's got his finger in everything." Raybould's car was no longer visible from the highway. "Let's go."

Mayer drove to the entrance, dousing the headlights before turning in, the big raceway sign looming overhead, dark and crusted with ice. Mayer said, "Which way?" Raybould's car had disappeared.

Hicks pointed to the right-hand corner of the main building. There was a light on over there. "Give that a try."

Mayer rolled ahead, guiding the van by moonlight toward a pair of snow-covered livestock trailers, side by side near the midpoint of the concrete building. He slipped the van between them, killed the engine and they both got out.

Mayer said, "Cripes, it's cold," knowing it was fear more than the temperature, wishing he'd stayed out of this. He kept hearing the old bull street cop who'd trained him a lifetime ago in Division: "Once you get dirty you never get clean. Keep your hands in your own pockets, boy, and you'll do fine."

Hicks drew his weapon. "Just keep thinking about all that money, Bry. Aruba, bikini thongs, colored drinks. Whatever you want." He raked back on the slide, chambering a round. "Now come on."

Mayer drew his sidearm and followed his partner. They got to the corner of the building in time to see Raybould, a hundred yards along the building's flank, handing his gun to one of Corsino's men, a big bastard in a white fedora and matching wool coat. The guy stuck the gun in his coat pocket then gave Raybould a quick frisk, taking his ankle gun, too. He opened a door and Raybould followed him inside.

Mayer said, "You see the size of that guy?"

"Big as a two-hole outhouse and twice as smart," Hicks said. "Fuck him. Let's do it."

They jogged to the metal door and flanked it. They could hear the guy through the door now, coming back down the stairs, big boots on metal-grate steps. The door opened and the guy stepped out, humming something, and Hicks cold-cocked him with the butt of his gun. As the guy fell Hicks plucked the hat off his head and put it on his own. "Hey, Bry," he said, "how do I look?"

"Like an asshole," Mayer said. "Help me get him out of the way."

Steve said to Kate, "This place is one of Toronto's best kept secrets. Only your hard core blues men even know it exits. You wouldn't believe some of the people who just show up here unannounced. Legends. John Lee Hooker, James Cotton, B.B. King. Dan Akroyd's a regular, and I saw Bruce Willis here once. Man blows a mean harp."

They were cruising north on Yonge Street in Steve's Cherokee, the Pantages Theater coming up on Kate's right, the theater crowd streaming out now, dispersing to clubs and cafés.

Kate said, "Who's playing tonight?"

"The house band, Bad 'n' Rude. Great musicians. They come on around ten-thirty, play a set, then open it up to any musicians in the crowd. And there's always a house full. You're gonna love it."

Steve turned right onto a narrow side street and had to brake to avoid a wino crossing the road, a khaki blanket shrouding his head. The man wheeled toward them, the Cherokee's low beams underlighting his face, and he scowled into the glare for a beat before weaving out of the way. Steve drove on, turning right again partway down the block into an unmarked alley. Kate shuddered as they bumped along the alley, the image of that wino still in her mind. She felt like she'd just come eyeball to eyeball with the Grim Reaper.

Steve said, "Here we are."

Kate had a look. Apart from the sign—The Blue Room, in cobalt neon—the place looked like the back end of a warehouse. Windows boarded up, crumbling brick, a beat up slat fence on one side of the small parking area, a couple of rusty dumpsters on the other. She said, "You go all out to impress a girl, don't you."

Steve smiled. "Have a little faith. You liked the restaurant, didn't you?"

Kate said she had, though her first impression of the place had been even more guarded than this, a seedy looking joint in the Asian district, no sign, down a narrow staircase littered with trash into what turned out to be a quaint Chinese outfit run by a fussy little guy named Jimmy Chan. Most of the other patrons had been Chinese, and once Kate got a look at the menu she understood why. Though she'd drawn the line at the deep-fried chicken feet she ended up enjoying herself, sampling all sorts of exotic fare. They'd stayed an hour longer than planned, listening to Chan tell stories about his days as a Hong Kong pimp in his giddy, broken English.

Steve got them parked, then looked over at Kate. "Still game?"

Kate said, "I'm game," and smiled. The guy was irresistible. She glanced at the entrance to the bar—a heavy, dungeon-style wood and wrought iron door—and saw two biker types in leather club jackets shoving a guy in jeans and a Jim Morrison T-shirt out the door, the guy not putting up much of a fight. She could hear the live music now, brassy and loud, pulsing out of the club through the open door.

"Bouncers," Steve said. "The place started out as a biker bar back in the seventies, now its owned by them. They're excellent peacekeepers."

Kate saw one of the bouncers talking to the guy, one hand on the guy's shoulder. The guy pushed the bouncer's hand away and the bouncer grabbed him by the throat. Kate said, "Did you bring your gun?"

Laughing, Steve reached across her lap—he smelled good, clean skin and shampoo, and Kate had the urge to kiss him on the neck—and opened the glove box. He took something out, a roll of tan felt or maybe cotton with something wrapped inside.

She said, "If that's a gun, I was only kidding."

"It's not a gun," Steve said, closing the glove box. He winked and opened his door. "It's a surprise. Now come on. And don't worry, I'm a cop."

Kate took his arm as they made their way across the parking lot, the night air cold, making her shiver. She tried not to look at the shoving match that had broken out between the bouncers and the guy in the T-shirt and of course she did. The guy wanted back inside for his coat and the bouncers wouldn't let him go.

Then they were inside, Steve taking her hand, guiding her through the crowd to a reserved table near the stage. Kate noticed the pleased smile on the singer's face when he saw Steve and as they sat she said, "You know that guy?"

Steve said, "Yep," and hailed a waitress. He asked Kate what she was drinking and Kate said she'd stick with white wine. She'd had a couple of glasses at the restaurant and was already feeling tipsy. She'd have to be careful. She was a cheap drunk and not a very graceful one.

She watched Steve order their drinks, the waitress flirting with him, and thought about calling her father; but it was late and even if she caught him awake he'd just chew her out for being a worry wart.

She looked up at the band, breaking into a fast shuffle now, an original, the singer said. A big group for the size of the place, Kate thought. Four horn players doing the old revue-style footwork, two black girls in pink sequins singing back up, three guitarists and the skinniest drummer Kate had ever seen. The lead singer was a balding redhead with big white Gary Busey teeth. His voice reminded her of calm blue water, deep and cool. Steve was right; they were great.

He touched her hand, leaning in close to speak in her ear. "So what do you think?"

"Nice," Kate said over the music. She looked at the thing he'd taken from the glove box, resting under his hand on the table now. "Are you going to tell me what that is now?"

"Nope."

"I'll lose interest."

Steve said, "I don't think so."

The waitress brought their drinks, wine for her, beer for him, and Steve paid her. They glanced at each other after the waitress left, comfortable together, then settled back to enjoy the music.

Raybould didn't like it, walking into a snake pit like this without his guns. At first he refused to give them up, but the goon in the hat insisted, telling him it was the only way he was going inside.

Now he stood where the goon had left him, in the delivery bay of the kitchen that serviced the dining lounge the heavy hitters did their betting from. The place was enormous, all stainless steel and cold green tile.

Twenty feet away, Connie Corsino stood behind an open grille cooking T-bones, a bib apron over his suit pants and shirt, seventy years old if he was a day. He looked up at Raybould and smiled, still some sparkle in those eyes. The steaks smelled good.

"Al," he said, like they were old pals. "Come ahead in."

Raybould approached the grille, his cop eyes taking in the layout. A three-by-ten stainless steel counter between him and the old man. A set of swinging doors back there for the busboys and waitresses, opening on the lounge. A wiseguy in a muscle-shirt sitting close to his boss in a tipped-back chair, eating a filet mignon sandwich and watching the news on a ceiling-mounted TV. Two other bodyguards loitering nearby in sunglasses and dark suits. Looking at them Raybould had to bite back a laugh. Guys like this broke him up. They worked so hard at the image.

Corsino said, "Guy runs this place's an associate of mine. I like to come up here sometimes and raid the freezer."

Raybould stopped a few feet shy of the grille, hands linked behind his back, waiting for the old man to finish his preliminaries.

Corsino said, "What can I fix you to eat? I got some Alfredo sauce over here." He kicked Muscle-shirt's chair. "One of these Dagwood sandwiches this garburator eats? Green eggs and ham?"

That got a chuckle out of the boys.

Raybould said, "I'm not hungry."

"Suit yourself," Corsino said. He flipped a steak, yellow flames sprouting up, eating the grease. "So, Al, tell me again why you don't just collect on this yourself?"

"It's like I told you over the phone. This punk grabbed the ticket from a civilian. Purse snatcher, didn't even know what he had. I happened to be in the vicinity so I went after him. All very public. Things got out of hand, I had to put the punk down. You know how it is. Problem is, my name's on the incident report. See? I can't just walk in there now and cash in the ticket, turn up a millionaire."

"So cash it and disappear."

Raybould smiled. "And leave all this?"

"Send a friend in to cash it for you then."

"You know me, Mister Corsino. I don't have any friends."

The old fucker nodding now, thinking it over.

Muscle-shirt turned up the volume on the TV with the remote. Raybould glanced up at the screen, a female anchor setting up the next news item:

"A story of misfortune from our neighbors to the north. Keith Whipple, a sixty-year-old Sudbury retiree—" A photo of Keith appeared behind the anchor "—recently realized a dream most all of us share. He won the lottery, ten million dollars on the six-four-nine. But on his way to Toronto with his daughter, Kate, to collect his winnings and spend Christmas with family, disaster struck." Kate's face appeared next to Keith's. Also shown was the mangled limo. "A head-on collision with an oil truck."

Raybould thought, Fuck. "So Mister Corsino. Are we on here or not?"

Corsino flipped another steak, glancing at him with those beady eyes. "Sure, Al. Relax."

He signaled one of his bodyguards, who dropped a gym bag at Raybould's feet. Raybould nudged it with his toe, testing its heft. It seemed a little light. He said, "And the other four?"

"Paulie's with my accountant right now, waiting for my call. When I'm satisfied the ticket's legit the money gets wired. You verify the transfer and we all go home happy. Sure you're not hungry, Al?"

Raybould shook his head. The idiot in the muscle-shirt cranked the volume up again. Corsino didn't seem to notice, his attention on the steaks.

"Though the Whipples survived the collision," the anchor said, "the ticket did not. It was stolen by a passing motorist, along with Mister Whipple's wallet and several thousand dollars' worth of Christmas gifts and cash. STV reporter Leo Lang interviewed Ms. Whipple earlier today at the North York Trauma Center, where her father is listed in stable condition."

Muscle-shirt said, "Boss, I think you oughta see this."

Corsino turned his head to look at the screen. Raybould came around the grille and stood behind him, watching, the next few seconds flashing in his mind.

Kate appeared on the hospital steps, the interview already in progress.

Leo Lang: "So Kate, if he's watching, what do you have to say to the man who robbed you?"

Kate: "What I'd like to say to him you wouldn't allow. But I want him to know this." The camera zoomed in on Kate's face, her eyes aimed straight into the lens. "My father's ticket is worthless to you now. If you try to cash it you'll be arrested. If you keep it, it's worthless to us all. Under the circumstances, we're willing to forgive and forget. If you return the ticket to us, we're offering a one million dollar reward."

Corsino kicked Muscle-shirt's chair. "Hey, Dagwood," he said, chuckling, "show me that part again. Where she says, 'If you try to cash it you'll be arrested'. It's my favorite."

Muscle-shirt hit the rewind button and Raybould noticed the VCR up there, a slim Sony unit mounted under the TV.

Corsino faced him, no amusement on his face now. "I taped this off the six o'clock news. This how you treat your friends, Al?"

On the screen Kate said, "If you try to cash it..."

Corsino said, "Air this fucker out."

Muscle-shirt came off his chair fast, weapon in hand, but Raybould was a split second faster, snatching a carving knife off the counter and grabbing Corsino from behind, holding the knife to his throat. Corsino's men closed in, guns raised.

"Back off, boys," Raybould said. "Nobody needs to get hurt."

"You're not gonna get hurt," the old guy said, no fear in him, "you're gonna die."

Raybould drew the blade lightly across Corsino's throat, breaking the loose skin. "That's the dotted line, you old prick." He faced the bodyguards. "Now put 'em down."

Corsino said, "Shoot this cunt!"

"Let him go," Muscle-shirt said, he and his two buddies closing in. These guys weren't backing down, they were just waiting for a clean shot.

Corsino spoke to Raybould over his shoulder, his bony, old man's body squirming with surprising strength. "Know what's in the bag, Al? A hundred grand—for the first man here puts a bullet in you. See how motivated these guys are?" He looked at his men. "Now *shoot* this sonofa—"

The stairway door banged open and Hicks and Mayer came in, sidearms raised. Hicks tossed the white fedora onto the floor and said, "Police, all of you, freeze!" And to the nearest bodyguard, "Drop it, meatball."

The bodyguard drew a bead on Hicks. "You drop it."

Corsino said, "Who're these guys?"

"Internal Affairs," Raybould said. "Fuck 'em."

Hicks said, "Bryan, get the bag."

The bodyguard shifted his aim to Mayer. "Touch it, I shoot you in the balls."

Hicks put a bullet in his temple. He said, "Bryan, get the—"

And the door to the walk-in freezer swung open, a guy with frost in his eyebrows popping out, cutting Mayer in half with a blazing Uzi. Every man in the room with a weapon was firing it now, diving for cover. Bullets spanged off pots and appliances.

Using Corsino as a shield, Raybould rushed Muscle-shirt and drove the knife into his chest, seizing the man's weapon as he fell. He shoved the old guinea aside, spun to fire and a slug plowed through his forearm. He hit the deck and fired at Hicks, catching him in the thigh, then shot the guy from the freezer in the ankle, the guy dancing around on one foot now, screaming like hell, the Uzi firing wild. Hicks finished him off.

"Rodney," Raybould said from behind the grille. The steaks were starting to burn, dense smoke spiraling up into the vent canopy. "Excellent timing."

One of the bodyguards opened fire on the grille and Hicks shot him in the neck. The bodyguard slouched to the floor, gun spinning across the tiles.

"Shit, Rodney," Raybould said. "Nice shooting. I should've stayed partnered with you—"

Corsino came at Raybould from behind, a fire axe raised over his head. Raybould twisted from his crouch and shot the old man in the belly, watching him fold, the axe flying wild.

"Hey, asshole," Raybould said to the surviving bodyguard, crouched ten feet away behind a big laminated chopping block. "Your boss's dead. You're out of work and my arm hurts. What say we call it a day? Maybe gang up on the copper over there by the door, wants to put you in jail."

The bodyguard said, "Meat eater, you're gonna die, motherfucker, and I'm personally gonna stuff your dick in your mouth when it's done."

"Nice image," Raybould said. "You hear that, Rodney? Your wife used to like my dick in her mouth. She liked it a lot. You with SIU now, Rodney? Is that why you're here?" He waited. "Cat got your tongue? How's that leg?"

Raybould raised up to fire a couple of rounds at the bodyguard and a couple more at Hicks, just to keep things going. Both men returned fire. Then, covered by the counter, he belly crawled to the swinging doors and silently slipped out, gunfire still raging behind him.

The band finished their first set at eleven-twenty, Kate's ears buzzing in the sudden lull. A Paul Butterfield tune came on the house speakers, "Walkin' Blues," the volume set low so people could talk. Steve excused himself, got up and said a few words to the lead singer, then came back to the table.

Kate said, "How do you know him?"

"I'm a regular."

"I gathered. Did you come here when it was a biker bar?"

"I was eight," Steve said, taking a sip of his beer. "But yeah, I hung out here all the time. Had to kill a guy to get in, beat him to death with a spoke wrench. It's an initiation thing, but hey—my motto? Whatever it takes."

"You look like a killer," Kate said, giggling, tipsy. "Something in the eyes..."

Steve gave her his Clint Eastwood squint and Kate threw her head back and laughed. She touched his arm and Steve put his hand over hers.

They chatted for a while about little things, getting acquainted, at ease with one another. Steve was a talker and Kate loved to listen. He used his hands a lot, and when he laughed a deep dimple appeared in his right cheek, the mild asymmetry adding to Kate's growing affection for him.

Somehow the subject of embarrassing moments during first dates came up and Kate told him about falling down a flight of stairs on her backside at the Sadie Hawkins dance in the ninth grade, the boy she'd taken standing on the top step with his mouth hanging open while she sat on the landing in a pair of her aunt's pumps—the reason she'd fallen in the first place—laughing herself sick.

"I waited a month for him to call," she told him, "but he never did."

"What's he do now?"

"Last I heard he's a surgical resident in Boston. Gonna be an orthopod like his dad."

"He didn't try to examine you? See if you broke anything?"

Kate laughed. "He didn't have that much imagination."

"Good story," Steve said, "but I've got it beat. In fact, I've got a first-date story so embarrassing there's no *way* I'm going to tell it."

"No fair," Kate said, giving him a poke. "Come on, 'fess up."

"All right, you asked for it. But this is under duress."

"Duly noted. Now give."

"I was nineteen," Steve said, "tending bar in a place called Shox on Queen Street. There was this upscale modeling agency next door and every lunch hour these tall, decked-out babes'd slink in for salads and wine coolers."

"Babes?"

"Yeah, you know. Babes. Mostly synthetic. There was this one in particular, had one of those Cindy Crawford moles on her upper lip—"

"The first thing you noticed about her."

Steve gave her an innocent look. "Of course. Anyway, I was young, she was bodacious, and I finally got up the nerve to ask her out. She smiled, gave me her phone number and said, 'How's tomorrow night sound?' Being cool, I told her that'd be peachy. The guys at the bar couldn't believe it. When we got off that night they took me out on the town. I hit it a bit hard and woke up the next morning with the mother of all hangovers. You name it, I had it. Mostly gastrointestinal, if you know what I mean."

"My father calls it the green apple two-step."

"You do know what I mean. By noon or so I was pretty sure I was gonna have to call her up and cancel."

"Did she have a name, this babe?"

"Greta. Or maybe Grechen. You want to hear this or not?"

Kate laughed. "Please, go on."

"By four o'clock I had myself convinced I'd be okay. I didn't want to blow it—what would you think, guy calls you up and says he can't make it, he's got the green apple two-step—so I gave her a call, made the arrangements, rode the Go train with her into the city and took her to the fanciest restaurant I could find."

"Chinese?" Kate said, smiling.

Steve laughed. "Continental. So during dinner, every ten minutes or so I'm excusing myself, running off to the boy's room. I'm sure she thinks I'm back there snorting cocaine or something; I wasn't exactly relaxed. We eat—salad and wine coolers for her, soup and crackers for me—the check comes and this time I've really got to go, but I don't want her to think I'm stiffing her for the check so I stay. Somebody she knows comes over, she's gabbing away and I'm thinking, If I can just sneak out this one bit of gas..."

Kate laughed. "Not gas, right?"

Steve made a face. "Right. So I'm sitting there on this...wet spot and it's time to go. Tan cotton pants and a short-sleeve shirt. No jacket. And what's her idea of a good time after dinner?"

"The movies? A nice dark theater?"

"Shopping. All the way to the Eaton Center on foot trying to hide my behind. We end up in The Gap, where I bought these tan pants, and I see an identical pair hanging on the rack. So while she's busy in the dress section I roll these pants into a bulky knit sweater and take them over to the cash, tell the cashier I don't want the sweater, just the pants and keep my eye on Grechen or maybe Greta while the cashier does her thing. We get back on the Go train and I excuse myself. By now she's used to it, but this time all I want to do is change my drawers; my gut's finally settling down. So I get in this cramped little cubicle back there, take off my pants and underwear, ball 'em up and throw 'em out the window. Then I open the Gap bag and there's the bulky knit sweater."

"No pants?"

"No pants."

"Oh my God," Kate said, her laughter loud enough to draw stares. "What'd you do?"

"Locked myself in 'til the train stopped, then pulled the sweater on like a diaper and ran like hell. Next day I quit my job at the bar and got on with the city mowing lawns."

Kate said, "Okay," tears streaming from her eyes as she pictured it, "you win."

Steve said, "It's not that funny," as the singer came on stage and called his name: "Steve? Can you come up here, man?" Showing those big teeth.

Steve picked up the roll he'd brought in with him and stood. "Be right back," he said. Then he was up on stage, the singer handing him a mike, Steve taking something out of the roll.

"Ladies and gentlemen," the singer said, "a special treat tonight." He looked down at Kate. "This one goes out to you, Kate..."

Then she saw what he had: a harmonica, Steve hunched over it now, eyes closed, body rocking, rich, throaty sounds coming from his cupped hands to fill the room, making the downy hairs on her arms stand on end. Kate knew the tune, "Whammer Jammer," by the J. Geils Band. The crowd went wild, jumping to its feet, clapping along with the beat. Kate joined them, wondering what other surprises Steve Seger had in store for her tonight.

Hicks had seen Raybould leave, crawling out through the swinging doors back there, but he couldn't get to the stairwell to go after him. Every time he tried Corsino's goon pinned him down. Hicks decided to negotiate. His leg was leaking a steady stream of blood and it hurt like hell.

He said, "Hey, listen up. I'm a cop and I'm expecting back up any minute. Raybould's already gone."

"Whaddya mean, gone?"

"I mean gone. Out those doors over there. Look, it's him I'm after. You want to get your ass out of here in one piece, do it now or I swear when the cavalry arrives I'll shoot you myself."

"You mean it? I can go?"

"I mean it. Put the gun down now and walk out of here."

"How do I know you won't shoot me?"

"I just fucking told you I won't shoot you. Now go!"

The goon tossed out his gun and stood up, fingers laced behind his head. Hicks shot him twice in the chest, the goon crashing into a silverware cart.

Hicks tried to stand up then, get down the stairs and cut Raybould off before he got to his car, but he never got past his knees; the room took a lazy spin and the lights went out. Hicks fainted dead away.

He came to a short time later, disoriented, his leg throbbing with pain. He got his belt around it above the bullet hole and yanked it tight with his teeth. Crawling on his hands and knees, he found a cell phone on one of the dead bodyguards, got the thing working and called for help.

He tried to get to the bag of money after that, hide it somewhere until the heat was off, but shit, he looked over at Bryan's bullet-riddled corpse and passed out again.

Steve wound up doing five songs, the crowd getting balky every time he tried to sit down. If it hadn't been for the appearance of Reese van der Heiden, a saxophonist for the Toronto Symphony and one of the best blues musicians Steve had ever seen, he'd've been stuck on stage until dawn. He'd played better tonight than he had in years, the energy of the band, the enthusiasm of the crowd, the whole atmosphere bringing it out of him. But none of it pleased him more than the sight of Kate's beaming face as he returned to the table through a gauntlet of backslaps and high-fives, her wide smile only for him, the sparkle in her eyes as she clapped along with the rest of them.

She put her arms around his neck and kissed him on the mouth and the smartass on the lights swung a spot on them, drawing a prolonged *ooh!* from the crowd. Then the band rolled into an old Muddy Waters standard and they were alone again, easing into their seats, holding hands across the table.

"That was fantastic," Kate said. "Where did you learn to play like that?"

"My grandfather, mostly," Steve said, feeling like the grin on his face would never go away. "A lot of it I picked up just listening."

Kate raised his hand to her mouth, brushing his knuckles with her lips. "Think I'd make a good groupie?" she said and Steve felt her touch all the way down to his boots.

"I'll turn my badge in tomorrow. Put a band together and go on the road." He stood, disengaging his hand from Kate's. "Save my seat," he said and took off to the boy's room.

He collected a few more kudos in the john, one enthusiastic drunk jostling him so hard in front of the urinal Steve almost peed on his own shoes. The Muddy Waters tune ended while he was washing up and then a strange thing happened, an old girl-group tune reaching his ears, "My Boyfriend's Back" by the Angels. As out of place in the Blue Room as a polka, but it sounded great. The crowd thought so, too.

Steve went out to see what was up, his own empty table visible before he could see the stage—holy shit—Kate up there now with a mike in her hand, singing lead with the girls doing back up, all of them looking down at him with smiles on their faces. She had all the right moves, too, sassy as hell. Steve sat in his chair and just grinned at her.

When the song ended the crowd surged to its feet, shouting for more, but Kate said, "Sorry, folks, that's the only one I know," and walked off the stage, face red as a beet, hiding in her hair. Steve stood too, pulling her chair out for her when she got to the table.

The singer announced a break, the lights went down and Steve asked Kate if she wanted another drink. She said no, then whispered something in his ear.

A minute later they left the Blue Room, Kate snuggled under Steve's arm against the winter chill.

Raybould found the guard Hicks had cold-cocked still unconscious, laid out on his back with his eyes half open, bald head haloed in blood. He took his guns back—helping himself to the guard's piece, too, a big chrome-plated Desert Eagle, three extra clips in the guy's pocket—then got in his car and drove to the exit, alert for an ambush, realizing only as he turned onto the highway that Hicks and his fat-boy partner had been acting alone. Not as cops, either, but after the money. Probably Paulie who finked on him. Or maybe IA working with SIU, the way it started, hoping to turn up some dirt on him, strengthen their case against him; then Hicks and fatso getting wind of what was going down and deciding, fuck it, retire rich. Leave a stack of corpses at the scene—one dirty cop and a bunch of mob assholes, nice work, fellas—pocket the ticket *and* the cash and walk away clean. Decent plan, if you didn't know about the sting on the ticket. Which made him doubt Hicks' actions had ever been official. Probably just Hicks with a four-year hard-on about his coke-whore wife, looking to get even and just lucking into the whole thing. Not that it mattered. He had a flight booked to Grand Cayman Island at five tomorrow afternoon and he'd be on it, ten million richer instead of only five.

It was time for plan B.

He pulled into a closed gas station a few miles from the racetrack and wrapped his forearm with gauze he kept in a first-aid kit in the glovebox. The wound was through and through, not bleeding much, and his fingers were all working, which meant no serious damage had been done. He had a bottle of Percocets in the first-aid kit and he chewed a couple of those, then drove back to the city.

Steve said, "You sure you're okay with this? Being here, I mean?"

Here was Steve's loft apartment, on the sofa, Nat King Cole crooning "White Christmas" in the background.

Kate looked up at him from her glass of wine, her second since the club for a total of six. Maybe seven. She said, "Hmm?" though she'd heard him.

"You seem a little distracted. I don't know, maybe it's too soon. I mean, maybe we should've just gone back to the hospital."

"No, I'm fine." Distracted, yes, but not for the reasons he might be thinking. "I was just..." But there was no way she could tell him what she'd been thinking. Was there? She giggled and held up her wine glass. "Too much wine," she said. "Could I have another?"

"Sure," Steve said, getting up.

Kate caught him by the wrist. "I was kidding. One more of these and...well, I've had enough. Let's watch the movie."

Steve said, "Good idea," and got busy queuing up the video.

They'd picked up *One Flew Over The Cuckoo's Nest* at a nearby video outlet, Kate surprised when Steve took it off the shelf and said he'd never seen it. It was one of her all time favorites. She and her dad had the dialogue practically memorized.

The suggestion to come to Steve's place had been hers—the wine talking, but Steve had been quick to agree. They'd snuggled all the way home in the truck.

Kate loved his place. It was exactly as she'd expected, spacious and neat, lots of natural wood and earthy colors. She'd always liked the idea of a loft, everything right there, no secrets. It was hard not to notice that big bed over there by the windows, so neatly made and inviting. Kate giggled at her thoughts.

Steve said, "What's funny?"

"Never mind," Kate said. She took the remote from him and fast-forwarded through the opening credits. "It's time to introduce you to R. P. McMurphy."

Stan Howson, Hicks' superior officer, walked alongside the stretcher Hicks was strapped to, a couple of paramedics wheeling it at a fast clip through a maze of squad cars to a waiting ambulance. The ride across the parking lot was bumpy, the morphine they'd given him not working yet, and Hicks listened to his boss rag him out with both hands clamped to the side rails. He couldn't believe he'd fainted like that. Raybould's bullet had only creased him, a through-and-through flesh wound, but shit, it hurt.

"Goddam cowboys," Howson was saying. "What were you thinking? Bryan's wife and mine go bowling together every Thursday night. What am I supposed to tell her?"

Hicks said, "You're right, Stan. We were out of line. I'll take the heat on this, all of it. Shit, it was me talked Bryan into it." He grabbed Howson's wrist. "But Stan, promise me, you've got to bring that animal down."

"He's going down, all right. Count on it."

"You got the tapes from the van?"

"Yeah."

They were almost to the ambulance.

"There's an alley on Stanton across from the liquor store," Hicks said. "Pop the manhole cover back there, you'll find more of his handiwork. We should've called it in then, but the scene was spotless." Easy to sound sincere with the pain in his leg. "We figured if we could nail him making the switch with Corsino, with the ticket in his hand..."

The paramedics hoisted the stretcher into the ambulance.

Howson said, "Don't worry, Rodney. We'll take it from here."

Kate closed the narrow gap of leather sofa between them, cozying herself into Steve's side. He looked away from the TV to glance at her, smiling, and Kate wet her lips, ready as she'd ever been. But Steve turned back to the movie, letting his arm slide off the back of the couch to encircle her shoulders, but that was it.

Rule number one, Kate thought. Never screen a film classic in front of a man you intend to seduce.

Steve laughed out loud. Kate looked at the tube and saw Jack Nicholson's character walking zombie-like into the common room from shock therapy, hamming it up for his cronies, who at the moment weren't quite sure if he was kidding or not.

Kate raised up and kissed Steve lightly on the corner of his mouth, feeling him shiver. That got his attention. He turned to her, looking for more, but now Kate was looking at the tube, saying, "Wait, this's my favorite bit."

On the screen, smiling that infamous smile, Nicholson said, "The next woman takes me on's gonna light up like a pinball machine and pay off in silver dollars."

"Jack," Kate said, her eyes on Steve again. "Ain't he the coolest?"

"Yeah," Steve said. He hit the pause button on the remote. "Except maybe for Clint."

Kate brushed her lips against his, the touch like silk. "Well, mister," she said, feeling more than the wine now. "Can you light me up like a pinball machine?"

Steve smiled. "Will you pay off in silver dollars?"

She kissed him again, a real kiss this time, finding his tongue, their mouths not able to get enough; not using their hands yet, but savoring this part, knowing there was so much more ahead.

"Didn't we talk about waiting?" Steve said, moving his lips against hers, keeping the thrill alive.

"We waited...twenty-four hours?" She checked her watch. "Twenty-seven."

Then they were gone, the movie forgotten, time condensed into their touch, their movement, their hunger. There was a sweet, urgent inevitability to their lovemaking Kate had sensed even in the limo, and every time since that she had felt his touch or heard his voice shape her name. She felt herself falling, letting it happen.

13

RAYBOULD PARKED IN FRONT of an apartment block on Jarvis Street. The place was a dump, trash poking out of the snow, crack vials crunching under his boots on the front steps. He went inside, down one flight to the basement level and knocked on the door to apartment 3. Somewhere down the hall rap music played at full volume, the bass track thudding like an urgent heartbeat through the cinderblock walls.

He flexed his hand while he waited, trying to prevent the arm from cramping up, the Percocets not touching the pain. He fucking hated getting shot.

He knocked again, harder this time, and a hoarse woman's voice said through the door: "Who is it? I've got a gun!"

"It's Al. Open up."

Bev Beauregard opened the door, smiling when she saw him, striking a pose in her ratty housecoat, obviously stoned. "Well, fuck me gently..."

"You kiss your mother with that mouth?" Raybould said. Bev was just another in a long line of fuck-ups Raybould kept like livestock, people like Swain who owed him favors or were just too shit-scared of him to balk. He shouldered past her into the apartment. "You alone in here?"

Bev stood behind him, lighting a cigarette with shaky hands. He turned to look at her, waiting for an answer, Bev eyeing him through veils of smoke, using whatever was left of her brain to puzzle out why he was here.

"Yeah, I'm alone. What's up, Al? Feelin' frisky?"

"You glanced in a mirror lately, Bev?" Fucking dummy. He showed her his arm, the gauze soaked through with blood. "I've been shot. Are you blind?"

"Why'd you come here, then?" Insulted now. "I got thrown out of nursing six years ago. You know that."

"But you're still a nurse, right? You can still handle a needle and thread?" He sat in an easy chair next to the phone table and rolled up his sleeve. "Now get a move on. I've got things to do. And get me something to drink."

Bev gave him a look but did as she was told, shuffling off into a back room, mumbling under her breath.

While he waited Raybould took a small address book out of his pocket and found a number. He dialed it on Bev's phone, letting it ring. Four times, five...

Elwood Smith rolled onto his side, ignoring the phone, trying to hang onto the dream he'd been having. He should've turned on the goddam answering machine. He'd had a snifter of brandy before retiring and had drifted into the sweetest dream... What had it been? Ah, yes, he and his son, Eric, sailing in Guadeloupe, the thirty-eight footer slicing the whitecaps... That had been three years ago, a month before Elwood was called to identify Eric's body in the city morgue, riddled with bullets from a drug pusher's gun.

Why didn't you tell me? Elwood thought, still half asleep. Why? Eric had been clean for six months, a half-year's distance on a brutal heroin addiction. The father and son trip had been in commemoration of that milestone. And what a time they'd had, sailing, girl-watching together, scuba diving off the yacht, eating like pigs. What had made him start using again? Get mixed up with that crowd *again*? Questions without answers, questions that would hound him to his grave.

Goddamn phone...

Elwood switched on the bedside lamp, squinting at the digital alarm: ten after twelve. The last call he'd gotten after midnight had been from his wife, telling him it was over between them. "Eric is dead, Elwood. When it happened it tore my heart out. But that was a long time ago. You and I, we're still alive. You go to the bank, to your job, the only thing that matters to you anymore. You come home, you drink, you go to sleep. There's no room in your life for me anymore. Well, I'm sorry, El, but I can't live that way any longer..."

He picked up the receiver and said hello.

"Elwood. It's Al Raybould. Sorry to wake you."

The cool, cadenced voice triggered a swell of emotion in Elwood, dredged up from the last time he'd spoken to this man on the phone. That call too had come in the night, only two words spoken, two sweet syllables that had satisfied a need in Elwood so powerful he wouldn't have believed it possible had he not experienced it first hand. Those words had been simply, "It's done."

"Detective Raybould," Elwood said. "Nonsense. It's good to hear your voice." A framed photograph of his son stood on the night table in front of the lamp, Eric at twelve, posing on the ice in his hockey gear. Elwood turned it to face him, saying, "It's been a long time."

"Three years. And call me Al. Remember?"

"Sure, Al. What can I do for you?"

"I don't like calling in favors unless I'm really strapped. But, you remember after I shot the guy who killed your boy, you said if I ever needed anything..."

"And I meant it, too. Every word. That savage fucker deserved to die and you made it happen. Name it, Al, and it's done."

It's done.

"Well, here's the thing. I'm about to come into some money. Quite a lot of money, as a matter of fact. My girl and I, we won the lottery—"

"That's fantastic." Elwood said, wide awake now. "How much?"

"Ten million."

"Nice number."

"Yeah, that it is. She'll be coming in to see you in the morning with the check. My girl. We'd like to get this done quick and quiet, if you know what I mean. Zero fanfare."

"I read you."

"Okay. Here's what I'd like you to set up..."

Raybould made one more call, a quick one, then hung up the phone. When he looked up Bev was standing in the archway with some first-aid supplies, waiting for him to finish. She approached him now, kneeling on the floor between his legs. She'd done a hasty make-up job on her face and Raybould had the sudden urge to kick it in for her.

She said, "Who's Archie?" and Raybould told her to mind her own business. Huffing, she came at him with a loaded insulin syringe. Raybould caught her by the wrist, twisting hard enough to make her cry out.

"What's that?" he said, letting her go.

"Demerol. It'll mellow you out, ease the pain." Massaging his thighs now. "But I'll need money for some more."

"Get it over with."

She snugged a rubber tourniquet around his arm, rubbed a vein with an alcohol swab and injected the Demerol in a big warm bolus. Raybould closed his eyes and let his head drift back, the drug pumping through him like an orgasm. He could feel Bev's hands on him again, grabby and hot, working their way up his thighs to his belt.

"Just patch the hole," he said.

Then he drifted a while.

Hicks lay in a St. James hospital bed with an IV in his hand and a surgical dressing on his leg, listening to the guy in the next bed snore. Bad enough, but he'd rather listen to the guy snore than talk. Jesus Christ. The guy'd practically chewed his ear off earlier, on and on about his prostate operation, the goddam anesthetist who stuck forty needles in his back, the crummy hospital food that'd make a goat puke.

They'd fixed Hicks' leg under local anesthesia. He'd insisted. He wanted to stay sharp. This thing wasn't over yet, not by a long shot. What he needed now was time to think. Three years partnered with Raybould, he knew how the man's mind worked. But damn, it was hard to concentrate, the old coot sawing logs, Bryan shot dead. He still couldn't believe it, Bryan like a brother to him, staging these great debates all the time about the dumbest shit, stuffing down junk food like there was no tomorrow. Bryan had trusted him, against his own better judgment, and now he was dead.

"Hey!" Hicks said. "Shut it!"

The old guy snorted and changed positions, quiet a few seconds, then started snoring again. Hicks grabbed the spring-loaded arm that supported the tiny TV and swung it around in front of him. He fit the earphone into his ear and turned the thing on, quickly scanning the channels. News everywhere. Or commercials. This was why he hated television—

Something...

He flipped back a couple of stations and saw a young woman on the steps of the North York Trauma Center, talking about a stolen lottery ticket.

"Son of a bitch."

When the spot was done he pushed the TV aside and got out of bed, gingerly, testing the leg. The doctor told him the local he'd injected should control the worst of the pain for about eight hours and so far it seemed to be working. The leg felt solid beneath him, only a dull ache when he put his weight on it.

He untaped the IV and pulled it out of his hand. Then he found his clothes. He was on the street five minutes later, hailing a cab, surprised no one had tried to stop him. His pants were a mess, crusted with blood, one leg hacked to hell by the orderly who'd taken a pair of scissors to it to get at the wound. The cabbie took one look at him and almost drove off, but Hicks showed him his badge. He gave the guy his home address and told him to gun it.

Raybould surfaced through a warm fog. He opened his eyes and saw Bev wrapping his wound with gauze. In spite of how low the poor broad had sunk, she was still a pretty good nurse.

When she was done she looked up at him, giving him a moist, pouty look that might've sold twenty years ago but tonight just made her look dopey. She started rubbing his thighs again, saying, "Now, baby, what've you got for me?"

Raybould stood up, almost knocking her over. "Some advice," he said. "Get off the shit."

He got his coat on and left, feeling fine.

Hicks had the cab driver wait while he went inside for a change of clothes and his other gun, a .45 Smith semi-auto he used for target shooting. They'd taken his service pistol at the scene. He had some Dilaudids in the medicine cabinet for the migraines he sometimes got and he brought these too, along with a pocket flask of Chivas Royal Salut, the last of a bottle Bryan had given him for his birthday last year.

He had the cabbie drive him downtown, ignoring the guy when he tried to get a conversation going, asking about his leg. He had a hard time getting out of the car, the leg beginning to stiffen up on him, and on his way into headquarters he swallowed a couple of the pain pills. He took the elevator to the garage level and limped over to the Vehicle Supervisor's window. Bob Grimard was on tonight, beergut straining against the buttons on his regulation blue shirt.

He turned the TV down in there and said, "Rodney. I heard you got shot."

"Flesh wound," Hicks said. "They patched me up and threw me out. Couldn't even wangle a free meal out of them."

Bob said, "Socialized medicine." He poked two fingers into a gap between the buttons on his shirt and scratched his belly. "Sorry to hear about Bryan," he said. "He was a good shit."

"Yeah, Grim, thanks. He was. Look, I need the keys to the van."

"Sure thing." Grim got the keys and handed them out. "You're not working tonight."

"No. Just some things in there I need."

Five minutes later Hicks pulled the van onto College Street, ignoring Grimard's surprised look as he sped past the window, the stout aluminum case containing Mayer's surveillance gear open on the seat beside him. He took the Don Valley to the 401 and got off at North York, just a short hop from there to the trauma center. He pulled into the parking lot of a fast food joint across the street from the hospital and shut off the engine. The dash clock said 1:02 AM. He'd give it a couple of hours.

He adjusted his seat all the way back and straightened the leg as much as he could. The sucker was really pounding now, keeping time with his heartbeat. He shook out a couple more pills and washed them down with a mouthful of Chivas. Shit burned all the way down, but man, it hit the spot.

Settling in, Hicks fixed his gaze on the main entrance. He jerked awake forty minutes later, wincing in pain. A spot of blood had soaked through the dressing to stain his pants. He looked through the windshield and saw Raybould climbing the hospital steps.

"Prick," he said, clearing his throat. "You're an open book."

He switched on the surveillance gear and had a look, trying to remember what Bryan had told him about it, wishing he'd paid more attention.

Raybould showed the receptionist his shield. "I need to see a patient," he told her. "Name of Whipple."

The receptionist pecked away at her keyboard. "Keith Whipple?" she said and Raybould nodded. "He's in Stepdown, officer. Bed six. Take the elevator to level three and turn right, follow the signs."

He kept his badge out, showing it to the nurse who intercepted him at the doors to the Stepdown Unit. "Detective Sergeant Raybould," he said. "It's urgent that I speak with Kate Whipple. Is she here tonight by any chance?"

"Actually, no," the nurse said. "But she left a number where she can be reached."

"Can I have it?"

"Certainly. Come with me."

Raybould followed her into the unit, waiting at the desk while she got the number off Whipple's chart and handed it over. He glanced at it saying, "Would you have any idea where this is?"

"I'm afraid not," the nurse said, "but her father might be able to help you. I brought him some juice just a short while ago. He's probably still awake."

She gave him a perky smile and told him to follow her. Nice fanny, working it for him as she walked. She left him at the cubicle door, saying, "Let me know if I can be of any further help."

The old man was awake, sitting up in bed with his reading glasses on, flipping through a copy of *Premiere* magazine. He looked like he'd been hit by a train.

Raybould got right into it, knowing it was best to hit them right away, shake them hard before they had time to think.

"Mister Whipple," he said, "Detective Sergeant Raybould. I don't mean to alarm you, sir, but it's urgent that I speak with your daughter. We have reason to believe she's in danger."

That was the look he was going for, shocked, afraid, ready to do anything to help.

"My God, Detective, what's going on?"

"It's got to do with the lottery ticket," Raybould said. "It's changed hands a number of times since it was stolen from you. Right now it's in the possession of a renegade cop by the name of Hicks. The thing is, Mister Whipple, I know this guy; he's a desperate, brutal man. And he's after your daughter."

"But, why?"

The ticket, sir. The sting you set up with the Lottery Corporation. Hicks found out about it, so now the only way he can get to the money is through your daughter. Or yourself, but your daughter's the more likely target. Now, I have officers waiting outside, ready to transfer her to protective custody, but we've got to get to her first. There's really no time to lose."

Keith pointed to Kate's note on the bedside table. "She's out with a young police officer she's become friendly with. His address and phone number are on that note."

Raybould picked up the note and read the address: 1123 Pine Street. Ten minute drive. He glanced at the name, Steve Seger, and smiled to himself, thinking, Small world. "Can I keep this?"

"Of course."

"Okay, let me go out to the desk and try this number." He glanced again at the piece of paper, a concerned cop on the job. "Then I'll be back with a couple more questions."

He left the old man with his mouth hanging open, pale as a ghost. He asked the nurse with the perky smile for the use of a phone and she led him to a doctors' dictating booth, nice and private. He closed the door and dialed Steve's number, got the answering machine and hung up. Two in the morning they were either out at a club, screening their calls or fast asleep. Not that it mattered. He'd catch up to them soon enough.

He leaned back in the chair, still glowing from the Demerol, and lit a smoke. Let the old boy squirm a bit, then finish the job. He smoked the Lucky Strike to the filter, his mind idling comfortably, then dropped the butt to the floor and crushed it under his heel. For fun he tried the number again—answering machine—then went back to Keith's room. The old guy'd been crying, busy wiping at the tears now, trying to show he was a man.

"No answer at this number, Mister Whipple," Raybould said. He gave Keith's shoulder a pat. "But I've dispatched a cruiser to Constable Seger's address."

"Kate said they'd be going out to a club...a blues club," Keith said. He gazed vacantly into space, searching his memory. "For the life of me I can't recall if she told me the name of the place..."

"That's all right, sir. Hicks won't have that information either. With any luck we can stay one step ahead of him." He brought out a notepad and pen and sat on the edge of the bed. "Now I need the names and addresses of your closest relatives, other people Hicks might use as leverage, you understand what I mean?" Keith nodded. "Especially the ones who live in the area. I understand you were on your way to visit family for the holidays when the accident took place?"

"Yes, my sister Lee, last name Merrick. She and her husband Dale live in one of those condominium complexes, twenty-eight-eighty-six Sayles Crescent, suite seven-eleven. It's just off—"

"I know Sayles," Raybould said, jotting it down. "Anybody else?"

Hicks watched him come out of the hospital, moving like he had forever. He paused on the steps and raised his eyes to the night sky, dull white up there with low cloud cover and reflected city light. He took a deep breath and let it out slowly, a frosty streamer that hung on the still winter air. Now he flexed his shoulders and lit a smoke, ritualized gestures Hicks recognized from their years together, Raybould psyching himself up, committing to a course of action. The son of a bitch was like a machine, never slept, nobody he cared about but himself. Hicks couldn't believe he'd once admired the guy. Those early days together, Hicks telling his wife about his new partner, the man like a god to him then. Streetwise and crafty, feared wherever he went, hallmarks of power Hicks secretly wished for but could never command. And as much as it tormented him, he understood why. At the bottom of things, where it mattered, Hicks was afraid. To lose what he had, to get hurt, to die. Raybould was encumbered by none of these fears. The fucker was barely human.

Hicks squinted through the windshield. Was he talking to himself over there? He turned back to the surveillance panel and adjusted some dials. Static. Fucking thing. He'd had it working nicely for a while, heard Raybould asking the receptionist where Whipple was, then he'd lost the signal. Shit...ah, there.

Not talking. Singing something...

Now he was moving, heading for his car a half block away.

Hicks started the van. He waited until Raybould pulled away from the curb, then fell in behind him, giving him lots of room. The trip was a short one.

14

SOMETHING COLD TOUCHED STEVE'S neck at the base of his skull. Even before he opened his eyes he knew what it was. His body froze.

A male voice came from behind him, oily smooth, oddly familiar in the dark. "You know what that is. I'm impressed."

Kate lay naked beside him, still sound asleep. Steve squeezed her arm, waking her.

"You lovebirds keep it down now," the voice said. "If I have to shoot you here, we're going to wake up the whole neighborhood."

"Who are you?" Steve said, feeling Kate tense beside him. He held onto her, doing his best to steady her.

"The lucky ticket holder," the voice said, "come to collect his reward. And Kate, I'd just like you to know, I'm not the guy who stole it from you. It just sort of...fell into my hands."

"If that's all this is," Steve said, "why have you got a gun to my head?"

"Two reasons, since you asked. The first is a matter of sincerity. I saw your news spot, Kate, and quite frankly it reeked of setup. In my opinion, you have no intention of paying that reward."

Kate said, "That's not—"

"Keep it down," the voice said. "The second has to do with the law, possession being nine-tenths thereof. I've got the ticket. I had to kill to get it and take a bullet trying to keep it. That thing has caused me nothing but grief since the moment I set eyes on it. So I figure it's mine. I've earned it. And I'm not giving up a thin fucking dime's worth. So now Kate, you've got a problem. To get that problem behind you, all you've gotta do is a little footwork. You do that and get it right, and by this time tomorrow you can be back on the workbench with Constable Seger here, doing whatever it is the two of you do. Are you catching my drift?"

Kate said, "You want me to cash in the ticket and give the money to you."

"Give the girl a candy apple. Exactly. You're going to cash in the ticket, then do some banking for me." He poked the muzzle of the gun into Steve's neck, startling him. "And while you're busy doing that, I'm gonna keep Romeo here entertained."

The bedside lamp came on and the man rose up from his crouch, showing himself in the sudden light, letting them see the gun. "But before we get to all that," he said, "we're going for a nice long ride in the country." He tucked the gun under his arm and clapped his hands together twice. "Okay, kids, rise and shine. Lots to do before sunup."

Steve got out of bed with his hands raised, his gaze ticking to his service pistol, hanging in its holster on the coat rack five feet away. He looked again at the man with the gun, placing him now as his eyes adjusted to the light. He said, "Detective Raybould."

Raybould smiled. "Good for you, son. Your mom'd be proud."

Steve looked over his shoulder at Kate, still under the covers, then back at Raybould. "Uh, she's naked. Do you mind...?"

"Tell you what, Constable. If I see anything I've never seen before, I'll put my hat over it."

"It's okay, Steve," Kate said. She sat on the edge of the bed, managing to dress without exposing herself very much.

Steve got his jeans off the back of the chair next to the bed, his gun just a short reach away now. His palms were slick with sweat.

Had he left a round chambered? The safety on?

Raybould said, "So near and yet so far, eh, Rookie?"

Steve felt the tension, the readiness to act, drop out of his muscles like a physical weight, replaced by a dull sickness in the pit of his stomach. He started pulling on his jeans.

"I've slept with mine under my pillow for the past ten years," Raybould said. "When I sleep." He leaned into Steve's line of sight, the gun back in his hand. "Put it out of your mind."

As Steve finished dressing he recalled the look on his mother's face when she introduced him to Raybould the other day, the intimidation so clearly registered there. His mother wasn't afraid of anyone and this guy had fazed her. That told him a lot. He'd have to choose his moment carefully.

When they were dressed Raybould walked them to the exit, telling them to bundle up warm, a smart-ass tone in his voice, the whole thing a game to him.

"By the way, Steve," he said, "a grade-schooler could pick this lock. You should invest in a good solid deadbolt." Giving advice at gunpoint. He pointed to Steve's keys on the table by the door. "Those your keys?"

"Yes."

"Okay, here's where we establish trust." He glanced at Steve. "And find out just how much your hide means to the little lady. Us boys'll go in my car. Kate, you follow in Steve's." He touched her chin, raising it. "And believe me, you can't even begin to imagine what'll happen to loverboy here should you decide to take a detour somewhere along the way. All set?"

Nodding, Kate picked up Steve's keys. Steve reached for her arm and Raybould tapped him on the back of the head with the gun, hard enough to make him stagger. He got right in Steve's face.

"I want you on your best behavior, Constable. I know ways to hurt people you never heard of at the academy. Understood?"

Steve nodded, trying to shake off the black dots that swirled in his vision, trying to remember his training and remain calm.

Kate put her arm around him and led him out the apartment door.

Hicks saw them come out of the building in single file, the first thin shafts of daylight angling in over the rooftops now. He'd caught snatches of conversation on the receiver, something about entertaining Romeo, hurting people at the academy, strange shit like that, Raybould doing most of the talking. Hicks had been set to say fuck it, bust in there with his .45 blazing, when Raybould said something about a drive in the country. Out of town suited Hicks better than playing OK Corral right here in the city, so he decided to wait. Learn something from the prick. Patience, following the path of least resistance, all the crap Raybould used to lecture him about during stakeouts.

They were splitting up now, Raybould leading the boyfriend to his car, the girl going the other way, around the building and out of sight. What the hell?

Hicks worked a couple of dials on the unit, trying to catch what Raybould was saying to the boyfriend. He could see the gun in Raybould's hand now, pressed against his thigh, screwing up the reception. He wished Bryan was still around.

Fed up, Hicks slammed the lid shut and slouched down in his seat, watching to see what would happen.

On the way to the car Raybould said to Steve, "I've gotta hand it to you, kid, that girl is fine." Goading him. "I may have to tear a piece off that myself before the day is out."

Steve spun on him. "You lay so much as a finger—"

Raybould hit him again with the gun, drawing blood this time, the kid seeing it on his fingers as he sank to his knees. That was good. Get his attention then take him to school. He hunched over the dummy and put the muzzle to his cheek.

"You're thinking with your dick now, Constable. That'll get you killed. You're of limited use to me, so I suggest you behave. Now get up and shut up."

The kid did as he was told. Raybould opened the passenger door for him and the kid got in, putting his seatbelt on like a good citizen. Raybould went around the hood and climbed in beside him. For peace of mind he handcuffed the kid to the door, both hands, nice and snug.

"Okay, chum," he said, leaning back in his seat, "I'll only say this once. I have a set of rules I give to all the creeps. I picked them up in grade school from this nasty little nun named Mary Aloysius. I hated the fucking things then, broke 'em every chance I got, but over the years I've come to see the sense in them. They're simple, but firm. Follow them and you'll do fine. Are you ready?"

Steve nodded.

"Number one, speak when you're spoken to. Number two, do what you're told, when you're told. And number three, don't give me any lip. Simple enough?"

"Simple enough."

"Good," Raybould said. He turned in his seat to look out the rear window. "Now, let's see what she'll do. Some women, you never can tell."

Kate's mind was a mass of white noise, her body running on auto-pilot, propelling her around the building to the Cherokee on legs she could no longer feel. None of it seemed real, but a nightmare from which she'd been only partially wakened. She felt sick, light-headed, the wine fermenting in her stomach, leaving a foul taste in her mouth. The morning air was bitterly cold, the light itself more dreamlike than real, fuzzy and dense with shadow. Her heels clocked against the sidewalk in a rising cadence, not quite a run, the sound coming back at her from the warehouse across the street like the reports of a small-caliber rifle.

She tried to unlock the Cherokee and fumbled the keys into the dirty snow. She picked them up and got the door open, banging her head on the jamb as she climbed into the seat. The truck was freezing, the upholstery stiff, the engine grinding heavily before it caught. Kate pulled on her seat belt and clasped it, a habitual act that suddenly seemed strange. Her heart was riding in her throat.

She paused a moment then, trying to think. What should she do? Go to the police? But the guy *was* a policeman, Steve knew him. And what was he doing with her father's ticket? Why would he do a thing like this to them? It was all so crazy...but she had little doubt that he was serious. Driving away now would mean certain death for Steve. She could see no other option. She'd have to do what he wanted and pray he let them go when it was done.

She put the Cherokee in reverse, touched the accelerator and the engine stalled. She started it again and gunned it, the engine whining in protest. She waited as long as she could stand it, letting the engine warm up, then shifted into reverse again. This time the engine held.

She backed into the street, teeth chattering, something throbbing painfully behind her eyes. She pulled up behind Raybould's sedan and saw him in his rearview mirror. Smiling at her. She'd never been more terrified.

The girl pulled up behind them in a green Cherokee, an early '90s model going to rust. Raybould found her eyes in the rearview and gave her a smile, thinking, Cute little pie. He pulled away from the curb, checking once to make sure she was following.

By six AM they were on the 401, a small convoy heading west out of the city, industrial sprawl giving way to scattered farms, flat fields blanketed in snow.

Raybould slowed and signaled on highway 91 west of Guelph, turning left onto a dirt road marked by a faded billboard that read AUTO WRECKERS and pictured a cartoon tow truck hauling a cartoon car. Behind him, Kate did the same. They'd been on the road just under an hour now, Raybould setting a casual pace.

He glanced at Steve, saying, "Almost there."

"Almost where?"

"Where we're going," Raybould said. In the early part of the trip the kid had tried some of the hostage negotiation techniques he'd learned at the academy on him and Raybould had laughed in his face. They'd driven in silence since then. He said, "Some advice, okay, kid?"

Steve said nothing.

Raybould backhanded him in the face. "You listening?"

"Yeah," Steve said. "I'm listening."

"Don't try to be a hero. You don't have it in you. Understood?"

"Understood."

The auto wreckers stood about a mile off the highway, a cluster of tin sheds and cinderblock buildings cresting a blunt hill. Behind the buildings stretched row upon row of snow-capped wrecks: cars, trucks, a few rusted-out antiques, a couple of school buses and some cannibalized heavy machinery.

Raybould parked at the base of the hill, told Steve to stay put, and walked the last hundred yards to the top. Archie was waiting at the gate like he'd been told, looking at his rubber boots, gaunt cheeks ruddy from the cold. Raybould rewarded his obedience with a fatherly pat on the head, though the man was at least a dozen years his senior. Archie accepted the gesture with a bashful grin. He stood about five-one, skinny as a rail in filthy blue coveralls with his name stitched on the pocket, a pale-skinned Jamaican with more East Indian in him than black. Raybould liked to get him talking—it was the accent—but Archie was a man of few words.

Raybould handed him a wad of cash. "Here you go, Arch, like I promised." Archie stuffed the cash into his pocket. "That's more than you make in a month. Now the yard's closed for the day, am I right?"

"I got no problem wit' dat, Mistah Rey-bould," Archie said. He shot a quick glance at the two vehicles parked down the hill, then went back to looking at his rubbers.

"You chain up that dog like I told you?"

"Yessir."

Raybould nodded. "Your parole officer tells me you've been a good boy. No urges?"

"No, Mistah Rey-bould. I don' even tink about dat stuff no more."

"Okay, Arch. Disappear."

Kate sat hunched over the wheel behind Raybould's sedan, wishing Steve would turn to look at her. Raybould was up the hill, at least a hundred yards away, and if they were ever going to get a chance to make a run for it, this might be it. But Steve was sitting at a strange angle, half turned to the passenger door, his left shoulder reefed way around. He'd been sitting that way the whole trip and it was only now, seeing this chance to escape, that Kate realized why. The son of a bitch had handcuffed him to the door.

Fucker, she thought. You fucker.

Raybould was talking to some runty guy up there, handing him something. Now the guy was walking away, climbing into a stripped-down flatbed, bumping toward them down the hill. He drove past without making eye contact, so short he had to crane his neck to see over the dash. He turned right and continued up the dirt road.

Raybould flipped over a board on the chain link gate, the word CLOSED painted on it in runny red letters, then started down the hill. Kate tensed as he approached her window, bending to tap on the glass. She rolled down the window a few inches and looked up at him, the chill wind ruffling his hair.

"Steve and I've got some things to do," he said, looking up at the drab cluster of buildings. "You're going to wait here 'til I wave you up, so pay attention. Shouldn't be long." Then he walked away, boots crunching on packed snow.

He got back in his car and drove up the hill, parking in front of a flat-roofed building at the rear of the complex, almost out of Kate's sight. She put the car in drive and rolled ahead a few yards, improving her view.

And waited. Nothing else she could do.

Raybould leaned over him with the handcuff key saying, "Your momma show you any moves?"

Steve said, "A few."

"Thinking about trying any of 'em out on me?" He wedged his right forearm against Steve's neck, pressing Steve's face to the cold glass. Up this close, Steve could smell cigarettes on him, and more faintly, cologne. "Because if you are, I gotta tell you, I love that shit. Fisticuffs. Shootin' the boots. Who knows, maybe we can fool around a bit while we're waiting for your honey." He pocketed the cuffs, taking his gun out again before relaxing the pressure on Steve's neck. "Your honey with all the money. Go ahead," he said. "Get out."

Steve did as he was told, staggering slightly on stiff legs. The wind was nasty, whooping between the buildings, whipping up twisters of dry snow. Oddly, Steve remembered the day his father had told his mother to take her brat and get out, his mother tugging him down the front steps by the wrist with his coat unzipped. It had been a day like this, the same kind of bitter weather.

Raybould slid out behind him through the passenger door, the gun jabbed into his ribs. "Remember what I told you," he said. "Best behavior. Now move."

Steve wanted to turn on him then, try dropping him with a spinning punch to that cold-fish face, but he held back, his mother's sensible voice in his head: "No point trying to tag him when he's ready for it. Wait for your moment, then don't hesitate."

They came to a steel door. "Open it," Raybould said. Steve did and Raybould shoved him into a dim room with a high counter, an ancient cash register and four walls of floor-to-ceiling shelves jammed with used engine parts, the whole place caked in grime. There was a calendar tacked to the wall over the register, open at August of the previous year, a stacked redhead stretched out on the hood of a '63 Impala, fire-engine red. "I had a Chevy like that in my teens," Raybould said. "Two-tone green and white." He pointed the gun at a door behind the counter. "Through there."

Steve went through the doorway into a cement-floored salvage bay strewn with radiators, gas tanks, stripped engines and scattered heaps of scrap metal. There were a couple of workbenches littered with tools, a welding station with two big acetylene tanks leaning on a mobile cart and a couple of hoists. It was cold in here. Steve could see his breath. He tried not to shiver.

"Okay, kid," Raybould said, "get those clothes off. I need you naked."

Steve turned to look at him. "Are you serious?"

"What do you think?"

The waiting was driving Kate crazy, every instinct telling her to flee, go to the police, let them handle it. She was risking both their lives by just sitting here. She should be doing *something*...

But what would he do when he came out and found her missing? Wait around for the police to arrive? Of course not. He'd move. And he'd kill Steve. She didn't doubt it for a second. He'd kill Steve, just to show her he was for real, then he'd go after her father—

It dawned on Kate then how Raybould had found them. He'd already gotten to her dad...and her news spot had shown him the way.

Something inside her sank like a rock into cold mud. She slammed the Cherokee into reverse, got halfway through a three-point turn and saw Raybould standing at the top of the hill, waving her up. She sat for several seconds, watching him, Raybould looking down at her with that smirk on his face. Daring her to run. *Do it, Kate. I'll kill your boyfriend, it's nothing to me. We've got a whole year to get this done.*

He motioned with his head. *Come on.*

Kate drove up the hill. She pulled up beside him with the doors locked and opened her window a crack, still ready to run if she had to. She said, "Did you hurt my father?"

Raybould said, "Of course not," acting insulted. "What do you take me for?" He opened his jacket a little, showing her the gun. "Now get out of the truck. We're on a tight schedule here."

Kate waited, staring at him, searching his eyes for the lie. Then she switched off the ignition and got out. Raybould led her through the office to the salvage bay.

She cried out when she saw Steve, duct-taped to a wooden chair, naked in this cold barn, the chair chained to a block and tackle rigged to an overhead I-beam. The tape across his mouth closed off part of his nostrils, forcing him to throw his head back and suck hard against it to get any air. He looked terrified.

Kate darted toward him. Raybould said, "That's close enough," but Kate ignored him, dropping to her knees by the chair, trying to peel the tape off Steve's mouth.

Then Raybould had her by the arm.

"There's one thing I absolutely demand," he said, turning her to face him, hurting her arm, "and that is obedience." He shook her once, as one might a rebellious child, then released her, pointing to a chair ten feet away, set facing Steve so she could watch. "Sit over there. Don't move until I tell you."

Kate walked over to the chair and sat down.

Raybould turned to Steve and started pulling on one of the chains, the heavy links clacking through the pulleys as he took up the slack. The chair rose slowly, tilting forward as it left the floor, Steve's body jerking at the sudden weightlessness. When it was up about five feet Raybould locked it into place.

Kate watched him roll the acetylene tanks over and get the torch going, adjusting the flame to a bright, unwavering blue. She watched him give Steve's chair a push, getting it swinging in a lazy arc. Watched him gaze lid-eyed at the flame, a whimsical half-smile on his face, head cocked, totally relaxed.

"This is one of my favorite places," he said, looking around the salvage bay now, taking it all in. "It's like a flea market in here for anybody with a little imagination and an appreciation for the uses of pain. Pain is bar none the best motivator known to man. Apply the correct amount of pain for the correct amount of time and I don't care who he is, there is nothing a man won't say or do to escape it."

Raybould gave Steve's chair another shove. "I want you to relax, Kate," he said. "I'm not going to hurt you. If you're smart, you'll walk away from this without so much as a stubbed toe." He turned to Steve. "But I am going to hurt him."

Steve swung toward him and Raybould raised the torch. Steve's bare shins passed through the flame, then back through it again. Steve screamed against the gag in his mouth.

Kate jumped to her feet. "Stop it! Please, I'll do whatever you want. You don't have to hurt him."

"I know that, Kate," Raybould said, smiling. "But I want to."

Steve drifted again through the hissing flame, his muffled screams making Kate's skin crawl. "Stop it!" she shouted. *"Stop it!"*

Raybould tucked the still-lit torch into its cylindrical holster and walked over to Kate. He took a wrinkled envelope out of his pocket and handed it to her. "All the information you'll need is in there," he told her. "Once you've got the check, go straight to the address on the envelope. It's a bank. A very big bank. Ask for the manager, Elwood Smith. He's expecting you. All you've got to do then is endorse the check. He does the rest." He gave her the ticket. "Tell him to put the cash in a bag. A million dollars. Don't bother counting it, I trust him. Are we clear so far?"

"Yes," Kate said, "I'll do it, just please, don't hurt him anymore."

"That's entirely up to you. You've got until noon. That should give you plenty of time. Take your car. When you get back, I make a quick call. If you've done your job, we drive to the airport and that's where our relationship ends."

Kate said, "You'll let us go?" She looked over Raybould's shoulder to see Steve, spinning slowly as his arc diminished, craning his neck to look at her, trying to tell her something with his eyes.

"You have my word," Raybould said. "Now—" He noticed Kate's gaze and turned to look at Steve. "Something you'd like to say, Constable? Some advice for the young lady?" He walked over and tore the tape off Steve's mouth, removing the gag. "Go ahead."

It broke Kate's heart to see him hanging there, fighting back tears, pain written on his face in deep furrows. "Run, Kate," he said, his voice breaking. "Don't come back here—"

Raybould stuffed the gag back into his mouth and gave the chair another shove, getting it swinging again. Then he looked over at Kate. "Bad advice," he said. "Time to go, Kate."

Kate took a last look at Steve, trying to tell him with her eyes not to worry, she'd get it done and they'd be free. She turned away from him then and started for the exit. Raybould's voice froze her.

"And Kate."

She didn't answer, didn't turn around.

"Kate, look at me."

Kate turned to see him raise a grimy red gas can and give it a shake. Heard the gasoline sloshing around inside, cool and deadly.

"If I even smell a cop, I'll set your boyfriend on fire."

Kate held his gaze for a long moment, her heart so full of loathing and fear she thought it might burst. Then she walked out the door.

She hit the yard running, heading for the Cherokee, tears freezing on her face in the cutting wind. She opened the driver's-side door, got her foot up on the running board and felt something hard jab her in the spine. She spun with a startled squeal, nerves stretched so thin now she almost wet herself. A complete stranger stood behind her, pockmarked face red from the cold, the hand not holding the gun tucked into the armpit of his overcoat.

He said, "Gimme the keys."

"Who are you?"

Hicks put the gun to her throat, raising her chin with it, oiled metal shockingly cold in the winter air. "Gimme the fuckin' keys."

Kate handed him the keys.

"Now get in."

Kate slid in behind the wheel, watching as the man limped around the hood. Before he reached the door Kate stuffed the ticket and the envelope into her bag and tossed the bag onto the back seat. She noticed the dime-size bloodstain on the man's trousers as he got in beside her. He closed the door and sat facing her, handing her the keys.

"Drive," he said. "You already know where we're going."

"But—"

"I hate repeating myself."

Kate lost it. "I want to know who the *fuck* you are!"

Hicks put the gun in her face and cocked the trigger.

Heart pounding, Kate put her seatbelt on and started the car. Hicks lowered the gun, keeping it aimed at her side.

"Just drive," he said.

Kate did as she was told, both hands clamped to the wheel.

15

RAYBOULD STOOD WATCHING AS the chair Steve was bound to slowed in its arc. He lit a cigarette off the torch flame and watched, his expression amused and mildly curious, a man pondering an unexpected gift, savoring its small mystery before peeling it open to see what's inside. Steve tried to keep his eyes on him but the chair twisted as it swung, first one way, winding up the chains, then the other, making him dizzy. It was worse when he couldn't see the man; he could hear the torch, its reptilian hiss, but he couldn't tell if Raybould was coming at him with it. His muscles shivered uncontrollably, bunching in spasm from the tension and the cold.

The chair stopped suddenly, Raybould turning it to face him. He was still holding the torch, the blue flame steady, almost eager. Steve looked into his eyes.

"I hated having to lie to her like that," Raybould said. "You know I'm going to kill you. Both of you. What choice do I have? You're a cop, you understand. It's really just bad luck." He cocked his head, giving Steve that quirky half smile. "You're probably the smart ass who set up the sting with the lottery people. Or was it that mother of yours? Yeah, I bet it was Liz. Slippery bitch. See? If you'd've left well enough alone, you wouldn't be in this fix." The smile disappeared. "Now look at you."

He gave the chair a brisk shove. Steve swung out into space, craning to see Raybould raise the torch, its hard light reflected in his eyes. The chair reached the end of its trajectory in a slither of chains, hung there an instant, then swooped down.

Steve screamed against the gag in his mouth.

The man with the gun fidgeted constantly, glancing behind them every few seconds as if expecting to see Raybould in hot pursuit. Kate hadn't really got a good look at him yet, afraid to make eye contact and risk antagonizing him. She felt like she was sitting next to an unstable explosive, hair-trigger tension coming off the man in waves of b.o. and nervous heat. She could see the gun at the edge of her vision, the only part of him not in motion, still aimed at her side. They'd been on the road about twenty minutes now, twenty minutes of strained silence, Kate trying to puzzle out who he was and why he was involved. Her arms ached from clutching the steering wheel.

The man laughed suddenly, startling Kate, an adrenaline junkie's whoop of a laugh. "That son of a bitch is gonna be so pissed," he said, and Kate took a quick look at him, seeing the wild excitement in his eyes. "That's a contract killer you've been messing with, Kate—it is Kate, isn't it?" Kate nodded. "I'm doing you a favor here, Kate. And hey, you can forget about your boyfriend. He's already dead."

Despite what he was saying, something in his tone, something almost conspiratorial, gave Kate permission to look at him. He returned her gaze in a frank, non-threatening way, wanting her to know he meant what he was saying, that he believed it.

"You'd've been dead too if you went back there," he said now. "Tell you what, though. You stick to the rule book on this and once we're in the air, I'll make a call. Sic the S.W.A.T. boys on his ass. Fuckhead put this hole in my leg. Probably aiming for my balls."

Kate said, "In the air?"

Hicks smiled. "Ever been to Fiji? That's where we're going. Halfway around the world. Who knows, you might even like it."

"I can't go to Fiji," Kate said, crossing an overpass now, traffic flashing past beneath them on the 401. "This is crazy. Look, he's got my friend back there and he's going to kill him if I don't come back with the money. I can't go anywhere with you. He'll kill Steve and then he'll go after my father and there's no way I can allow that to happen."

"That's where you're wrong, Kate. There's no way you can stop it from happening. Didn't I just tell you who you're dealing with?"

Kate veered right off the overpass onto the cloverleaf feeder lane, driving too fast, the rear deck breaking loose on the snow-packed surface.

"Hey," Hicks said, bracing his free hand against the dash. "Take it easy."

Kate glanced at him and thought, *No seatbelt.*

"Okay," she said, taking a shot in the dark. "What about this. You're a cop, right?"

"What makes you say that?"

"You're a cop and you hate that sick freak back there. I have no idea why, but I know I'm right. So—"

"So how about you just drive, okay?"

"Please," Kate said, "hear me out." She merged into traffic on the busy four-lane, heading east toward the city. "I'll give you the money, all of it, you have my word. I don't even want it anymore. But please, call your friends on the force right now. We can pull off at the next exit and find a phone. Send them back there with some kind of attack force, something, and get my friend out of there..." Tears stung her eyes.

Hicks said, "Look at me, Kate," his tone hard now, like Raybould's a half hour earlier. She looked and Hicks showed her the gun. "You see this? I'm not your friend. I'm not your partner. You've got something I want and if you don't fuck with me, the only favor I'm gonna do for you is I'm not gonna shoot you. Now zip it, okay? You're giving me a headache."

All right, you bastard, Kate thought. All right.

She maneuvered the Cherokee into the left-hand lane, traffic moving fast in spite of the sloppy road conditions. She tucked them in behind a big Dodge Ram and rode its tail.

Hicks said, "Where's the ticket?"

"In my bag," Kate said, scenes from a hundred B-movies flashing in her mind. "In the back seat." The right lane was clear now, only a big orange snow plow a few hundred yards ahead, half in the lane, half on the shoulder, its huge blade sending up a curl of wet crud.

Hicks turned in his seat, reaching for Kate's bag. "I want to get a look at—"

Kate veered hard-right around the Ram and gunned it, throwing Hicks off balance. He shouted at her, threatening, trying to get the gun trained on her again, but Kate didn't hear him, heard only the roar of the engine, the thrum of her own determined fury.

She aimed the Cherokee at the back of the plow and gunned it, at the last second closing her eyes—

And felt the steering wheel wrenched from her grasp, cranked to the left with brutal force. She opened her eyes and saw the snow plow tilt away from her in a flash of orange metal, the Cherokee's front bumper grazing one huge tire. Hicks' arm was braced across her body, working the wheel.

"Crazy bitch!" he shouted, swerving to the right now to avoid the braking Ram. The Cherokee canted sharply with the move, the driver's-side wheels leaving the ground, and by instinct Kate's hands went back to the wheel. "I've got it," she said and Hicks let go, Kate correcting for the skid, the wheels slamming to the pavement as Hicks flopped back into his seat.

Then they were clear, riding the right-hand lane in front of the snow plow, the driver's airhorn a solid bellow behind them. The guy in the Ram gave them the finger as he blew past.

"The fuck you tryna do?" Hicks said. "Put me through the windshield?" He jammed the gun into her side. "Fuckin' mental case. You'd've killed us both." He put his seatbelt on one-handed, the hand shaking badly. "Slow the fuck down."

Kate eased up on the accelerator. Christ, what a stunt. What had she been thinking? Movies. She'd been thinking about scenes from movies. How many times had she seen it? The good guy under the gun, sending the bad guy through the windshield by slamming the car into a tree or a handy wall, then driving away in a wreck that somehow still ran. But this was no movie. He was right, she would have killed them both. And she was no use to anyone dead.

"Fuck me," Hicks said, breathing hard. "If you're gonna be a bitch about this, I can play it just as rough as Raybould."

"No," Kate said, "I'm just scared," and realized she wasn't. Not anymore. "I didn't realize how fast I was going…"

"Just stick to the posted limit," Hicks said. Kate looked at him and noticed the bloodstain on his trousers had gotten bigger. He was rubbing the leg now, wincing. "Look," he said. "I'm not a prick. Cooperate and I'll make sure you don't go home empty-handed. When we get to Fiji, I'll look after you. Okay?"

"Okay," Kate said. "Okay."

She looked straight ahead and drove.

They pulled up to the curb in front of the Lottery Corporation at five after nine. The morning traffic on Bloor Street was still heavy and within seconds a Toronto Transit bus chuffed up behind them and the driver leaned on the horn. Hicks rolled down his window and waved the guy around. No dice. The guy just sat there, glaring.

"Fuck him," Hicks said to Kate. "Put on your flashers and park it right here."

The bus driver got out and came along the sidewalk toward Hicks' window. Watching his approach in the sideview mirror, Hicks holstered his gun and got out his badge. Kate thought, I knew it. Before the driver could say boo Hicks showed him the badge and told him to go the fuck around. The bus driver made a show of examining Hicks' ID, bent right in close to squint at it, then said they'd have to move ahead a few feet so he could go around. No problem, Hicks said.

"Sorry, Officer Hicks," the bus driver said, "I had no way of knowing," and went back to his bus.

Without being told Kate drove ahead a few feet, turned on the emergency flashers and switched off the ignition. Hicks watched the bus roll past, then turned his attention back to Kate. He left his gun holstered.

He said, "This is the easy part, so please, don't be stupid. From here on in, you fuck with me and I will shoot you. I don't care who's watching. Do you believe me?"

"Yes," Kate said. "Officer Hicks."

"You gonna crack wise on me now, Kate?"

"That's your name, isn't it?"

"Yeah, that's my name. Happy?"

"Yeah, I'm happy."

"Good. Now when I tell you, you're going to get out of the car—carefully, don't for Christ-sake get run over—then walk around the hood to the sidewalk. I'll follow you in from there. You smile, tell them how embarrassed you are, all that fuss and the ticket turns up in your father's coat pocket. If they want to know who I am, I'm your police escort. You tell them it's been a rough couple days, can we please get this done without the usual horse and pony show. If they need publicity shots, whatever, you'll be happy to come back in a week or so and do it then. Clear enough?"

Kate nodded. Hicks unlatched his door, holding it partway open against the wind, and said, "Okay, let's do it."

Kate grabbed her bag and opened the door, a gust of wind almost breaking her grip on the handle. She got out, closed the door without locking it and went around the hood to the sidewalk. Hicks was waiting for her, favoring his leg. He nodded toward the entrance, fifteen feet away across bare cement.

Holding her bag in front of her, Kate put her head down against the wind and walked, Hicks falling in behind her. Five feet from the entrance she reached into her bag and tore a sheet off her note pad; at two feet she let the sheet fly over her shoulder into the wind.

"Oh, shit," she said, spinning to face Hicks. "The ticket!"

Hicks leaped after it with a curse, almost snapping it out of midair; it danced through his fingers—"Motherfucker!"—and rose on a sudden updraft, spiraling back toward the street. Hicks pivoted on his bad leg and almost fell. He stumbled toward the curb, crashing into three executive types with leather attaché cases and navy wool coats, then dropped to his knees to chase it under the Cherokee.

Kate bolted, heading east on Bloor, running full out. Behind her Hicks peeled the piece of paper off the Cherokee's front wheel, looked at it and cursed again. One of the execs confronted him as he stood and Hicks punched him in the face. The guy pinwheeled into his buddies, the three of them tumbling to the sidewalk in a heap of blue wool.

Hicks went after Kate, shouting her name into the wind.

Kate tore blindly around the first corner she came to, running headlong into a Salvation Army Santa soliciting change with a brass bell and one of those plastic globes on a red metal stand. Santa tumbled over backwards, letting out a huge grunt as Kate landed on his enormous belly, the real thing.

"Hey," Santa said, trying to grab Kate's arm as she scrambled off him. "Slow down."

Kate got to her feet and picked up the metal stand. Hicks hobbled around the corner and Kate swung the thing with everything she had. The plastic globe, already more than half full of change and crumpled bills, caught Hicks on the chin. The globe exploded, change flying everywhere, and Hicks went ass over tea kettle, striking the pavement with the back of his head.

Lights out.

Kate dropped the metal stand and bent to reach inside Hicks' coat. The ruffled Santa grabbed her by the collar and Kate rose, turning on him with Hicks' gun in her hand.

"Fuck off," she said.

Santa put up his chubby hands and did just that.

Kate ran back to the Cherokee with the gun in her hand, startled pedestrians giving her a wide berth. She got into the truck, started it up and peeled out at speed.

Normally Raybould didn't mind hurting people, especially when there was something to be gained by doing it. Sometimes he did it just for the sport, when the mood was on him and he had the requisite privacy. But this kid, he was a cop, and though Raybould had strayed about as far as a person could beyond the bounds of acceptable behavior for a cop, there was still a part of him that acknowledged the honor involved in being a member of the profession. Hurting him in front of his girl, he'd had a reason for that.

Hurting him now, without giving him a fair shot at defending himself, well, today he just couldn't see the sport in it. Today he was a millionaire, and he felt too damn good about that to be ugly. He'd spooked the kid with the torch after the girl left, just to let him know he could do it. There was a second there, as the little fucker swung toward him looking all fierce and wild in the eyes, when it seemed like a hell of a good idea: barbecue the chump like a spring lamb just for looking at him the wrong way, not to mention the trouble he'd already caused. But the feeling passed. Lucky day for these two. When the time came he'd make it quick and painless. Leave them for Archie to work his magic on. *Poof*, no more Kate and Steve.

Raybould got out of the chair he'd been sitting in, the same one Kate had sat in during his demonstration of the uses of pain. He'd been thinking about the freedom this money would bring, imagining some of the things he would do with it. The kid had been hanging there so quietly, Raybould had almost forgotten about him. But he was struggling now, making the chains rattle. Raybould walked over and tore the tape off his mouth, removing the gag.

"Something on your mind, kid?"

"Cold," Steve said, teeth chattering. "Can I get dressed now?"

"You want to get dressed." He stood behind the chair and gave it a playful push, pushing it again as it swung back, a dad amusing his kid on a swing. He said, "I don't think so. Men don't like to fight when they're nude, isn't that strange? Somebody breaks into the house, starts plugging a guy's wife while he's in the tub, ten to one he pulls on his drawers before he goes out to help her. Personally I don't give a shit, I'll fight a fucker with a ribbon on my dick."

Steve said, "How about me?"

"How about you what?" Raybould said. Pushing the chair.

"Before, remember you said when she's gone, maybe we could mix it up, you and me?"

Raybould chuckled. "You want to *fight* me?"

"Let me out of this chair, I'll fight you."

Raybould stopped the chair, turning it to face him. "Shit, I'm game."

He lowered Steve to the floor and brought out a pocket knife, going to work on the tape, freeing his legs first, then his arms and chest, finally his neck. Steve sat there a few moments, flexing his hands and feet, trying to coax the feeling back into them. Raybould backed away from him and removed his coat. He slid his Glock out of its holster and set it on top of a rusty oil drum.

"This'll be the championship belt," he said. "Right here. Winner takes all."

Steve stood up and Raybould smiled.

"You sure you want to do this, kid? You look like Bambi over there."

"I'm not a kid," Steve said. He hobbled to his clothes, left in a heap on the floor, and pulled on his pants.

Raybould grinned, saying, "See? A man just won't fight with his balls showing." He chose a patch of open floor and stood at ease, waiting for Steve. "Come on, kid," he said. "This shouldn't take long."

Steve did up his belt, moved in closer and got his fists up.

His legs were killing him, the burns across his shins stinging in the cold. He was lightheaded, dizzy from spinning up there with nothing to look at but the floor, and he could barely feel his fists, clenched now into bludgeons the way his mother had taught him. But this was it, the only chance he was going to get.

He picked his spot, three feet from Raybould, and dug in, bare feet rooted to the floor, fists up and ready. Raybould smirked at him, hands still hanging by his sides, and Steve hit him in the chest with everything he had, getting his hip into it, catching the look of surprise on Raybould's face as he reacted, too late, his block glancing off Steve's forearm. Raybould flew back a good four feet, the smirk gone from his face now, but he didn't fall down. Shit.

Steve lunged without hesitation, aiming a kick at the man's groin, and Raybould came alive, deflecting Steve's kick with ease. Anticipating the block, Steve countered with a knife hand to the throat and saw Raybould shrink back with amazing speed, felt iron fingers clamp his wrist followed by pain of paralyzing enormity, his wrist bent back just shy of the breaking point, forcing him to his knees.

Raybould sank to one knee behind him, cranking Steve's wrist even harder, his lips, his hot breath, close to Steve's ear.

"You didn't tell me you wanted to play rough," he said, grabbing Steve's voice box between the fingers of his other hand, wrenching Steve's head back, squeezing. "My round, wouldn't you say?"

Steve shook his head yes, his larynx on the verge of collapse.

Raybould released him, backing away. Steve slumped forward onto his elbows, coughing, the pain in his wrist flaring all the way up to his neck. He looked up at Raybould and saw him rubbing his chest, smiling, like they were pals sparring in the gym.

"Man," he said, "you hit hard. Your mother taught you that?"

Steve got up, rubbing his wrist. The crazy fucker was having a good time.

"You want to get back in the chair now, or you want to play some more?"

Steve put his fists up. "Let's play."

Raybould shrugged and came at him saying, "You've got heart, kid, I'll give you that." He threw a jab, Steve blocking it easily, then kicked him in the shin with the toe of his boot. Steve stumble back, almost falling. "Smarts, don't it," Raybould said and kicked him again, this time in the thigh. Steve sat down hard on the grimy cement floor, rolled once and stood, unsteady, tears filming his eyes. He put his fists up.

Raybould moved, gliding with a boxer's graceful menace. Steve waited for him, pushing back the pain, blocking hard, up and under when Raybould threw a punch at his face, striking simultaneously with an elbow to the detective's ribs. Raybould's air barked out and Steve took the advantage, driving a vicious kick into his knee. The bastard went down on that knee and Steve kicked out with his heel, connecting with Raybould's forehead, dropping him flat to the floor. Steve turned and ran for the oil drum, not sure what the explosion behind him was until white fire ignited in the back of his leg and his nervous system short-circuited, sending him to the floor in a shivering heap.

He looked back and saw Raybould up on one elbow, dazed, a small revolver in his hand drawn from an ankle holster, still aimed at him.

"You little fucker," he said, no trace of amusement in his voice now. "Get your ass back in that chair."

"Dad, it's me."

"Katie, thank God. A detective was here—"

"I know. He found me."

"Where are you? Are you all right?"

"I'm fine, Dad. I'm downtown, in a phone booth."

"The detective—"

"Raybould."

"Yes, he said you were in danger, said something about protective custody."

"I've been with him since early this morning, then another detective. I just dropped him off."

"So you're alone now?"

"Just for a while. I'm going to meet Raybould again very soon. How are you doing?"

"Worried sick. Better now that I hear your voice."

"I love you, Dad."

"I love you too, sweetheart. This damn ticket..."

"I know. Maybe something good will come from it yet."

"When will I see you?"

"Soon, I think. Dad, I gotta go."

"Where are you going now?"

"Shopping."

16

THEY HAD THEIR BACKS to her when she came in, Raybould sitting with his legs crossed, smoking, Steve dangling in the air in front of him, the chair rotating slowly on its axis of chains. Steve had his jeans on now and when Kate saw him—limp and motionless, blood staining the denim a wet maroon—something staggered inside her. She froze in the doorway with a zippered tote bag in her hand, leaning against the jamb to keep from falling, certain he was dead.

"That was fast," Raybould said without turning.

"People bend over backwards for you when you're rich," Kate said, trying to maintain her focus. "You bastard."

At the sound of her voice Steve raised his head, his face coming into view as the chair continued its lazy spin. Relieved, Kate walked into the salvage bay, trying not to look at him, the dazed warning in his eyes.

Raybould said, "Did you get it done?"

Kate tossed the bag on the floor at his feet, the Wal-Mart tags still on it. Raybould picked it up and stood, resting the bag on the arm of the chair to unzip it. He looked inside and chuckled. "Cute," he said, reaching inside, pulling out a loose roll of toilet paper. He held it up for Steve to see. The bag was full of them.

Reaching behind her, Kate drew Hicks' gun from the waistband of her jeans and aimed it at Raybould, her grip clumsy because of the cast. With a steady voice she delivered the line she'd been rehearsing all the way back from the city.

"You'll be needing that, you bastard, because all you're gonna get from me is shit."

Raybould held his arms out to his sides like a benevolent Christ. "Okay," he said, "you got me, Kate. You got me." Using his thumb and forefinger he unholstered his gun and set it on the chair, then returned his hands to his sides.

Kate said, "Now cut him loose."

"All in due course," Raybould said, grinning. "My, aren't you the fireball." He took a casual step toward her, in no hurry. "But you know, Kate, if you'd've come through that door shooting, that would've been a lot more convincing."

He kept moving, backing her into a corner.

"I'll shoot you," Kate said, "I swear it."

"And so you should. God knows, I would. But I've got to tell you, Kate, to kill a man in cold blood, most people would have to reach way down inside for the heart to do something like that." Still moving. "Personally, I've never understood that. For me it's purely mechanical. "Just aim—" he pointed his index finger at her, sighting down his arm "—and fire."

Kate cocked the hammer. "Stop now. I mean it."

"You might want to flip the safety off there, Kate," he said, showing her his open hands. "Right by your thumb."

"Bullshit."

"Suit yourself." He took another step, leaning forward slightly, studying the gun. "That's a forty-five you've got there, isn't it? That is a nasty weapon. Do you have any idea the kind of damage that sucker can do?" His hand shot out and snatched the gun, quicker than Kate's eyes could track it. "Here, let me give you a little demonstration."

He put the gun to her forehead and pulled the trigger. Kate screamed, drowning out the dry snap of the hammer. She looked at him with tears in her eyes. Raybould thumbed the safety off, gave her a "Duh," expression, then turned his back on her and aimed the gun at Steve. Finished with her.

"Now a gut shot from a forty-five," he said, approaching Steve, aiming at his exposed belly, "that's a terrible thing. Tears you all up inside." He shifted his aim to Steve's knee. "Kneecap? I don't even want to think about that." Raising the barrel to Steve's head now. "A head shot from a forty-five, that's almost humane. Forget about the furniture, though."

He ticked his aim randomly over Steve's body, Steve flinching with each move, waiting for the bullet to come.

"Let's start with your balls," Raybould said. "That should demonstrate my point well enough." He drew a bead on Steve's crotch, saying, "You see, Kate, one way or another you're going to get me that money. If I have to kill every friend you've got, every member of your fucked-up family, your bitch aunt Lee—"

Raybould glanced black in time to see Kate come whirling toward him in the classic, spinning wind-up of the discus thrower, her extended right arm lashing around in a blur of white plaster. Before he could get his hands up the cast struck him on the bridge of the nose. Kate heard a wet crunch and saw Raybould drop like an express elevator, blood gouting from his nose. She stood over him, ready to fight him if she had to, the fierce determination in her eyes dimming only gradually to disbelief at Raybould's utter stillness.

She looked up at Steve with wide eyes. He was trying to tell her something through the gag, pointing with his eyes. Then Kate understood.

The guns.

She picked up both weapons, threw Raybould's as far as she could into a heap of junk and tucked Hicks' into the back of her jeans. She went to Steve on wobbly legs, looking from the smear of blood on her cast to Steve, pointing now with his chin to the control box for the chainfall, a remote with two buttons on it, a red one and a green one, hanging nearby from its cable. Kate pressed the green button and the chair came down at full speed, chains slithering through pulleys. "Oh!" she said and punched the red button, the thing stopping an instant before the chair hit the floor.

Kate left him there and found an Exacto knife on Archie's workbench. She ran the blade out, a new one, glanced at Raybould's still shape as she passed him, then started in on the tape, hacking Steve free. He fell the short distance to the floor, wrists still bound behind him, grunting behind the tape Kate now coaxed off his face. Using his tongue, he pushed out the oily rag Raybould had stuffed into his mouth, dry heaving a couple of times before taking a breath. His body, curled in a fetal position, shivered on the cement floor.

Kate leaned over him to cut his hands loose. Breathless, Steve said, "Check the inside of his left ankle, under his pants. He's got another gun."

Kate drew Hicks' .45, aiming it at Raybould as she approached him. He lay on his side with his arms flung up, the way he'd fallen, his head resting on his shoulder as if in repose. Kate squatted at his feet, pointing the gun at him while she got his pant leg up and worked the .38 snubby out of its holster. She backed away from him quickly, returning to Steve with a gun in each hand. Steve was sitting up now, clutching his wounded leg. His head was bent forward and he appeared to be crying. Kate set the guns down, draped her coat over his shoulders and sat beside him on the floor, both of them facing Raybould now, twelve feet away.

"It's okay," she said, hugging him, kissing his face. "It's over…"

Not crying, Kate realized—laughing. Hysterically.

"What's so funny?"

Steve looked at her with red eyes. "'Because…all you're gonna get from me is shit?'"

Kate started laughing too, releasing the pent-up tension. She said, "I thought it was pretty good." Then: "No, okay, you're right. I watch too many movies."

They laughed a while longer, crazed, edgy laughter, holding tight to one another. When it tapered off Kate looked over at Raybould and said, "Shouldn't I tie him up or something?"

Steve said, "Kate, I think he's dead."

"Dead?"

She picked up the .45 and walked over to Raybould, poking him in the ribs with her toe, half expecting his hand to snake out and grab her ankle. But he didn't move. Blood leaked from his nose without vigor, a dark plum color. Kate bent over him to feel for a pulse. There was none. She tried again—to be sure—but felt only cool skin.

She turned to Steve and felt the blood drain from her face, delayed shock settling over her like a wet blanket. Steve got to his feet, limping, and met her half way, Kate clinging to him in a near faint, glad to feel his arms around her.

"He was going to kill us, Kate. You realize that, don't you?"

Kate nodded. She knew it, yes, had never doubted it. But she had just killed a man...

"He even told me so after you left," Steve was saying, his voice soothing. "God, you never should have come back here. Not without the police. That was the craziest, bravest thing I've ever seen." He touched her chin, raising it, finding her eyes. "Thanks, Kate. Thanks a lot."

Kate smiled, then started to sob, pressing herself into Steve's arms.

Epilogue

THE REPORTER FROM THE Toronto Sun, a petite blond with a husky smoker's voice, said, "Any word on Detective Hicks? We haven't been able to get within a mile of him."

"Last we heard," Keith said from his wheelchair, parked by the windows in his private room, "he's still over at Saint James Hospital, eating his meals through a straw." He smiled at Kate, using the same stock answers he'd used with the dozens of other reporters he'd talked to in the five-and-a-half weeks since Raybould's death. Not to mention the charities—legitimate or otherwise—lawyers, investment types, real estate brokers and just plain whackos that had shown up at his bedside, all with some scheme designed to separate him from his fortune. He said, "Babe Ruth over here whacked him so hard they had to wire his jaw shut."

"And what about you?" the reporter said, aiming her microphone at Kate. "How's the investigation going?"

"Just about through," Kate said, not wanting to get into it. She'd had lawyers, district attorneys and detectives grilling her almost nonstop since Steve dialed 911 from the auto wreckers office, waves of them showing up with their questions, deadpan and officious. Endless questions. She wondered how many times they needed to hear it before it finally sank in. The only break they'd given her had been on Christmas day, spent in this room with as many of her family members present as the nurses would allow, the rest of them filing through in shifts. Keith had envelopes for each of them.

The reporter said, "Weren't you afraid when—"

"Look," Kate said, "Can we wrap this up? I'm pretty tired."

"Sure," the reporter said. "Just one more question for your father." She turned to Keith and gave him a smile, a little flirtatious, Kate thought. "What are you going to do with all that money?"

"Well, we've consulted a financial adviser," Keith said, "but I'm thinking of getting into crop circles. Very big right now. Or maybe orthopedic hardware, see if I can't come up with a more comfortable way to mend broken bones."

The reporter said, "None of my business, right?"

Keith only smiled.

"We're going to have fun with it," Kate said, ticked off by some of the things already in print about this whole ordeal, bald faced lies most of it. "But you should know my father has generously taken care of his family, and that he's donated a million dollars to cancer research."

"How very nice," the reporter said, but her tape machine was already off.

Steve came in as the reporter was leaving, using his crutches and doing a pretty apt job of it. He kissed Kate on the forehead then settled into a chair across from Keith, rolling a narrow table on wheels between them. They'd been into a heated cribbage tournament since Steve checked in down the hall. Raybould's bullet had lodged in his femur, shattering part of it, requiring one operation for its removal and another, five days ago, for a bone graft taken from his hip. Kate watched them play a while, then turned on the TV. Oprah was on, introducing a very large woman—

Kate said, "You guys, check this out."

Keith and Steve looked up from their game to the twenty-inch screen.

"I'm calling it *Nine-Tenths Of The Law*," the big woman was saying, "as in possession being nine-tenths of the law? It's about the ten million dollar lottery ticket that was stolen from me by a purse snatcher—he's dead now—and the wild ride that money took, *my* money, before it ended up in the pockets of some hicks from Sudbury who *claim* it was theirs to begin with. It's an incredible story, everybody dying who got their hands on it." She grinned, showy in a floral silk dress and matching brimmed hat. "Except for me," she said and the crowd tittered, happy for her. "There was a huge bidding war for the book rights, went on for a week."

Oprah smiled. "And Doubleday took it for how much?"

The big woman smiled back at her. "One point two million dollars."

The crowd cheered. "Sensational," Oprah said.

Keith said, "Who the hell is she?" and Kate shrugged.

Oprah said, "And tell us about Hollywood."

"Oh, I'm holding out on those guys," the big woman said, preening for the camera. "I've had reams of movie offers already, but I told them all, the only way it's gonna happen's if I get to play myself." She turned to the studio audience, opening her arms to it, giving her vast bosom a shake. "After all, who else could fill the role?"

Laughter and cheers from the crowd.

Oprah said, "How exciting." She touched the big woman's hand, giving her a sly, girlfriend look, saying, "Money, fame, and something else..." She winked at the audience. "Romance."

A bashful grin from the big woman. "Oh, Oprah, you promised."

Leaning toward the audience, Oprah said, "And he's right here in the studio."

The camera panned the crowd, zooming in on a beefy guy in a short-sleeve Hawaiian shirt, a pair of Ray Bans dangling from one ear. He grinned self-consciously, spotting his mug on the monitor.

Steve said, "That guy's the spitting image of..." He snapped his fingers, trying to remember.

"Father Karras from *The Exorcist*," Kate said. "Uh..."

"Jason Miller," Keith said.

The big woman blew a kiss at the guy and Kate shut the thing off, silencing the whistles and cheers.

Keith turned back to the card game, shaking his head. "God damn," he said. "They're coming out of the woodwork."

"Got room for a third?" Kate said, and pulled up a chair.

About the Author

Sean Costello is a practicing physician who lives and works in Sudbury, Ontario, his home since 1981. *Finders Keepers* is his fourth novel.

For information on previous and upcoming titles, visit the author's website: www.seancostello.net

Printed in the United States
1431700003B/65